The School of 1

Theresa Crater

M000087283

Crystal Star Publishing
1303 Alexandria St.
Lafayette, CO 80026
https://crystalstarpublishing.wordpress.com
School of Hard Knocks
by Theresa Crater
Digital ISBN: 978-0-9971413-3-7[1]
Print ISBN: 978-0-9971413-4-4[2]
Cover art by Earthly Charms
Edited by Historical Editorial
Copyright 2017 Theresa Crater
Printed in the United States of America
Worldwide Electronic & Digital Rights

1st North American and UK Print Rights

For Lois & Mamie

Prologue

C aroline
     Even before we are born, the story of our life has already been written. We spend our days trying to live up to that story. We measure our success or failure by it. Those of us who fill out the original outline skate through life accepted, surrounded by family, colleagues, and friends, but with a hollow feeling, a sense that there's something missing, something waiting just on the other side of some boundary we cannot cross, because if we did . . .

Those of us who fail to live up to that story never fully embrace our real life. We miss its treasures because we measure ourselves against the phantom we can barely imagine. If only . . .

I did not live up to my story. I tried to find my way back to it by doing the right thing by you. But there was no going back from that. How can a mother make up for such a betrayal?

My own mother thought she'd found her story when she married my father, that siren dream calling out to her from the glossy pictures in *Ladies' Home Journal*. But her wildness snuck in like a stray cat. And try as she might to catch it and turn it out for good, there was always some hole somewhere, and it would slink back inside.

Strangely enough, Maggie had it best of all until the inevitable happened. Then she had the worst of it. I tried to ease her way in the end.

No matter what you do, it will all be turned inside out at the finish. You will have sung the descant rather than the melody, worn the label on the outside, irretrievably harmed the one perfect thing you ruined yourself to save. We all did the worst thing a mother can do.

But I'm getting ahead of myself. For me, the story starts when my father disappeared that day, but really it begins with Maggie and what Mother told me about her.

M aggie—1890s
I couldn't rightly say when I was born. Nobody kept no records of such things back in that time. My momma told me it was late and the woman from the next plantation came over to help. Most people was gone by then, left old Mr. Winters and traveled up north somewhere or got themselves some land and struck out on their own. The century had just about run its course, and some folks had they hopes up that the next one would bring better times. But of course, I didn't know nothing about all that. The leaves was turning all colors like they do—them reds and yellows and the gold that shines out at you from the woods and lifts your heart right up out your chest. And the full moon hanging in the sky, big as a lemon meringue pie set out to cool. 'Least that's what they told me, and every time I see that harvest moon, I think back on it.

I couldn't say who was my blood and who wasn't, and I would've been better off never to have found out. Momma had a weakness for babies, almost like a sweet tooth. Couldn't pass one by without stopping to cluck in its face, talk to its momma, tell her how to fix up colic, how to keep the baby from crying when it was teething, how to get away from a man who'd done gone crazy from being beat or worked half to death or who was just plain mean. She took in strays—babies left behind when they mommas went north, saying they couldn't carry them all that way. Saying the young'un would die on the trip, which was likely true. Saying they didn't know what they'd find to eat themselves. Or just leaving 'em on the doorstep. Some she just took for a while till their mommas got themselves straightened out. Sometimes she took on the mommas, too. Mr. Winters's house was big, and he didn't seem to mind, 'long as we stayed in our place, cooked his meals, and kept everything shining and nice. It was a lot of work keeping up that house. Momma was glad of the help. And the company.

With all them women around, there was plenty of hands. We babies stayed in a big room with the bottom half of what they call a Dutch door pulled closed. One of the older children would be set to watch us. We crawled and played, slept where we nodded off, and finally learned to walk. When we could toddle along pretty good, we took to following our mothers 'cause that's how we thought of all those women, some who came and went, some who stayed—our mothers. We followed them on their chores if they let us.

The first thing I really remember—it must have been canning season. Momma kept calling the girl who was watching us to come help, and she finally forgot to close the door good. I remember reaching for that big, shiny knob, leaning against the door, and it just pushed open. I fell through and landed in the hall. I cried, but all that noise and laughter covered it up. So I tottered toward the sound. Down that long hallway—it was long to me then—I fell and crawled the rest of the way. Finally, the carpet turned to well-scrubbed wood. The smell of peaches and sugar filled the air, and the rise and fall of women's voices. Momma stood over an enormous shiny pot, her face wet with steam and sweat, her eyes intent.

The girl who was supposed to have been watching us came in, arms full of wood. She dumped it in the box next to the stove and shook the bark and wood chips out of her dress. Momma jerked the door to the wood-burner open. Heat blasted out. Red squares of burned-down wood glowed inside.

"Add another log. We need to keep this hot for the next batch." She glanced over her shoulder at the group of women crowded along the long counter.

"'Bout ready, Miss Jenny," one of them called over.

The girl picked up a small log and thrust it into the belly of the cast-iron stove. The log smoked, then red fingers of flame danced along the edge. I reached out for it, but Momma slammed the door shut. Then she wrapped two thick cloths around her hands and grabbed that pot and lifted. She took a step back and ran smack into me, lost her balance, and screamed. Scalding liquid spilled over, hitting the floor, splashing my arm. I shrieked. The women at the counter all ran over at once, another of them tripping over me. But one of them grabbed the pot from Momma and carried it over to the sink.

"How'd this baby get in here?"

Arms reached down and picked me up. Lottie carried me out back to the well, Momma right on her heels, and Old Joe pumped the handle, bringing up that sweet, cold water. Momma held me and her own leg under it. I reckon I stopped screaming then because that's all I remember. I have this little scar on my forearm to show for it. Momma used to tell the story, though, in the kitchen after I'd gotten big enough to string beans or shell peas or whatever it was we was having for supper that night. She carried a scar from it, too.

When we got big enough, the women took us outside to teach us those chores. I loved the chickens, the colors, the sounds of clucking. Until one pecked me hard on the hand. Then I was afraid of them for a while, but I got over it. And the horses and mules with their big hooves. They scared me, too, when I was little.

When I got a little older, I'd wander down to the stables and follow Mick around, and he'd explain everything he was doing— mucking the stalls or nailing a shoe on, which terrified me until he explained it was just like our fingernails, and it didn't hurt to cut them, now did it? He let me lead the horse, but now that I think on it, I'll bet he had a hold of the rope farther up. I loved it when they'd put their velvet noses into my hand, snuffling for a treat. Yeah, he taught me good.

We children had the run of the place, at least our part of it. We loved going down by the creek and picking up rocks, then watching

the crayfish scurry for cover. Or making piles of leaves and jumping
in them, climbing trees, sneaking up on deer, watching the beavers
down by the pond.

Mr. Winters owned the place, but he was getting soft in the head,
so they said. Only they said it in the kitchen, not to his face. His wife
had died after the war, and he never remarried. Took that baby with
her in a mess of blood and wailing. Momma used to tell the story
when somebody new come to stay. 'Course she was a young'un then,
so I don't know how she remembered it. Mr. Winters's son, he'd gone
off to war in his shiny gray uniform but never came back. Shot or
died from his wounds or some fever that burned through the camps,
most likely. But the war had been over so long by the time I come
along that nobody talked about it much anymore. Things had gotten
a little wild what with colored folks running for office and Yankees
coming down here to try to tell us our business, but now it was almost the new century. White peoples was determined to put us back
in our place. That's what they called it.

I heard all this in the kitchen or out slopping the hogs or feeding
the chickens or working in the kitchen garden. Momma didn't let me
work the fields, though. Said that was for them others. Most folks on
Mr. Winters's plantation didn't sharecrop. They did what they called
communal farming. Said they did better thataway. Took their noon
meal together when they was plantin' or harvestin. We fed them out
back.

When I was tall enough to lift the big ladle, I helped. The men
lined up, dusty and sweating, let the mules out of the harnesses, and
turned them out to graze, those big rubbery lips nosing under everywhere for what grass they could find. The men brought they tin plates
and cups and held them out, they hands rough and dry as the hooves
of those mules. Shuffling in line, too tired not to—and it was only just noon—wiping their heads with their red bandanas, smiling at
me, calling me Miss Maggie. The colored folk called me by that name,

but Mr. Winters, he called me Pearl. Said that's where the name Margaret come from. It took me years to figure out what he meant by that. I never really knew my full name was Margaret and Maggie was a nickname. I didn't know how I come to have so many names when most folks do with one. But I'm running ahead of myself.

One morning we was out back helping with the laundry. A bunch of younger kids sat around playing in the mud, but I had to work. A whiff of lye come from the damp shirts when I shook them out and handed them up to be hung on the line.

"Mas'er say come," Tim called across the backyard. They still called him that. Better to be safe than sorry.

Momma asked Lottie to take her place at the tub, took off her apron, and straightened her skirt.

"He say bring Maggie."

Momma stopped short, her mouth wrinkling in a frown, then turned to me. "Well, come on then."

In the kitchen, she took a tiny bit of bacon grease from the jar on the stove and rubbed it into the skin of her chafed hands. Then she studied me, her eyes narrowed. She pushed my loose curls behind my ears, tugged the wrinkles from my dress, and told me to follow her. We walked through the dining room, where the morning light glinted off the gold trim on the rows of round dishes in the walnut sideboard. The silver candle holders gleamed from a recent polish, and the dark wood of the table gave off a faint scent of beeswax.

"Now you keep quiet," Momma said. "Lord knows we can't be wasting the time of an important man like Mr. Winters." We reached the hallway with its long stretch of carpet. Momma said this was from Turkey, but I never could make out any birds in the design. And the turkeys was meaner than the chickens by a long shot.

"He was a senator, you know, Mr. Winters was."

"I know, Momma." She was always saying this. I didn't know what it meant. We walked to the door of his library, and Momma knocked.

"Please come in, Jenny." Mr. Winters sounded like the flow of deep water.

Momma walked right in, but suddenly I was afraid to step over the threshold. I hung back, studying that rug in the hallway.

"Yes, sir, Mr. Winters?" Momma asked.

"Where's Pearl?" Mr. Winters looked around the room.

Momma turned and saw me standing in the hall. "You git in here." She reached out and grabbed me when I came close, pulled me to stand beside her. I twisted my arm in her steel grip. "You hold still now, you hear?" she hissed at me, her voice pitched for my ears only.

"Let her go, Jenny." Mr. Winters sat back in his big cushy chair next to the fireplace.

Momma dropped her hand, and I rubbed my arm where she'd grabbed me, stared down at a new carpet, this one scarlet and blue, big tears surprising me.

"Pearl." Mr. Winters's gentle voice reached me across a great expanse. "You're not scared of me, now are you? Do you remember how you used to play on this rug you're studying so hard now, right here in front of the fireplace?"

I remembered a rag doll, the feel of heat on my back, the sound of my mother's laughter. My eyes lifted to his, the blue of a winter sky, his gray eyebrows bushy below that high forehead and neatly trimmed silver hair.

"That's better." He switched his gaze to Momma. "She's nine now, isn't she?"

I slipped behind Momma's skirts.

"Will be this October."

"I'm going to need some help, Jenny. My eyes aren't what they used to be."

I snuck another look. They seemed the same to me, pale and distant, but ready to kindle up when he laughed.

"Yes, sir," Momma murmured.

"Miss Grayson here—" He nodded toward the sofa. I found a woman sitting there, one of those pretty rose teacups in one hand, her blue shiny skirts pooling around her, a bright white blouse all buttoned up to her chin with big poufy sleeves that ended in cuffs that started halfway up her forearm and buttons all the way down to her wrist. I'd sure hate to have to iron that. "—has agreed to come twice a week to teach Pearl to read and write."

Momma couldn't quite disguise her gasp. She reached around and touched my arm as if to reassure herself I was safe. "Mas'er, you knows better than me" sometimes she talked like that in front of strange white people, "but ain't that 'gainst the law, sir?" She ducked her head. I was standing by her side now and saw her eyes cut to that Miss Grayson, then back down to her shoes, where they belonged.

"Now, don't you worry, Jenny. You know all that's changed. What I'm proposing is perfectly legal, and Miss Grayson's family has suffered some hardship lately." He nodded at his visitor, and she lowered her eyes. "It's a good position for a lady, and it seems to me," he looked me up and down, from my bare feet, one tucked behind the other, to my skinned knee where I'd slipped in the creek, and up my dress, damp and stained, "like our Pearl could use some lessons in deportment."

Momma didn't know what that word meant. I could tell by how her back stiffened. She hesitated to speak up in front of this lady. Ordinarily, she'd tell him just what she was thinking, polite and all, but still. They was like that. But in front of company, she had to act her part. "Whatever you say, sir. 'Long as" Miss Grayson couldn't conceal her surprise that Momma had more to say, so Momma studied her shoes real good, "Maggie still learns how to keep a house," she ended in a whisper.

"Quite correct." Mr. Winters smiled at Miss Grayson like he was soothing down a hen who'd taken objection to someone searching her nest. "Our Pearl here must learn to keep a house, cook, clean, all your marvelous skills." Now he was soothing the other hen. "You're doing an excellent job of teaching her that, but I require her assistance in my work." He looked right sharp at Momma, who nodded her head, but I could tell she'd have more to say later on.

When we got back, Momma told Ellie she was going to start supper early. When Momma helped cook, it meant something special was goin' on. "Maggie, go get me one of those guinea hens Mr. Winters like so much."

"But, Momma," I started.

"I don't want no lip from you, girl." She used that tone that promised a hand to my behind if I didn't do just like she say right then.

I hated killing chickens, but them tiny hens was worse. You had to be careful wringing their necks, and they weren't hardly worth the plucking after all was said and done. Just a couple of mouthfuls, looked like to me. I ain't never had one. They was special for Mr. Winters and sometimes company. When I got back to the kitchen, Momma was rolling out dough for pie crusts, and she sent me for some canned peaches, like the ones that had spilled all over the kitchen that one time. I helped her mix up pies, and then she set me to stringing beans out on the back stoop.

That night, while we served dinner to Mr. Winters, who sat alone at that long table with one candelabra lit, dressed in his fine blue suit and starched white shirt—thank heavens it didn't have all them buttons like Miss Grayson's blouse did—Momma served the soup, then that hen, all trussed up and filled with her cornbread stuffing, slipping in a few questions as she set down a plate or took one away. I only heard the sound of voices through the kitchen door where I was crouched until he raised his. "Times have changed, Jenny. And I have plans for that girl. Now do as I say."

Momma came huffing back into the kitchen and then served the peach cobbler in a silence as crisp as her starched white apron. But later on when I was lying in bed, voices reached me from the open window in the downstairs library where he took his sherry of an evening. The clink of glasses told me Momma was having some, too. I heard a low, muffled laugh, playful and full of a promise that disturbed my childlike understanding, with a hint of something deep and rich, like the dark earth in spring. The scent of his big cigar drifted up, mixing with the heavy jasmine on the trellis on the side of the house, and I fell asleep knowing everything was all right.

"Ow." I tried to squirm away. "Stop."

"You hold still now. I don't know how that man expects me to get you ready with all the work I got left to do."

I jerked my face out from between her two soapy hands, but she grabbed me by the ear. "Ow, Momma, that hurts."

"Hold still, then." She took up her wash rag and started scrubbing like I was a soup pot with a crusty bottom. I squeezed my eyes tight.

"Well, that will just have to do," she finally said.

I opened my eyes just as she upended a sauce pan full of cool water over my head. I shook just like that old sheepdog does when us kids coax him over by the well and douse him with a bucket. I decided then and there never to do it again.

She grabbed my hands. "Let me see them nails."

"Momma?" I looked around for a hammer. Was she going to drive nails into my hands just like they done to Jesus, who died for our sins?

Her face softened. "Fingernails, you crazy girl."

My face scrunched up. Maybe Momma done lost her mind like that runner we'd had a few winters back. She took up a paring knife. "Momma?"

She ran the edge of the knife under the nail of my forefinger and held the result up to her face. "Where do you get this dirt?" I shrugged. She repeated the process on each finger. "I swear I could use this to plant a garden with."

"Yes, ma'am." Best to placate her.

She paused and considered me, one eyebrow cocked. "Don't you sass me, girl."

"No, ma'am."

She chuckled. "Well, get yourself dry, then."

Filled with relief, I grabbed the strip of old flannel she'd laid out and rubbed off the water, then wrapped it around me and ran down the hall to my bedroom. I pulled on the clean underclothes she'd laid across my bed, glad nobody else was there. I was reaching for the dress when she appeared. "Don't put that clean dress on yet. Come into my room."

She had the best room in the slaves' quarters, at least the ones in the house, and the cabins weren't nothing but square rooms, some with a potbellied stove. I was supposed to call them servants' quarters now, though, since it's been more than thirty years since Mr. Lincoln declared us free. Some say Mr. Winters hisself voted for our freedom when he was a congressman, not that things had changed all that much. I heard tell that Mr. Winters had always been kind and kept overseers who were easy with the lash. Mostly anyway. Only difference was we didn't have no overseers no more. George ran things for him. Some rednecks in town talked bad about George 'cause of it, but we didn't pay them no never mind.

Momma's windows, hung with white lace curtains, thin as a wisp of cloud but swirled into the shape of roses, looked out on a garden, this one fully fleshed out with the reddest roses ever. Pink, too, and yellow, but the reds was my favorite. Those grew right close up to the window, which was open at the bottom. A faint breeze brought the heavy sweetness of damask roses and wisteria, almost masking the strong musk of the tobacco fields. The prettiest quilt ever, a log cabin pattern made with castoffs and some old drapes that had been replaced, covered her bed. The feedbag patterns went to the others.

She nodded at her dressing table, that shrine of hair brushes, a bottle of scent, two pairs of earrings, and her prize pearl necklace. "Well, come on. Let's see what we can do with that hair."

She covered my shoulders with another flannel, and I braced myself. But her fury must have been quenched in the water of the bath. She took her own special hair oil, rubbed just a bit of it in her palms, and massaged my scalp. Then she started parting and combing, creating braids that magically grew along my head like neat rows in the garden. And she talked—lectured, more like it—on how to behave with Miss Grayson. "You got to be a bit careful with these white ladies now. They ain't used to our ways here."

I nodded, but a strand of hair pulled too tight, so I set right still. "Yes, ma'am."

"Listen to everything she say and don't talk back, no matter what kind of nonsense come outta her mouth—you hear me now?"

"Yes, ma'am." She droned on about not looking her in the eye, about calling her Miss, about not using no rough words—all stuff I knew already. I closed my eyes, enjoying the gentle scrape of the comb, Momma's fingers digging out the next bit of hair for the braid. Her voice blended with the honeybees busy outside the window, with the murmur of voices in the dining room, where Lottie and Suzie polished the silver—no matter that Mr. Winters never used it no more.

A finger poked me in the ribs. "Wake up and look."

I opened my eyes and found a tidy young girl looking back, her hazel eyes set off by tiny green ribbons at the end of each neat braid.

"Momma." I turned my head this way and that in front of the three-paneled mirror. "It's beautiful."

Her eyes gleamed, and she nodded her head. "Let's get that dress on you, then."

I ran back to my room, still empty since this time of day everyone was helping clean the upstairs rooms. Momma slipped a green plaid dress over my upstretched arms, put my one pair of good, shiny shoes on my feet, and started to repeat everything she'd already said. I threw my arms around her and kissed her smooth cheek. "It'll be all right, Momma. You'll see."

"It better be," she said, but she dabbed her eyes with the handkerchief she kept folded in her apron, so I knew she weren't really mad. "Now, let's go."

Mr. Winters sat in the library at his huge rolltop desk, sorting through papers, his pipe sending up a trail of white smoke. I looked around but found the room empty of other humans. One of the cats perched on top of a bookcase, head cocked, prob'ly at a spider.

"Where is she?" Momma asked.

Mr. Winters looked up, pipe clinched between his teeth. "Who?"

Momma stifled what would have been a sigh. "That Miss Grayson, that's who." She looked around and found me teasing the cat. "Leave that critter alone. Get over here so Mr. Winters can see you."

I skipped over to his desk.

"And walk like a lady. You'd think I ain't taught her nothing."

Mr. Winters took my hand and nudged me closer to his chair. He smelled like tobacco and musk. The leather of his chair and the dust of books made my nose crinkle. "She's all dressed up for church, Jenny. You didn't have to go to all that trouble."

"The child's got her Sunday meetin' clothes and then work clothes. Nothing in between. If you want her to dress different—"

A knock on the library door interrupted her and was quickly followed by the sonorous, practiced tone of Simon announcing my tutor. I pulled my hand from Mr. Winters's and moved behind the potted palm that took up most of the corner beside his desk. He stood up, his chair creaking. "Miss Grayson, please do come in. We'll have tea, I think. Yes?" He looked at his guest, who stood just inside the doorway, her little feet close together in their button-up shoes—that woman loved her some buttons—her wide skirts almost hiding them.

Momma eyed his pipe.

"Oh yes." He put the pipe down in its little tray.

"You don't need to go to any trouble for me." Miss Grayson's voice was soft, not sweet soft, but quiet, like she wasn't used to talking much.

"Tea and—" he looked at me and smiled "—some cookies, I think. Milk for Pearl."

Momma's nostrils flared, but not so anyone else but me and maybe Mr. Winters would notice. Simon looked straight ahead just like a piece of furniture. Momma nodded, then started toward the door but came up short. Miss Grayson's wide skirts blocked the doorway, but the lady didn't seem to notice. I wondered how many crinolines she was wearing. She unpinned her hat and handed it over to Simon without really looking at him, then stepped forward.

"Pearl." Mr. Winters looked around for me. "Where'd that child get to?" He spied me behind the plant and gently pulled me forward. "You remember Miss Grayson?"

I nodded, looking down at my shoes.

"She's here to teach you to read and write and do your sums."

I hazarded a look at her, but she was studying Mr. Winters, not me. "Yes, sir," I said. Couldn't go wrong saying that.

"Good girl. I'll be right here answering my correspondence, and I've set up a table over there for you two to work." He pointed at the window where another large potted plant used to stand, but in its place now was a small pine table painted white with two chairs pulled up on either side of it. Mr. Winters escorted Miss Grayson over to it just like she was too dim-witted to find it herself, pulled out the adult-sized chair, and she fussed around with sitting down, spreading her skirts just so. She started to take off her gloves, pulling a little at the top of each finger, then tugging them off.

I watched, mesmerized by the process.

"Pearl." Mr. Winters's voice startled me out of my reverie. "You can seat yourself, can't you?"

I slipped into the little chair and slumped down, trying to get smaller. Simon's arrival with tea, cookies, and some milk saved me. He placed the glass in front of me, then a pretty dessert plate, paused just long enough for me to look up. He winked, then turned his face back to stone so fast I wondered if I'd imagined it. But it cheered me. I had a conspirator.

He poured out tea for Miss Grayson, who demurred, then accepted, and bolted two cookies so fast I reckoned she was starving. Simon moved on to serve Mr. Winters, and Miss Grayson asked me in her flat, cold voice, "Do you know your letters yet?"

My eyes strayed to Mr. Winters's desk, where he answered letters every day in the afternoon. "I don't get no letters, ma'am."

"No, I mean the alphabet."

I stared at her, blank as the small slate lying on the table in front of me.

"Your ABCs?" she tried again, cocking her head in unconscious imitation of the cat behind her, biting her lip to keep herself from laughing at me.

"No, ma'am."

"Well, we'll start there." She picked up a white stick and held it up. "Do you know what this is?"

I suppressed a heavy sigh. "That's chalk, ma'am." She smiled like I'd said something clever. This was going to be a long hour. "I'll write the letters and pronounce them, then you'll draw them underneath and say each one in turn. The first letter in the alphabet is *A*." She drew two lines coming down like my stick figures, but put a line between them about at the knees. Next, she drew two pillows together on a bed. *"B."* A sliver of moon. *"C."* She kept going for two more.

Then she handed me the little piece of slate. I laid it down on the table and tried to draw, but the chalk gave off a screech like a gutted pig. I dropped it right quick.

"Here." Miss Grayson reached over and laid the chalk between my thumb and forefinger. "This way it won't make that noise."

I tried again, and she was right. Looked like she knew something after all. I drew the letters and tried to remember the names. I got the first three right, then forgot. And so we passed that first hour, her repeating the letters as she wrote them in groups of about five, me drawing them and trying to remember. I remembered about a dozen by the time she sat back and, for the very first time, smiled at me.

"Pearl is smart for a little Negra," she said to Mr. Winters.

His head came up with a snap. He took a breath and smoothed the frown off his face. "Sorry, you startled me," he said, but I knew it was what she'd said. "Yes, our Pearl is the most promising of the children academically. That's why I picked her for you to teach."

Miss Grayson studied my hazel eyes and high yellow color. At least by the calculating expression on her face, I reckoned that was what she was studying. "I see," she said.

"Once Pearl has learned, I'm going to open a school for colored children."

Miss Grayson's hand flew up to her mouth, but it didn't catch her gasp.

"Just to teach them the three *R*s. I think everybody should be able to read their Bible. Don't you agree, Miss Grayson?"

She clasped her hands together so tight the knuckles showed white, but her tone was honey sweet. "That's very progressive of you, Mr. Winters. I hope the others can see your point."

"Oh, everyone will get used to it, I'm sure, just like we've had to get used to so many other things."

"I hope so since you've decided to involve me." Her jaw tightened. "Not that I don't appreciate your help for my family."

"I'll be sure you're well out of it before that happens, Miss Grayson."

She hesitated, then said, "Thank you," stumbling just a bit on the words.

"There's talk—" she started to say, but glanced at me and stopped.

Mr. Winters pushed his papers away and stood up. "Come here, Pearl."

I sprang up and ran over to him.

"No running," Miss Grayson said almost automatically, like she'd heard that all her life.

My eyes must have gone wide because Mr. Winters answered my unvoiced thought. "Miss Grayson is also going to teach you how to act like a lady, so you'll have to mind her."

I slowed my steps but reached the relative safety of his presence soon enough. He bent down to me. "You've made an excellent start, wouldn't you agree?" He wasn't asking me, though. He looked past me at her.

"Yes, certainly acceptable," she answered.

I set my shoulders. I remembered fifteen letters. I bet she didn't remember so many after her first lesson.

"Now you go see your mother."

Dismissed, I headed out of the room, trying my best not to run.

"What kind of talk have you heard?" he asked just before the door closed all the way. I stuck out my foot so it didn't click shut.

"Some of the men are starting up those," she paused for the right word, "nighttime visitations they used to have so often. They seem to think some of the niggers—" she didn't hesitate to use that word now she thought I was gone "—are getting a little too uppity."

"Anyone in particular?"

"You should talk to my father. They don't discuss such things in front of ladies."

"I see."

"I thought you ought to know since you're considering started a colored school. People might not take to it."

Mr. Winters took a breath to say something but noticed me peeking through the door. He shot me a look that promised a licking, so I let it shut quiet and went to find Momma first thing. I knew she'd have my hide if I messed up this dress.

2

I found Momma in the kitchen telling cook what to do, as usual. Momma saw me and held her hand up, palm forward. "Don't you even think of coming in this room with that dress on."

I stopped dead in the hall.

"I think we'll have mashed potatoes and your special gravy, Ellie. You do make some fine gravy." This brought a sullen smile to Ellie's face, like the sun behind a dark cloud. Momma turned to me. "Now, let's get you out of that dress."

I chattered away about *A*, *B*, *C*, and how to hold chalk so it didn't squeak while Momma took off my dress and took the special ribbons out of my hair. When I looked up, she had a bemused look on her face. "Well, I guess these lessons ain't gonna be so bad after all."

"No, ma'am." I told her the story, all about how I was going to teach the other children how to read, too.

"Is that so?" Her eyes grew thoughtful.

"But I don't like her," I whispered.

"Well, we all got to put up with something. Best you start learning how to get along with ornery white folks 'cause you'll be doin' it all your life."

"She's mean, talking about how colored folks is getting' uppity."

She asked me the same thing Mr. Winters had asked. "Anyone in particular?"

"She say her daddy don't talk about that in front of the women-folk."

I carefully repeated what I'd overheard about the nighttime meetings. Momma's hand flew to her mouth and her eyes got big. "Mm, mm, mm," she said, shaking her head. "Well, now." She stood there thinking so long I had to tug on her hand.

"Go on and get your work clothes on." She didn't say nothin' about doing no work, though, so I skipped out to the barn to visit Mick.

He had a new horse he was healin' and I liked to watch him soothe them down. It soothed me, to tell the truth. He told me all about moving slow, talking in a low tone, not trying to touch them before they was ready. This old bay had some deep cuts across his hindquarters, and his mouth was tore up something awful. Mick dabbed salve over his sores. I reached out to daub my fingers in the ointment, but he stopped me.

"He ain't ready to let anybody else touch him yet. Soon as he is, you can help me, all right?"

I tucked my head and dug my toe into the dirt, disappointed.

"See how he's perking up his ears? That's a good sign. He'll be all right soon enough." He shook his head. "I don't know why them peoples got to be so cruel. That Billy Grayson got hisself a mean streak."

"Miss Grayson teachin' me to read."

"Is she now?" I saw his eyes hood over, which meant he was hiding something from me, thinking I was too young.

"I don't like her," I said, hoping to pull his secret out of him.

He looked at me like he studied a horse, figuring out how best to approach it. That always took a while, so I watched the old bay's eyes close and his lips start to droop. He cocked his big hind hoof, ready to go off into dreamland.

Finally, Mick said, "I reckon that Miss Grayson had it hard, growing up in that family."

"Really?" It was a new idea to me that white folks might have it hard. I thought for them the crooked was made straight, and the rough places plain, like it say in the good book.

"Could be. Peoples that's mean to animals is usually mean to other people, especially ones they think are beneath them." He sat down on a hay bale, pulled a piece loose, and stuck it in his mouth.

I knew I was in for one of his teachings, so I sat down beside him. "You mean like us?"

"That's right. And womenfolk. I bet that Miss Grayson been treated rough. Ole Mr. Grayson, they granddaddy, he worked for Mr. Winters's father as an overseer back when we was slaves. He was a mean one. Took pleasure in tying men to the whipping post. The more blood, the better he liked it." He eyed me to see how I'd react.

I hunched up my shoulders. "I'm glad slavery is over."

"It over and it ain't over."

"What you mean?"

"We ain't property no more, but it be hard to make a livin' on your own, 'specially these days."

I waited. I knew he'd answer all my questions, and he didn't like to be poked and prodded. Just like his horses that way.

"See, right after Mr. Lincoln set us free—"

"I thought it was Mr. Winters in the Congress done that," I said, forgetting not to interrupt.

He snorted a little, like one of them high-steppin' carriage horses, then waited a minute until he figured I'd settled down. "After Mr. Lincoln and Mr. Winters set us free—" I ducked my head, realizing how silly it sounded "—they was colored folks runnin' for office, startin' stores, like Daniel Carter did. Some got they ten acres and a mule and started farmin'."

He shook his head at this last part like there was some joke, but I didn't get it. I didn't interrupt him, though. Once was enough.

"But most folks stayed where they was at 'cause they didn't have much choice. They was free. They got paid some money now. Things was a little better. But when them Yankees come down telling white folks what to do and how to run things, well that was just about the last straw."

He leaned back and gazed into the distance, remembering, I guess. "Now the white folks figure things has settled down. It's been well over twenty-five years, so they think those Yankees has forgot about us. Now they want to go back to the old ways."

"They gonna own us again?"

Mick pushed his hat back and smiled. "Not own us, but they want to put us back in our place, 'specially those who's got something, like a store or a farm."

"That's what that Miss Grayson said."

He studied me a minute, his fading brown eyes sharp all of a sudden. "What she say?"

So I repeated my story to Mick. "Mr. Winters say I'm gonna teach the other children to read and write. 'Rithmetic, too."

"Is that right?"

I nodded and tried not to puff out my chest like some rooster.

"So she say they goin' back to those nighttime meetings?"

I was a little put out everyone was worried about these meetings and not thinking about me becoming a teacher, but I just said, "Yes, sir."

"Mm, mm, mm," he said, exactly like Momma.

"What's it mean?"

"You better ask your Momma about that." He stood up. "I got to feed all these animals and put stuff up for the night, so you run along now."

"Can I put salve on his lip tomorrow?"

"Who? Oh, this old bay? We'll see."

That evening after we'd washed up the dishes and scrubbed the countertops and stove, Momma went down to the cabins and sat around the campfire with the folks as really run the plantation, letting me tag along. I tried to start a game of drawing ABCs in the dirt, but the other kids wanted to play hide-and-seek. I hid behind a big rock near where Momma was telling George, Suzie, and Mick about what that Miss Grayson had said. George pretty much managed the farm, at least that's what Momma said. He was tall and skinny as a fence post. Some folks in town called him Red 'cause of his hair being like the sky at sunrise, but he didn't like it, so nobody said it to his face.

Suzie ran the house. She was a little bit shorter than Momma, rounder, her hair a gray cloud above her mocha face. Her shoulders sloped like a soft hill, but she was always remembering and straightening up, sometimes with a soft little grunt, like something pained her. Like Momma, she wore flowered work dresses, some from store-bought fabric. Suzie took her orders from Momma, but nobody else.

"Sound like the Klan is startin' up again," Mick said.

"If that child heard right, then that's what it sound like all right." Suzie rocked back on her log, hands on her knees. "Bad times comin'."

They sat in silence for a while. Some pine sap sizzled in the fire they burned to keep the mosquitoes off. I forgot about hiding and sat with my back against the rock. Their shadows danced against the cabin walls, long and strange.

"Question is, who they goin' after," Momma said. Their faces all gradually turned to her. "Nah, can't risk it. She's too young."

"We can't say nothin' to her, but you know how white peoples talk in front of us like we ain't got no sense," Suzie said. "It might just come out."

"'Course I'll listen to what the child says, but I got a better chance with Henry."

George shook his head. "They ain't gonna tell him. They knows he ain't like them. Leastwise, not much."

"Thank the Lord," Momma muttered.

"We'll spread the word. Tell everybody to watch out," Mick said. "Somebody will say something that'll give us a hint."

"We'll get everybody listenin'." George clapped his hands down on his knees and strained to stand. Momma took his elbow to steady him. "Think we can post some watches?"

"I'll see about it," Mick said. It was easier for him to travel around. Lots of folks called him to shoe they horses and such.

"I's got to get these old bones in the bed," George said. He stopped dead when he spied me leaning against the rock. "Jenny."

Momma spotted me just as I stood up.

"What you doin' listenin' to us talk?"

I started digging at the ground with one toe. "I didn't mean nothin' by it."

"You keep your mouth shut about this, you hear me? You can get hurt behind this."

I looked up at the three adults, their faces creased with worry. "I'll listen to Miss Grayson, but I won't say nothin', Momma. I promise."

She straightened up, surprised by my tone of voice.

Seems like I grew up some that night, but not as much as later.

I learned the whole alphabet in no time flat and, as summer turned to fall, progressed to copying passages out of the Bible. I sat at the small table, studying that small writing, trying not to tear the onion-thin sheets when I turned a page. I'd write out a passage on my slate using my chalk, concentrating on getting each letter just right and not letting the chalk squeak. Mr. Winters had hisself what he called a fountain pen, but he didn't let me use it. He promised when I mastered my lessons I could use it to write letters for him, which made Miss Grayson sniff a little the first time he said it. Mr. Winters waggled his eyebrows at me, which almost made me bust out laughing.

After I would finish writing, Miss Grayson would read it first, showing me where I'd missed letters. Once I fixed it, she'd hand the slate back to me and make me sound it out, demonstratin' how the letters made words. Those letters sounded different when you put them together. It was kinda tricky sometimes. I loved recognizing words I already knew, but some of them was long and complicated.

She showed me how to see words I already knew inside those long ones, but that didn't always work. Then she'd asked me what the verse meant, which was the hardest part because, well—I don't mean no disrespect, but sometimes those verses didn't make no kind of sense whatsoever. Mr. Winters would help out more often than not, and he could explain something so it made me feel like I was rising up out of my little chair, my heart swelling with mystery and just a touch of glory.

While I copied out my verses, Miss Grayson would talk to Mr. Winters. At first, just from her seat at the table, but soon she just got up and plopped herself down next to him if he'd finished his letter writin' and was readin' his paper or a book. Well, she didn't plop. She perched on the edge, one hand cupping the other in her lap, her back straight as a tall pine tree, her voice kind of breathy. Momma say that was 'cause her corset was too tight. Thinking about that made me want to laugh, and I'd have to hold my breath and stare at the Bible verse until the urge passed off.

My verses got longer and her conversations with Mr. Winters did the same. She had herself a little fan from China, she said. A soft apricot background featurin' birds with long tails dotted with blue and purple spots the color of peacocks, deep summer-green trees, and gold trim all the way around. I coveted it, even though the Good Book told me not to. She'd unfurl it and laugh behind it, cock her eyes at Mr. Winters, then snap it back together and tap her left hand with the ivory handle. She'd taken off her oyster gloves so as not to spoil them with the chalk. Apologized to Mr. Winters for her bare hands.

"Oh, of course, Miss Grayson. You must be practical."

This day she laid her gloves on the side of the table, picked a long, thorny passage for me, and started to get up.

"I ain't got—"

"Haven't, Pearl. I haven't got."

"I haven't got enough room on my slate, ma'am."

"Well, then." She looked around the room vaguely. "Just do the first half." She dismissed me with a small wave of her hand and picked up her gloves.

But by the time I'd filled up my slate, she weren't paying me no never mind. She had herself scooted up close to Mr. Winters and was telling him some story that I couldn't rightly hear. They was talking low and laughing together, Mr. Winters's head tilted toward her, a half-smile on his face.

"That Miss Pritchett, she can hardly contain herself with Miss Watson now engaged to Mr. Smith. She thought she'd won him, but—" Miss Grayson put her hand, once again covered with her white glove, to her chest, looked down demurely "—I really shouldn't talk like this."

"Yes?" The smile didn't quite reach Mr. Winters's eyes. I knew because when he was really happy, his eyes sparkled like the sun reflecting off the waves on a lake.

"Well, I hear the Smith family is having money trouble." She said this in a whisper, but I'd moved a little forward so I could hear. "Have been for some time. Can't find anyone to work for them hardly. These days what we have to pay these niggers is a downright shame."

Mr. Winters didn't take exception like he usually do. He made some clucking sound as if to encourage her. I scooted back to my chair, picked up my slate, and studied the writing. Best to be invisible when white folks talk like this.

She was encouraged all right. "Used to do what you told them. Knew their place. Now I hear tell they want a nickel to plow a field, plus extra if they have a mule. Can't find anybody to pick tobacco for less than that. Mr. Smith said he'd rather let it rot in the field than give the niggers that much of his profit."

"Mm, mm, mm." Mr. Winters shook his head.

A hot flush ran up my neck.

"Why, Miss Pritchett's maid talked back to her so bad the other day their overseer took her out and tied her to the post. She won't talk again for a while, I hear." She laughed kinda mean like.

Mr. Winters's eyes went sharp, then he gave hisself a little shake. "Looks like those meetings might be coming just in time. I heard there was an incident on a farm over by Walkertown."

I took a breath, but when Miss Grayson looked down, he pointed his pipe at me to keep me still.

Miss Grayson didn't see. She opened her apricot lace fan with a little snap. "Why, Mr. Winters, I'm surprised to hear you say that. People say you are a nigger-lov—" She smoothed out some wrinkle only she could see on her skirt. "I mean, you seem to sympathize with the colored." She left this statement hanging like a hook luring a fish. And blast if Mr. Winters didn't take the bait.

"Lately, I've had cause to rethink my position. Some of my own niggers have been overstepping their bounds."

I couldn't help myself gasping.

"You get back to your studies, girl," Miss Grayson snapped, as if to demonstrate.

I opened my mouth to tell her I'd finished but thought better of it. No use being whipped. Mr. Winters nodded at me, and I stuck out my tongue at him. He frowned and pointed at the math book he taught me from. I sighed and dragged it over to me.

After I seemed to be paying them no mind, Miss Grayson whispered, "Tonight, I think. If you want to come."

"Hardly the thing for a gentleman to do, but tell your father he has my support if there's any trouble from it."

"I will." She stood up and gathered her umbrella. Weren't a cloud in the sky. And her fancy lace string purse that matched the fan. She'd done forgot all about me.

Mr. Winters stood up and walked her out into the hallway, leaving the door to the library open.

She gave a little curtsey. "Thank you for your help, Mr. Winters. My father will be happy to hear you're coming around to his way of thinking."

"My pleasure." He looked around for Simon, all self-important, then opened the door hisself. "See what I mean?"

Miss Grayson just shook her head like it was the most awful thing in the world.

I wondered where Simon was. Wondered if he'd get tied to the post like she say the maid had been. We had a post to tie the horses to. Mick didn't hold with whipping them, though.

Mr. Winters walked down the hall, his brown boots ringing out even over the carpet. I had to warn Simon to hide. I slammed the math book and followed, slipped through the dining room, hoping to head him off in the kitchen, but he got there afore me.

"Jenny, call George and Mick in, please. We have a situation."

"But you ain't gonna beat Simon?" I blurted out.

Mr. Winters snorted in surprise, and Momma looked at me like I'd taken leave of my senses. "What you talkin' about, girl?"

"Mr. Winters had to open the door hisself," I said.

"What she talkin' about?" Momma asked Mr. Winters.

He waved his hand at me like he was shooing flies. "Go get them. There's something important to discuss."

Momma looked between me and him, then headed out the back door. Mr. Winters sat at the kitchen table and gathered me between his knees. "Now, Pearl, you know I don't think like the Grayson family, don't you? I was trying to find out what their plans are, that's all."

I peeked up at him.

"Nobody's going to get hurt around here."

I melted into him for a hug. He pulled me up on his lap.

The screen door opened, and Momma stuck her head in. "Mick say he too dirty to come dropping straw and worse all over my clean floor."

"We'll meet on the veranda, then."

"Ellie," Momma hollered into the kitchen, "bring Mr. Winters some lemonade out to the veranda."

"For everyone, Jenny."

She hesitated, then added, "For all of us."

"Yes'm." Ellie managed to conceal her surprise.

Mr. Winters set me free. "Now you go run along and play."

"You get out of that dress first," Momma said.

I pulled at that dress so fast I was surprised no buttons flew, but I knew Momma would tan my hide if I ripped it, so I slowed down and undid a few, then slipped it over my head. I threw on my work dress and snuck into the upstairs back bedroom, takin' a detour to go outside to play. Okay, to eavesdrop.

". . . who they're after."

"Yes, George, but you can spread the word. Tell people to stay inside. Lock their doors."

I pulled the curtain back so I could see.

"We appreciate it, Mr. Winters, but the Klan will break into anybody's house." George took a deep breath, glancing at Momma. She nodded at him to go on. "Peoples need something to defend theyselves with. If you could see your way clear to give them some . . ."

"What George is tryin' to say is that they could do with some rifles," Mick finally said.

"Now hold on. You know I can't allow something like that. If a white man got killed and they figured out who gave them the guns, they could come after us." Mr. Winters looked from Mick to George.

They faces closed up. It weren't somethin' a white man would see, but I knew by the way they stiffened up and they faces got still. Only Momma wasn't havin' it.

She sat forward like she wanted to give him a piece of her mind but gave herself a little shake. She took a deep breath and reached for his hand. "Henry, they're coming after us already."

Mr. Winters held her hand for a minute, then returned it to Momma's lap like he was handling a fragile bird. "If anyone needs to hide here, that will be acceptable. I would rather not know for certain. As usual." He met each person's eyes. "I'm under a lot of pressure none of you are even aware of."

"Hm." Momma shook her head afore she could stop herself.

Mr. Winters pointed his finger at her. "Now, Jenny, I know you all hear things. I'm grateful to you—" he looked up, remembering his audience "—all of you for bringing matters to my attention in the past."

He gazed off into the distance at the low, sloping green lawn, the horseshoe drive that led out to the road lined with magnolias and dogwoods. "I'm sorry to mention this in front of you all. There's been a lot of talk about me not having anybody to inherit. Nasty talk about Pearl."

Momma's hand flew to her mouth.

"If it keeps up like this, I might have to marry that nitwit who teaches Pearl just to keep the peace."

Momma drew herself up, her back straight as a razor.

"If anybody suspects we armed anyone—" He took out a crisp white handkerchief and blew his nose into it. I drew back in surprise. If he knew how much trouble it was to clean and iron those . . . but his next words drove all thought from my mind "—they might kill our daughter."

Who was he talking about?

But Momma knew. She flew at him like a wet cat, raised her arm, and just caught herself before she slapped his face. I was too shocked to move. I was sure she'd be killed for raisin' a hand to a white man, Mr. Winters or not.

"I told you not to let that woman into your house. I knew this was gonna lead to trouble, but you wouldn't listen." She stood over him like some kind of ancient prophet I'd copied out of the Bible onto my slate. Or some dark angel announcing disaster. "Trying to turn our child into some kind of teacher. Pearl ain't white, Henry. Ain't nothing you can do to make her white."

George and Mick tried to make themselves invisible, but they didn't look surprised. They knew. They'd known all along. Everybody knew. 'Cept me. Now I had a daddy. I stared down at my two parents.

Mr. Winters didn't argue with her or even react to her raising a hand to him. He just lowered his head. "Tell me what to do, Jenny."

I ran into the kitchen and bent in front of the woodstove, holding the wick of the candle to the red coals, my knuckles smarting in only seconds. The flame stood tall and orange, and I stuffed the white taper into a small glass holder. Carried it into Momma's room, hands shaking. If I dripped wax on Suzie's clean floor, I'd be on my hands and knees cleaning it up. Settled in front of Momma's fancy dressing table, I put the candle down next to her porcelain hairpin holder, close to the mirror, and leaned forward, studying my face. The flame fluttered in the breeze from the open window. Reflected back in the mirror was all the evidence I'd ever needed to figure it out.

'Cept I'd never thought about it before. We took in so many children, ain't nobody got a daddy hardly. Children had been sold off during slavery, taken away from they mommas, raised by somebody else—if they was lucky. Now if folks married, they had a cabin to themselves with their kids. Or they got themselves a farm or had a business like Mr. Carter. There weren't too many of them.

The nursery burst with so many of us children, I never thought nothin' about having no daddy. But now I did. I'd had one all along. Right here in this house. And he was white. I thought back on how me and Momma used to visit with Mr. Winters pretty near every evening, sitting in the parlor, the veranda, or his library. That was my favorite, on that big rug he had in front of the fire or next to an open window come summer. I played with little wooden blocks, brought my dolls down. Momma and Mr.—well, Daddy, I reckon—would talk and laugh. More often he'd smoke his pipe and read by the oil lamp while she sewed or mended clothes, a quiet, companionable silence punctuated by the sizzle of pine tar from a log on the fire or children's voices down by the cabins or the low, distant hoot of an owl.

He used to hold me on his lap before they sent me off to bed and read to me from those big books, show me drawings and such. Then it had died down. Momma and him still got together of an evening, but I was off with my friends, like as not, running around the cabins, playing games, or sitting out watching the stars or the bats hunting mosquitoes.

Why hadn't she ever told me the truth? I stared at my face, the color of fine-ground wheat bread. Not walnut like Momma's or coal-black like Ellie. Hazel eyes. Not the pale blue of Mr. Winters, but not sparrow-brown like Momma's neither. At least five children I knew had eyes like mine. Did that mean they was all Mr. Winters's children? That weren't hardly likely. I never seen him down by the cabins at night, and nobody talked bad about him like they did some white men at other plantations. I used to think they was just treatin' the women bad, like white folks do to coloreds. Lately I'd been realizing it meant something else, something that made my stomach turn a hot pit of shame and my shoulders hunch over. White men had a special kind of torture for us. I felt like a dunce. I knew other children had white daddies, but it ain't never occurred to me that I did.

But Momma liked Mr. Winters. Leastwise, it seemed that way to me. She weren't afraid of him. Heck, I'd just seen her almost hit him, and he hadn't raised a hand to her. If we was at Miss Grayson's place, Momma would be dragged off and tied to the whipping post. Might never see the light of day again. Momma and Mr. Winters still spent lots of evenings together. She told him about the house, what they needed. Even told her how the crops was doin' and what George said. She was careful with him, though. Didn't tell him the whole story most of the time. But they seemed friendly enough, at least as friendly as anyone could be with a white man.

I wondered if she stayed in his room. My eyes went wide thinking of them—you know.

The door opened.

"Whatchu doing in here?" Momma asked.

I froze like a rabbit caught up against a fence.

Momma's eyes narrowed. "What's wrong with you?"

"Nothin.'" I scrambled up from the dresser seat and ran out of the room.

"You better not be messin' with my pearl necklace," Momma hollered after me.

A couple days passed before Miss Grayson came to give me more lessons. Mr. Winters—I still couldn't call him Daddy, even in my mind. He was still Mr. Winters to me, the owner of, if not us, then at least this plantation. We worked for him. Our lives was in his hands. Anyway, Mr. Winters sat at his desk, same as usual, greeted me with a big smile, same as usual, but I avoided his pale blue eyes. I tucked my head, walked over to the table by the window, and sat down.

"Good morning, Pearl." Miss Grayson had already arrived. She was wearing herself a red dress, this one with buttons all down the front and a big poof in the back. She couldn't hardly sit on her chair. She squirmed sideways, then forgot and sat back. A loud crunch came from her bustle.

"Blast," she whispered, then looked up at me right quick to see if I'd heard.

I stared down at my Bible to hide my smile.

She snapped her fan in irritation. "You're looking pleased with yourself, Pearl. Let's find a challenge for you today." She picked up the Bible and started leafing through it fast, almost tearing those thin pages, the tip of her tongue caught between those little pink lips I'd come to despise. I made fun of her, mimed her white lady ways to my friends, but now I was half-white. I glanced over at Mr. Winters and gave myself a little shake. I was the same as I'd always been.

Miss Grayson hadn't noticed my distraction. A look of triumph lit her face. "This one. See if you can figure this one out, you little monkey." She said this low, so Mr. Winters couldn't hear.

"Yes, ma'am," was all I said in answer. I'd show her.

Miss Grayson walked over to the fireplace. Her bustle stuck out lopsided now, making her look like she had half a behind. A hot delight filled my heart, wicked and satisfying. Mr. Winters looked up from his desk and kinda started. He glanced over at me to see if I'd noticed, and we shared a guilty smile. I forgave him that very minute. We were conspirators again, in league against the Miss Graysons of the world that wanted to beat the fun out of their maids, who approved of their men hunting down people like George and Mick, who ain't never done her a lick of harm, who wanted to replace my momma, I realized with a jolt. Ain't Mr. Winters said he might have to marry her? I made up my mind then and there I'd learn everything this crazy woman knew so Mr. Winters could tell her good-bye and send her back to her own house and never come back.

I turned my eye to the passage, filled with begots—whatever that meant—and a whole string of hard names. I wrote slow and careful like, checking each letter in each word before I moved on. Mr. Winters sat at his desk, his pen scratching across sheets of white paper that I yearned to try out. The clock ticked in the corner. The cat slept on a high shelf. Miss Grayson sat staring at the little fire, looking lost.

"I finished, Miss." I carried my slate over to her, but she hardly gave it a glance. Kept looking over at Mr. Winters. I waited a minute, shifting my weight from one foot to the other, then finally asked, "I got it all right, didn't I, Miss?"

Her high pink forehead wrinkled in irritation. She looked back at the slate, her eyes sharp as a robin looking for a worm. I stood next to her, the fire slowly heating my right side. She tried hard, but couldn't find any fault. But then her lips curled up in a mean smile. She pointed at the very last word. "You didn't finish the sentence, Pearl. You haven't learned about sentences yet."

I stood straighter, a trickle of sweat running down my side under my good dress. "I ran out of room, ma'am."

"You should space your words better. Plan ahead." She straightened her spine, prim and proper.

I raised my voice just a touch and said, "Maybe I'm ready to use Mr. Winters's paper. Maybe I done learned everything you know."

Both their heads came up at that. Miss Grayson raised her hand to strike me, her face flushing red as the coals at the bottom of the fireplace.

I took a step back, knocking against the fire irons.

Mr. Winters jumped up so fast his chair made a loud scrape and the cat dove from her perch, brushing a lamp on her way out the door. It wobbled, then righted itself.

"That will be all for today, Pearl." His voice froze Miss Grayson's hand. "Go to your room. I'll deal with you later."

I hightailed it for the door, following in the cat's wake. Didn't hang around to listen neither.

I ran to my room and took off my good dress, hands shaking so much I gave up on the buttons. At least they was big buttons. Not like that . . . I couldn't think of a good word for her. Maybe one of those the field hand had screamed when he dropped a sledgehammer on his foot. I laughed at the thought, calling her one of those names to her face. She'd pop all her pretty little buttons.

3

Time passed, and Miss Grayson's visits grew fewer. Momma seemed relieved and nervous all at the same time. But I was a child and didn't pay it no never mind. Childhood can be an ocean of time, golden, eternal moments of monarch butterflies flitting in summer fields, their orange wings etched in black like those stained-glass windows I saw once when Mr. Winters took Momma and me with him on a trip. We played hide-and-seek during evenings lit by fireflies and that river of light above, the Milky Way. The aching back of autumn harvest leaving us piles of squash, pumpkins, ears of colored corn. The cold snap of frost of a winter morning, breathing out a cloud, the icicles hanging off the gutters. Once Tim froze his tongue to one. Then the sweet surprise of snowdrops in early spring. Those first robins and the cardinals, all red and proud.

One winter evening stands out like an island in that childhood ocean. Snow fell all day, muffling ordinary sounds, wrapping us up in a magical world like the globe Mr. Winters had in his library. After supper, the snow stopped and a sickle moon lit the white fields. We finished scrubbin' down the kitchen, then grabbed feed sacks from the barn, and when those ran out, I snuck out old sheets with holes that Momma had stacked up in the sewing room. "Just in case we need 'em," she always said. We took all this down near the lake where there was a good hill.

Old Joe made up a fire, and everyone gathered around it, holding out their hands to warm them, laughing when one of the boys pushed too hard and ended up sliding all the way into the lake. The thin ice wouldn't hold a dragonfly if there was any around in this weather. Old Joe threw out a rope and they pulled themselves in, stripped off their wet clothes, and got wrapped in horse blankets, standing next to the fire so as not to catch their deaths, as Momma said. We all swam in the river in summer every chance we got, so I'd already seen everything there was to see. Folks lived on top of each other anyway.

Mick come running down from the stables, shirt flying out behind him. He slid on a patch of ice, and Old Joe grabbed him. "Jenny, come quick. We got us another runner."

Momma hesitated, so Mick said, "This one's 'fraid of menfolk. Screams every time I come near her. Looks tore up sumpin awful."

Momma looked around for Betty, who knew some healing. Found her jumping up from a log near the fire.

"I'll go get my things," Betty called over her shoulder. "Meet you in the barn."

This time Momma gestured for me to follow. I stood wide-eyed, thinkin' I'd seen wrong.

"Come on, now. We'll need you to heat water and such for us. Don't dawdle."

Momma took off across the field, and I had to run hard to keep up with her. I followed Momma down the aisle of the barn, stopping to pet Duke's soft nose. "Come on," Momma said.

Mick had the woman stowed in a back stall, fresh straw laid out in big pillows of gold. A hurricane lamp flickered on a stool just outside the open door. Whimpering come from a dark corner. Momma stepped inside, and the woman commenced to screaming.

Momma held out her hand. "Be quiet, now. We don't want nobody to know where you are, do we?" The woman quieted, so Momma took another step forward. She opened her mouth and screamed again.

I stuck my head around to see her better, and she turned her face to me. She was buck naked. Dark blood smeared the insides of her thighs, and her breasts was scratched and bleeding. Her face was swoll up like a ripe tomato, one eye closed and crusted over, the other desperate, pleading. That eye latched onto me like I was the last hope she had in the whole wide world.

Momma stepped back, and the woman took to whimpering again. Momma took another step back, and the woman stretched out her arm to me. "My baby," she mumbled. "My baby's alive."

"Go to her," Momma whispered.

A terrible dread weighted my feet to the ground, heavy as those irons Mick used to hammer out horseshoes, but Momma patted my shoulder. "It'll be all right. I'm right here. Go on, now."

I took a step forward, and the woman reached out both arms, one bent at a sickening angle. "Baby," she whimpered, even though I was ten years old by this time. She grabbed me and pulled me into her lap, wrapped her good arm around me, and commenced to wailing all over again. "You's alive," she sobbed out.

Her chest was thin, her collarbone almost sharp against my cheek where she'd pulled my head down, but I didn't dare move. I half lay, stiff as an iron rod, trying not to breathe in the scent of sweat and blood and worse. A deep gush of relief rose off her when I put my head on her shoulder. She patted my arm. "You's alive."

Betty crept up to one side and started murmuring to her, crooning a spiritual as she dipped a rag into hot water and started washing away the blood. She cleaned her face, using the woman's tears to help loosen the crust at her eye, clucking at the cuts on her cheek. "We gonna have to stich that one," she whispered to Momma, who hovered at the door, keeping an eye on the woman and me.

Betty cleaned her neck, then tore a fresh rag and started to wash the skin around me, slowly pushing the rag down between me and the woman's body until she loosened her grasp. I got my legs under me and pushed away, but the woman's eyes flew open, and she grabbed me against her again. That woman was strong for somebody so beat up.

"Slow and easy," Betty murmured, "just like Mick do with the horses that's been hurt."

Betty kept cleaning around me, and soon enough the woman gave out a long moan and laid back in the straw. I rolled off her. Then, when she kept her eyes closed, I scooched up and leaned against the wall of the stall, watching Betty wash and sing.

"Mick, get me some of that salve with the honey, purple coneflower, and marigold."

"Right away."

The woman's eyes flew open at his big voice, even at a whisper. She opened her mouth to yell, but Betty started singing again. With her eyes, she asked me to join in. I took up the tune.

"Swing low, sweet chariot." My voice shook.

"Jenny," Betty said, her voice running beneath my singing like a crosscurrent in a river, "see if you can get Mr. Winters to give us some strong spirits or even that medicine he keep for emergencies like this. I'm a-feared her arm's broke."

The woman didn't react to this. She seemed beyond words, beyond meaning, like a wounded animal, jerking up when there was sudden movement or a male voice. Shucks, Mick wouldn't hurt a fly.

I just kept singing.

"You all right?" Momma asked.

I nodded.

"Be right back."

Betty turned the woman on her side, her good arm beneath her, and cleaned off her nether regions just like she was a baby. She'd shit herself a few times, and some was dried and crusted, but Betty didn't act like it bothered her. She tore more rags, gently spread the woman's legs. The woman came up crying, pushing at Betty, but she was weak now. "It's all right. I ain't gonna hurt you. No more'n I have to." She mumbled this last part.

Betty cleaned and shook her head. "Mm, mm, mm. She tore up bad."

I didn't look. I couldn't. Instead, I sang. I run all the way through the verses I knew of "Chariot" and started on the next song that sprung to mind. Mick returned with a jar of salve and handed it to Betty without saying a word. She screwed off the lid and dipped her fingers in the golden gel. She spread some on the woman's breasts, the scent of honey and flowers replacing some of the rancid waste. Betty bundled up the rags full of blood and shit, wrapped them in a sheet, and handed them to Mick. "We should burn these."

I wondered if it was for sanitary purposes or to hide the evidence. Prob'ly both. Momma came back with a basket. She lifted out a jar of broth, a clean cotton shift, and a brown bottle of medicine. I gasped when she pulled out the next bottle. She'd done stole Mr. Winters's best brandy.

Momma fixed me with a look. "She needs it more than he does."

"Yes, ma'am."

Betty handed Mick a bucket and asked him to fill it for her. She followed him outside, and I heard water sloshing out on the ground. She came back, her hands dripping but clean. She dried them on another rag she hadn't used yet, then took the liquor bottle and pulled a glass from the basket. She poured a good bit of brandy into it, then added two pinches of the white powder and stirred it up good with a spoon.

"Lift her head up, Jenny."

Momma moved behind the woman, slow and quiet, then put her hands under her shoulders and pulled her up. She struggled a little, now lanky and weak as a newborn foal, but finally fell back against Momma's chest. Momma cradled her like a child. Then, when she settled, tipped her head back. Betty put the glass to her swollen lip. "Drink it all up. It'll take all the pain away."

The woman looked around desperately for me. I moved in front of her face. She saw me and then drank, wincing at first when the brandy touched the cuts on her lip, never taking her eyes off me. Soon the medicine took effect, and she fell back on Momma, asleep.

"Mick," Betty called out. "Let's set this arm."

He walked into the stall, his bulk taking up all the space.

"Maggie, you can go on out. You don't have to see this part."

I retreated down to Duke's stall, peering into the gloom. His snuffle reached me through the dark. Weight shifted, then he stuck his face over the half-door, searching my hands for treats. I opened the door to his stall and leaned against his solid mass, hot tears surprising me. He stood still for me.

A screech of hot agony erupted from down the aisle of the barn.

"I got it," Momma said.

"Hold her, Mick."

The woman cursed, words I'd never heard before, then her stream cut off.

"Good. Let's finish while she's out," Betty said.

I huddled closer to Duke, who turned his head around and tucked me to his shoulder. My shivering stopped, and after a while, Mick found me there. "It's all over now. She passed out from the pain, which is a blessing. We got her arm set, and Betty's stitching up a few cuts. We'll keep watch over her."

Momma appeared behind him. "Come on, now. Let's go get you cleaned up."

I followed her up to the house, meek and subdued. When we reached the kitchen, Momma got a bowl of hot water from the pan Nellie kept on the woodstove. I went back outside, stripped off my soiled clothes, and washed myself down, the cold winning out over the heat of the water. I ran back in, and Momma handed me a flannel nightgown, which I pulled over my head. "Let's get in the bed. Best you sleep with me so you can stay warm."

I cuddled up to her like a much younger child. "What happened to her?"

"Some men got ahold of her, that's what happened." Momma rocked me a little. "Looked like they'd had her for a while. Some of them bruises was old, and she had cuts that was half-healed."

I shivered.

Momma tightened her hold on me. "I know. I know. But we got her now."

"Why she think I was her baby?"

"Don't know. She's not in her right mind now. Might never come back to it."

"What happened to her baby?" I thought the child must be a girl since she'd mistaken me for her. I tried not to imagine her caught by these same men, all tore up or layin' dead somewhere in a ditch like a possum somebody shot.

"We'll try to find out. Now hush up and go to sleep."

I must have dropped off quick 'cause next thing I knew Betty was whispering to Momma. I squinted at the window. The sky outside was lightening up, pink streaks faint behind the lace curtains.

"She woke up crying for her baby," Betty said. "I can't get her to settle. She done tore out a few stitches."

Momma frowned, then studied me.

"You want me to go?" I was already swinging my legs out from the warm cover.

"I's got to see to breakfast and the cleaners," Momma said.

"I'll go," I said.

"Mick'll be there," Momma said. "Now all you got to do is sit with her. Let her think you's her child. Just soothe her down like Mick taught you. If we can get some more of that medicine into her, she'll go off to sleep. Soon as she does, you two come back and get you some breakfast."

I pulled on my work dress quick in the cold, followed Betty down the hallway, and pulled on some old boots from the pile of shoes by the back door. Cook handed Betty a basket, and we hurried down to the stables.

Mick carried an old feed sack around, and the horses was up, stomping their big hooves and bobbing their heads, pushing up against their stall doors. Mick dipped an old can into the sack and gave Duke his morning oats. Quiet munching descended in Mick's wake.

He pointed. "She in there. You call me if'n you get scared, now, you hear?"

"Yes, sir."

Betty stood by the stall, hands on her hips, the basket by her feet. She opened the half-door and stood back. I crept in, searching the gloom for the woman.

She started up from the corner. "My baby," she said, her voice rough and scratchy. The yearning just about tore my heart out. She reached out her good arm to me.

"Go on, now. She won't hurt you," Betty murmured.

They'd bandaged up her broken arm and tied it to her side so's she couldn't move it much. I crept to her good arm, and she grabbed me to her, tears leaking outta her puffy eyes. I hummed a little tune, something I sang to soothe the babies as was teething or missing they mommas bad.

"My baby," she kept saying, patting my arm. Then she settled back, quiet.

"Let's get some broth into her." Betty unscrewed the lid of a mason jar of broth, and the warm aroma of chicken and a touch of sage filled the stall. The woman's head turned to the smell. Betty held it up to her mouth, and she drank, her eyes unfocused like infants do when they sucking a bottle. She drank the whole thing down.

Betty mixed more white powder into a little bit of brandy and held it under the woman's mouth. She jerked her head back. "It'll soothe the pain," Betty whispered.

A flicker of understanding passed over her face. She drank, sputtering a bit, then sat back, her dull eyes watching me.

"What's that powder?" I asked Betty.

"Poppy," Betty said. "Mr. Winters call it opium or something like that."

"Like them orange flowers?"

Betty shook her head, her eyes still on her patient. "He say they different."

The woman watched us, her eyes drooping.

"What's your name?" Betty asked, but she didn't answer. Soon enough her eyes closed and she slept.

"I got to restitch her wound there," Betty said. "You go fetch me some hot water from Ellie."

I hesitated.

"Go on. She'll sleep now."

I ran back to the kitchen, slipping on an ice patch near the back door, but I didn't fall. The windows was all steamed up from Ellie's cooking, and three women were helping her, stirring this, kneading that.

"Whatchu need, Maggie?"

"Betty needs some hot water."

"How's that woman doing?"

"Looks bad."

Ellie shook her head, muttering something about white trash. I glanced over my shoulder, but Mr. Winters never came back here. He kept to his library mostly, reading, answering letters. Ellie poured water into a bucket, took a clean cloth from the stack by the sink, and handed it to me. "Wait, take this here." She handed me a sliver of lye soap. "You's a good girl," Ellie said.

She surprised me. Something warm filled my chest, replacing the cold dread I felt.

I helped Betty fix u p h er s titches, t rying n ot t o w ince myself when the needle went through the woman's soft flesh. She'd twitch a little with each prick, but didn't wake up. Betty bandaged her with the clean cloth I'd brought. "You's doing good, Maggie."

"Thank you."

"Now go get youself some breakfast, then come on down here about midmornin'. She'll be wake again by then. We'll see if she can talk some sense."

She was awake when I got back to the barn, both eyes open now that her face was healing a bit. But both those eyes followed my every move, and when Betty asked her any questions, all she'd do was start to whimper and reach for me. All week she was like that, and Momma sat me down and explained that it was the right thing to do for me to help her. "She still think you her child, and that's the only comfort she got in this world right now." So I spent most of my time in the stables with her.

I'd sit by her and hum gospel songs. We had to feed her like a baby, Betty or even Momma bringing down a plate and feeding her one bite at a time from a big spoon. She sat, her eyes looking out at something only she could see, opening her mouth when we coaxed her, chewing automatically, swallowing, sometimes opening her mouth again for the next bite, sometimes only responding when we touched the spoon to her lips.

When she'd had enough, she'd rock herself, curl up in a little ball, and lay down in the straw Mick kept clean for her. She could tolerate Mick's presence now, didn't jump when he talked. When she slept, which was most of the time to tell the truth, I followed Mick around. I didn't realize at the time he was healing me as much as I was helping the woman.

"They found her baby yet?" I kept asking.

He'd shake his big head slow like. "Nobody's heard nothin'. We's asking around."

"You think they'll find her?"

Mick studied me a minute. His brown eyes looked as sad as the bloodhound's after he'd been out all night huntin' runaways. "Most likely she dead."

That's what I thought, too. If those men had treated a child as bad as they'd treated her mother, they'd have killed her for sure. "Why they so mean, Mick?" I asked for the hundredth time.

And every time he'd answer the same. "Some people's been taught we nothing better than animals. That we they property they can do with as they like."

I'd reach to pet a horse's soft nose or scratch a cat's ear, if they'd let me, and say, "But why they want to hurt an animal?" I couldn't. I even hated killing the chickens.

"You good. You ain't got that meanness and anger in you."

"What they so mad about?"

He'd shake his head. "I don't know, Maggie. I can't figure it. Got the devil in 'em, I reckon. Leastwise, that's what Reverend Terry would say."

One morning Betty came down to feed the woman lunch, and after she ate, she laid down and stuck her thumb in her mouth just like a baby. Surprised the dickens out of me. I tried to pull her hand away like Momma did when a child was too old to be doin' that, but she started thrashing around, so I left it.

Betty just shook her head. "I sure hope she comes back to herself," she said. "Can't take care of no invalid forever."

I waited until the woman settled again, then wandered out looking for Mick. He was taking a break in a patch of winter sun, a piece of straw stuck in his mouth, his eyes closed. I picked a good spot beside him. After a while, I asked, "Why she act like a baby? She's a grown woman."

"What she do?"

"Sucking on her thumb," I said.

Mick grunted to let me know he'd heard me and sat on for so long you'd have thought he'd forgot about my question, but that was Mick's way. He never done nothing fast. Moved slow and deliberate around the horses and white people.

"I seen it afore." He took the piece of straw out of his mouth and pointed at the yellow tomcat laying beside us. "See how the tip of his tail is wet and a little bald?"

"Uh-huh," I said.

"He sucks on it."

I laughed. "Why he do that?"

"Got took away from his momma too soon. Still needed to suckle, so he pulls on the tip of his tail. It comforts him. He's going on six now and ain't never grew out of it."

"Think he will?"

"Prob'ly not. Saw a grown man who'd been beat as bad as that woman back there. He did the same as she. Turned back into a baby for a while."

"Why?"

"It's a way folks and animals has of healin' theyselves. Rememberin' the comfort of bein' a baby, being rocked and nursed, bein' loved. They go back to it till they can face the world again."

"Did that man ever do that? Face the world again?"

"Yeah, he did." Mick stretched out his leg and started rubbin' his knee where a mule had kicked him last summer. "Took him a while. Think he was ashamed when he came to hisself, so he was quiet for near on a week afore he talked to us. Told his story. Then Mr. Winters gave him a job, and he's fine now."

"He still here?"

Mick looked down on me for a minute. "He still here, but you wouldn't want me telling tales on you, would you?"

I shifted around, disappointed.

"Well, would you?"

"I reckon not."

"That's a good girl."

People kept sayin' that to me, but to tell you the truth, this whole thing was wearing on me.

4

That Sunday, all us from Salem Spring prayed for her at our church, a white clapboard cabin that used to be slave quarters on an abandoned plantation. The house had burned down during the war. The family moved to Georgia and nobody ever came back to claim it, so we didn't have to worry 'bout usin' it. Joseph saved a real painting of Mary at the tomb from the old mansion, and we had a cross made by Thomas down by Kernersville. Reverend Terry preached on the miracle of Lazarus, and I figured healin' this woman would be a lot easier for Jesus than that. I sure hoped he'd get on with it, then I felt bad and prayed for forgiveness.

The choir took off singing and we all started shouting and clapping. June got the spirit and talked in tongues for near on twenty minutes. We finished up with another prayer for us all, then the men moved the pews to the side, brought out long planks, and set them on sawhorses. The women went out to the wagons of folks as had come from farther away or fetched they baskets if they'd walked. They brought in tablecloths, some checkered red, some old and stained white, some just old sheets with a couple of holes in them, and spread them over the rough boards. Then they carried in the food, pride filling they faces, the men sniffing and saying, "That sure smells good, Mrs. Jones." She made the best fried chicken in the county. It was 'bout time 'cause it was well past midday, and my stomach was grumbling.

I grabbed a leg and a thigh before Momma spied me, some of Ellie's potato salad, collards, and ran back to where I sat with my friends every Sunday we could come. Momma made us all take turns coming to church. Said somebody had to feed Mr. Winters after he went to his service at the Episcopal Church, which lasted only an hour. I ain't never been there on a Sunday, but I had stopped in once when I was out with him. They had some fine stained-glass windows, all royal blue and scarlet, gold and emerald, showing Christ talking to the disciples or performing miracles. We only had rough glass in our church windows.

I settled in and filled my mouth with Mrs. Jones's fried chicken.

"Up and left in the middle of the night," Daisy was saying.

"Who?" I asked around the chicken in my mouth.

"The Browns. The white folks down on their place done lost they minds."

"White folks is crazy," Faith said.

We all stiffened and looked around, then laughed, realizing where we was. Weren't no white people within earshot.

"What they doing?" I asked.

"Beat Mr. Brown till he couldn't stand up. And for nothing," Daisy said.

"I hear they're fixin' to put us in our place," I said. I'd heard it from Mick when he come back from blacksmithin' one day.

Faith snorted. "They always saying that."

We turned our attention to cleaning our plates so we could get seconds before the food ran out. We jumped up as a group and crowded around the tables in the middle, shoveling more chicken, collards, corn, and potato salad on our plates, all the while eyeing the chocolate cake.

"You leave that cake alone," Momma said from out of nowhere.

"Leave some chicken for the reverend," a woman beside her hollered. "Them children act like nobody never feed 'em."

We ran back with our bounty and dove in. It could be a long afternoon. Some folks would stay all day, singing, reading the good book, Reverend Terry preaching another sermon.

Daisy took a few bites, then went on acting like the town crier. "Charlise is missin'. Them boys had her down in some shack. Got away a few nights ago."

"Who?" I asked.

"She came a few years ago. I hated laying there at night listening to her suffer."

I shivered. "They had her for all that time?"

"Nah, just a couple of months. Her baby—"

"You know where her baby is?" I blurted out.

Daisy studied my face. "Y'all got somebody down at the Winters's place?"

"I don't know nothin' about it," I said and pretended one of my shoelaces had come undone.

"You do, don't you?" Daisy said.

"What you girls talking about?" Momma's voice shut Daisy up fast.

"Nothin'," everybody said at once.

"What you say about a baby, Daisy?"

She hunched her shoulders. "Sammy Lee done took hisself a woman down to the shack."

"I see," Momma said. Reverend Terry had joined her and stood by her side. We all put our plates down, folded our hands in our laps, and looked up at them.

"This woman got a name?" Momma asked, her voice gentler now.

"Charlise," Daisy whispered.

"That's a good girl, Daisy. And the child?" Momma coaxed.

"Sammy Lee busted its head against the cabin wall. Say it cried too much."

Tears filled Momma's eyes, and Reverend Terry closed his eyes and started a prayer. "Lord, help these children, so young. They's seen so much sin. So much hurt. Lord, help this child who's passed on come to you. It was innocent."

Two big tears ran down his face, and I shut my eyes, unnerved to see this rock of a man moved like this. Reverend Terry went on for a while, praying for all of us by name, for our community, for the baby, for Charlise, even Sammy Lee, which made Daisy squirm. We all kept our eyes closed until he said, "Amen," which took a while. He studied us all one by one after he finished. "I reckon I don't have to tell you girls how dangerous this is, now do I?"

We all shook our heads.

"I would hate to have to preach a funeral for any of you."

I hugged my legs to me. A tear ran down Daisy's face.

"All right, then. Let's talk to your mommas. Make sure everybody understands." He went to get them.

Momma knelt down in front of Daisy. "I appreciate the information, sweetheart. Now never say nothin' about it again."

"Yes, ma'am," she said, subdued.

Momma wiped Daisy's face with her apron and kissed her cheek.

After our mommas was all told and they fussed at us about not talkin' to anybody, even colored folks, we took up our plates and pushed our food around some. I didn't want no chocolate cake after all.

We left church after that, packing up our food, Momma sayin' her good-byes. It took near on another half hour. Us girls went out back to a tall maple where somebody'd hung a swing and took turns pushing each other up high toward the branches. Soon we was laughin' again, daring each other to go higher, to grab for a leaf. Faith near about fell out and broke her neck, but she hung on. We'd mostly forgotten about Charlise until Momma came to get me. That heaviness came down on me again, making my feet drag shallow runnels in the red dust of the road on the way back home.

Next morning, I was up before the sun, even before Momma, so I cleaned up and dressed myself, then headed down to the kitchen to take breakfast down to the barn. Ellie was up, as always. Come to think on it now, seemed like she never slept. She gave me a good bowl of grits, which I ate up, then filled another one for the woman, and I carried it down through grass stiff with frost, my breath clouding in front of me. A full moon sat on the horizon, waiting for the sun to say hello from the east before it sank down to bed. The bowl kept my hands warm.

I could smell coffee from Mick's room, so I went on down to the woman's stall and opened it up. She was sitting bolt upright, staring at me, scared to death. I stopped in my tracks.

"Where am I?" she asked, clutching her blanket up around her chest with her one good arm. "What it this place?"

I didn't know what to say. Didn't know if I should tell her Mr. Winters's name in case it got out she'd been here, so I just said, "We been taking care of you, ma'am. You was hurt when you run here."

"I ran here?" She looked around at the boards of the stall and the straw.

"We'd have put you in the house, ma'am, 'cept we didn't want nobody finding you."

Her eyes flew wide, so I held out the bowl of grits to distract her. "I brung you breakfast."

It took her a minute to calm herself. Then she asked, "What's your name?"

"Maggie."

"Well, thank you, Maggie." She took the bowl, looked at her left arm still tied to her side, then settled the bowl awkwardly in the nest of blankets and started to feed herself.

I backed up a step, and she looked at me, spoon halfway to her mouth. "I'm gonna go get my momma."

She smiled at me, and it near about broke my heart. I walked a few steps up the aisle of the barn, the horses reaching out to me with their noses, looking for breakfast, too, then I broke into a run.

I found Momma and Betty in the kitchen eating. "She's awake."

"Whatchu mean, awake?" Betty asked, but Momma had already pushed her plate of grits and eggs back and was standing up.

We walked back, Betty and Momma listening to me tell what had happened. "She didn't treat you like her child?"

"No, asked my name and was polite and all."

"Well, Lord bless us, maybe she's gonna be all right."

Mick carried a big bucket of oats down the aisle, filling each horse's feed box. The ones waiting shook their heads and moved around their stalls, restless.

"She's awake," I whispered to Mick as I passed.

He frowned at me, then his head snapped up in surprise when he realized what I meant.

Momma and Betty stood at the door of her stall and introduced themselves like she ain't never met them. I snuck up behind them and peeked at her. She looked like some gentry receiving guests in her parlor, nodding her head at each of them. Or Mother Mary in the stable. "My name's Charlise. I apologize, but I don't recall how I got here."

"Mick found you. You were hurt," Momma said. "Betty here stitched you up and the two of them set your arm."

"How you feelin'?" Betty asked.

Charlise stretched out her legs and winced. "My ribs hurt some." She started to stand, and Betty settled her now empty bowl in the straw, pulled down the old shirt she'd dressed her in, and helped her to her feet. Charlise took a tentative step, her face wrinkling up a bit when she put her weight on her left ankle. "I can walk okay."

"Let's get you up to the house and give you a proper bath," Momma said. "We'll find a bed."

"This your girl?" Charlise pushed her chin out to indicate me.

"That there's Maggie. She's my daughter," Momma said all soft like.

"She's a good girl. Brung me my breakfast."

Mick had snuck up behind us, and we all waited to see if she'd reach out for me like she'd done before or call me baby. She didn't, though. She just looked at me for a minute, her forehead wrinkled in confusion, then she shook herself like she was waking up completely from some dream and nodded at me when she walked by.

She never did say nothing 'bout her lost baby again. Momma let her heal another week or so, then found some light work for her to do. She grew stronger and settled in nice. Come spring I came into the kitchen one morning and she was peeling potatoes with Ellie and the other girls, laughing, her head flung back, her eyes sparkling. It was a miracle to see.

She never could remember how she got to our place. Didn't seem to remember what had happened before that. And we didn't press. I asked Mick about it one day while I was watching him tend to the hooves of the horses. He looked up at me, sweat dripping off his face in the growing warmth of the season. "Sometimes forgettin' is for the best, Maggie."

5

S pring came, then summer, just like it always do, and Charlise became a member of our big family. We was close to harvest time,
and Salem Spring buzzed with anticipation. I'd gone from taking
lessons to helping Daddy with the ledgers and reading the business
letters that come in. I'd grown used to thinking of him as my father,
although I never called him that to his face. I finished up checking his
numbers and put everything back. Daddy said he had some business
to attend to.

I changed into a patched work dress, then went out in search
of Mick, but the barn was empty of humans. The horses drowsed in
their stalls, nosing at hay or sleeping, their big lips drooping down,
one hoof cocked. Mick must be away shoeing horses or something.
All my friends was out in the back fields picking tobacco. We'd hired
in extra help. "Lucky to get 'em this time of year," George had said.
Soon we'd be wrapping twine around the leaves and hanging them in
the shed to cure, the whole place filling up with that musky scent.

I could go pick tobacco, hide out in the woods, or go to the
kitchen and help fix lunch. A cardinal at the top of an evergreen sang
full throated and joyful, tempting me to go hide beneath my favorite
oak near the stream, but I knew if I did that Momma would give me
a sore behind for not helpin' out. She'd argued with Daddy about
me going to the library this morning already. Said she needed me.
Cookin' was easier than field work, so I trudged off to Ellie's domain,
where steam rose from six pots and three girls was shucking corn. Ellie just pointed to a pile of green beans near the corn, and I moved
toward it.

"Wash them hands first," she said, pointing a wooden spoon at
me.

"Yes'm." I went out back and pumped the handle on the well, enjoying the cool water, throwing some on my face, then ambled back,

resisting the urge to scratch behind the old bloodhound's ears, who was stretched out in a patch of autumn sun. I settled down with the beans.

After feeding all the farm help, we ate a big meal in the kitchen, stuffing our faces with okra, corn, green beans, fresh sliced tomatoes, and fried chicken. I liked the gizzards. They crunched good when you bit into them. I tried to grab another biscuit, but Suzie slapped my hand as soon as I reached for one. Momma had Charlise serving Mr. Winters, hovering just outside the dining room, watching her every move to see if she'd be all right. She musta been doing fine 'cause Momma came and sat down with us, finishing up her plate.

We stretched out in the mild autumn sun to digest, the older women gossiping about Miss Grayson coming to call last week, which darkened Momma's eyes, so they switched off to the latest goods in Mr. Carter's store and new babies they daughters and cousins had, marital disputes and suchlike. Soon enough I was re-cruited to wash up, and we only got in about another half hour's gos-sip on the back stoop before we had to start cooking all over again for supper.

The next morning, the tobacco crew was one man short. The whole place buzzed about loud voices coming from near his little house at the end of Turner Street late last night. Loud voices and torches.

"It don't bode well," George said. "Go get Mick."

Ted took off running, and I started after him, but Momma called me back. She hugged me to her. "Lord, keep my baby safe. Keep all my children safe. All the menfolk." I peeked around her arms and saw the others had all joined in, eyes closed, whispering "Amen" and "Help us, Jesus," rockin' and swayin'. She finished up and let go of me.

Mick come as fast as his bad leg would let him. "What hap-pened?"

"Rufus is missing."

"Who?"

George explained it to him.

Mick shook his head, then stared at the ground for one whole minute. Everybody knew not to interrupt him. He looked up, more fire in his eyes than I'd ever seen. "Moses," he called.

The plantation had a long string of bloodhounds named Moses. The first was named by an overseer who said it was the dog's job to "bring my people home," or so Mick told me. That took me a while to figure out, but now the dogs was our friends. So's we just kept on naming the best puppy Moses.

The old bloodhound lifted his head, sniffed the air, then ran over to him. "George, you comin'?"

"Yeah."

He pointed to the workers standing around. "Pick a couple more."

George pointed to two big men, who moved over to stand by Mick. "You know where he lived?" Mick asked them.

I noticed he was talking like he weren't alive no more.

"Yes, sir."

"Let's go, then."

They moved off, Moses taking up the rear.

We all watched them go, then Momma said right snappy, "All right. We still got tobacco to pick."

The helpers followed our own men down into the fields.

"You get to the kitchen and help," she said.

"But, Momma—"

She popped me on the leg, not hard enough to hurt, though. "I ain't got time for your mouth, Maggie."

The kitchen turned out to be a good place to get news. All the household servants had been recruited to cook for the hired help. Lottie knew Rufus's family, so she told us about him, his wife, they five children. "He a good man. Hard worker. Goes to meetin' every Sunday."

Ellie shook her head, her sullen looks lit by a burning anger beneath. Charlise dropped a pan, then spilled some water.

"Charlise, honey," Ellie said.

Betty and I looked at each other, surprised by her soft tone. Usually she'd chop off somebody's head for making two mistakes in a row.

"I believe ain't nobody tending to Mr. Winters. Would you go check on his room? See if it been cleaned."

"Yes'm," Charlise said.

"After that, see if Simon need some help."

Usually Momma gave such orders, but we was grateful Ellie had thought of something to take Charlise's mind off what was happening. We all knew Suzie done cleaned up after Mr. Winters, but we took care of our own as best we could. After she left, Lottie told a couple more stories about growing up with Rufus nearby, playing in the creeks, catching fireflies, that kinda thing. Then silence fell for a time, me peeling potatoes, Gladolia cuttin' them up.

"Why they got to go after Rufus?" Lottie asked nobody in particular.

"Ain't make no kinda sense," Ellie said.

"Maybe he looked some white man in the eye," Betty said.

"Or didn't jump outta the way fast enough when Billy Grayson was walking down the street."

"I hate them Graysons," I mumbled.

"It ain't Christian to hate, Maggie," Suzie said.

Ellie blew out her breath loud enough for us all to hear.

"Could be they was after one of his daughters and he kept her safe," Lottie said.

I looked around before I remembered Charlise had left.

"You reckon?" Betty asked.

"Ain't no rhyme or reason to the meanness of some white folk," Ellie said. She was unusually talkative today, which made me wonder what had happened to her in the past. I eyed her face and arms for scars but only saw little stars and other burn marks that come from cookin'. I couldn't see her back, though. And some injuries don't leave no visible marks.

After a while, Betty started humming her favorite spiritual, and we all took it up. Soon the kitchen was filled with voices in harmony, the clatter of pots and pans, and the wholesome smell of fresh bread rising.

We was getting' ready to carry pots outside to serve the workers when Moses come running into the yard and plopped down in his spot. Mick, George, and the two men he'd picked to help him walked up, their faces stern, eyes hooded.

"Oh no." Lottie wrung her hands in her apron.

The men stood together, and finally George told us the news. "We found him back in the woods hanging from an old maple tree."

"Oh, Lord." Lottie shook her head, tears flowing down her plump cheeks.

Momma grabbed me and started to push me out of the kitchen.

"Leave the child be, Jenny," Mick said.

Momma stiffened.

"She's old enough to hear. Needs to know what happens so she'll be careful."

George shook his head. "We carried him home. His wife was right grateful to us for cuttin' him down. Said Billy Grayson had talked to Rufus on his way home from here yesterday. Billy was right mad he weren't workin' for his family this year. Said Mr. Winters takin' everything from his family."

The women muttered and leaned against each other for comfort. Ellie stood alone, stiff and unyielding, her dark hands clenching into fists.

"Went by Reverend Terry's and told him. He's gone on over to be with the family. Funeral day after tomorrow."

"We'll all go," Momma said.

And that was that. We went back to work.

Momma weren't gonna let me go to the funeral, but Mick spoke up again, sayin' as how I was almost grown. He let me sit by him in church. I was sheltered by him, a big, solid block of a man, his big hand raising up to wipe away a tear every so often. He didn't sing no hymns, just tapped his foot some. He didn't let me go up front to view the body, though. For that, I was grateful. I could see from halfway down the aisle Rufus's face was all swoll up, his lips purple. A big red welt run all around his neck. It made my stomach churn. I was relieved when Reverend Terry closed the lid.

Some menfolk stood outside all around the church keepin' watch. You never knew what them Graysons might get up to. Or any of them white men for that matter. Except Daddy and a couple of others who was decent. At least most of the time. I saw one man under a tree holdin' a rifle. I was right glad of it.

I worked in the kitchen for the next few days, then went out and helped sew tobacco leaves together. Soon the sheds was all full of tobacco hanging from the rafters. I loved walking through the dim as the leaves turned from bright green to oak brown, smelling the musk that gathered in the back of my throat and almost turned to a cough. George talked about this being a good crop and how we'd make out fine in the fall auctions.

"Can I go this year, George?" I asked.

He laughed. "Ain't no place for womenfolk."

"But I want to hear them talk fast." Tim had come home last year and mimicked the auctioneer, crowding his words together in such a blur we couldn't make heads or tails out of it, throwing his arms around. "I-got-ten-I-got-ten-do-I-hear-fifteen? Ten-going-once.

Twice. Fifteen. Fifteen-from-the-gentleman-in-the-bowler-hat-do-I-hear-twenty?" Something like that. I tried to say it for George.

He just laughed and shook his head. "Naw, you got to stay home and study."

I sat down abruptly on a wooden crate.

"You seen that Miss Grayson lately?" he asked.

"I hate the Graysons."

"Now you know what Suzie say about hatin' people."

I hunched my shoulders. "She only comes by to see Mr. Winters now. Sometimes we read together." I wrinkled my nose. "She likes Shakespeare. Read something called *The Taming of the Shrew*."

"Shrew?"

"Like some mean woman. But in the play she falls in love with the man and gets all sweet." I made a face.

"I reckon she got her bonnet set toward him."

"Momma ain't gonna like it."

George studied me a long moment.

I watched dust float in the air, my stomach queasy from the thought of Miss Grayson being in the house all the time.

"Mr. Winters ain't gonna like it neither," George said softly.

I looked up at him fast. "I know," I said.

He gave me another long look, then patted my shoulder. "I was wonderin' when you'd figure it out."

"I heard," I said, "that night when you all was out on the veranda talkin' about helping folks out with rifles and such."

"I see." George rubbed his hands together, the calluses showing gray on his gnarled fingers, the nails rough. "You know, Mr. Winters cares about your momma—in his own way. As much as he can, least-wise. Of all the white men around, he's the best."

"I reckon."

"He loves you, too."

I nodded, hot tears surprising me. "Why he got to get married, then?"

George sat down beside me. "I reckon to keep folks settled down. He ain't got nobody to inherit. We got the best fields in the county. It's a rich plantation."

"Only white folks can own it?" I asked, but I already knew.

"That's right. And Mr. Winters can't spend all that much time with the colored before people will start doin' something about it."

I blew out my breath like old Duke did sometimes.

"He's trying to do his best by you. Teachin' you to read and write. Do you numbers. So's you can make your way in the world and not spend it cleaning somebody's house and takin' care of other people's children."

A tear escaped, and I rubbed it away so he wouldn't see, but he did.

"You'll be all right. You got spunk."

I smiled to show him I'd try.

When Suzie ironed out the newspaper in the mornings to get it all crisp and snappy for Mr. Winters, she kept lookin' for his picture on the society page where the white folks printed they gossip. She took to making me read it all to see if there was an announcement, but to our surprise, nothing came out. It sure were taking him a long time to ask Miss Grayson for her hand, as they put it. It had been near on two years. But we were in for a bigger surprise that next week.

The Virginia branch of the Winters showed up.

6

They sent they servants on ahead. Six of 'em. They was a tight-lipped bunch, heads down, eyes on they shoes. One of 'em limped pretty bad, and another had a wound had festered so much it stank. Momma sent him to Betty right off. They answered questions with yes'm or no ma'am. When we asked anything about the family, they just said, "I couldn't rightly say, ma'am." Looked like these Virginia Winters was hard on they coloreds.

We was sitting at dinner out in the servants' room just off the kitchen. Charlise was taking care of Mr. Winters right regular now. I reckoned Momma was punishing him for all this talk about marryin' by not waitin' on him her own self, but Charlise was doing pretty good. Learnin' the right manners and which fork went where. I never could figure why white people needed so many different forks and spoons and knives to eat with. Just made more work washing up, is what I thought. But ain't nobody asking me my opinion.

Ellie brought in another platter of her buttermilk fried chicken, and I reached for a thigh. Momma slapped my hand away and took the platter from Ellie. "Anybody want some more chicken?"

"I do," I said.

She ignored me. "Our Ellie makes some of the finest chicken in the Carolinas."

One older man shot his eyes at the platter and started to speak, then put his head back down.

"Jedidiah, you want some more?" Momma didn't wait on an answer. She plopped a big breast down in front of him. His eyes near about popped out of his head. Momma walked around the table, serving each of the Virginia coloreds a big second helping. Then she gave me a wing. Little bitty thing. She sat back down and asked, "What is Mrs. Winters like?"

"I couldn't rightly say, ma'am."

"Oh, come on, now. Help us out. How we s'posed to make her happy if we don't know nothing 'bout her? What she like to eat?"

"She likes her beef rare. Likes roasted beets and potatoes," Ruth ventured.

"Now, see, that's helpful."

Naomi leaned in conspiratorially. "She like my lemon meringue pie."

Momma smiled big. "We'll just have to get you to make some."

They loosened up a little under Momma's ministrations, but she didn't have enough time to finish the job. The Winters was due in two days, and they was bringing company. There was the main family, Mr. Winters, who was our Mr. Winters's cousin, his wife, daughter, and son, plus another lady who was friends with the daughter and her aunt, who was to chaperone. Weren't enough to have two other adults to watch out for her, it seemed. Plus they was all bringing maids and valets and such. Looked like the house was gonna be full to the rafters.

Momma 'bout bust a gut ordering everybody around. We had to pull out all the furniture, beat all the rugs, wash all the linens, get them ironed, dust each room, and polish up the fixtures. The list went on and on, it seemed. Ellie ordered extra food, talking 'bout how we didn't have enough chickens and complaining she'd have to slaughter a bull she'd hoped to keep through winter. Mick opened up a whole section of the barn he usually kept empty. I went down to visit. He stood in the middle of a stall throwing straw around, sneezing and sweating even in the cool weather. Even Moses moved from the middle of the yard where he liked to lay and took off for a corner in the woods where nobody'd bother him.

Momma brought out the old black uniforms for us all to wear while the Winters was in town. They was simple house dresses, really, but made from fine cotton. We dressed 'em up with white collars and wore white aprons over them. We'd need a whole pile of aprons to stay clean all day. She set a girl to sewing more.

"We want to look like a real fine house," Momma said.

Readings with Miss Grayson was canceled. Momma told Mr. Winters she needed everybody to work, and hadn't he said I needed to learn her housekeeping skills as much as the three *R*s?

"I believe Pearl has made enough progress to be dismissed for a while," he said, his nose in his newspaper. They was being all cold and formal with each other on account of him havin' to marry. She turned her back, and he dropped the paper, watching her stiff back as she walked out of the library. I followed, but at the door, I shot him a sympathetic look. He looked startled. What he think? I couldn't figure nothin' out?

I celebrated my release with a slice of apple pie Ellie give me when I told her we'd dispensed with Miss Grayson. I was exaggerating, but I figured I could pretend. Ellie had herself a slice, too, and topped both of them with some cream she'd whipped up for dinner. Neither of us told Momma.

Around dawn the next morning, a road wagon pulled into the drive leading to the barn, and a swarm of servants piled off. Momma sent Suzie to get them assigned to cabins and offer them breakfast. Just past lunch, the Virginia Winters arrived in a four-wheeled brougham pulled by a team of perfectly matched grays that made Mick salivate. A smaller version of the same carriage pulled by big, gleaming bays came in right behind them. The Virginia servants in regular work clothes started to unpack the trunks and boxes so quick I hardly had time to see them from my perch in one of the front bedrooms upstairs. Gladolia and me was so busy oohing and aahing over their luggage we almost missed it when Jedidiah and Joshua, dressed in tails and shirts so white they hurt my eyes to look at, moved in perfect choreography to open the doors, put out a block for the ladies to disembark, and bowed down until their noses almost touched their knees.

Gladolia grabbed my arm when a hat with purple and peacock-blue feathers appeared at the carriage door followed by a body covered in purple brocade. Jedidiah reached out his white-gloved hand, and the woman grasped it and pulled herself out, stepping down to the dusty drive and looking around imperiously. A tall reed of a man followed wearing a bowler hat and tweeds. A little boy jumped out dressed in a sailor's suit. He ran around to the horses, almost spooking them. Mick had to grab ahold of one to settle 'em. "Easy now," Mick said to the boy.

"Don't tell me what to do, nigger." He said it loud enough everybody heard, but nobody did nothin'. 'Cept Mick, who straightened up and turned into a stone statue.

An older girl climbed out, dressed in the same purple as her mother, minus the hat, and stood by her parents, copying their stance by sticking her nose up in the air.

The next carriage disgorged a big fat lady, her body covered in forest-green brocade so stiff she looked just like a sofa, her wide-brim hat just about knockin' Joshua in the face. This must be the aunt.

Next, an elegant white buckled boot with a little heel appeared on the block, revealing just a glimpse of slender ankle afore it got covered again. Then a white glove reached out to take Joshua's white glove, and a young lady unfolded from the carriage dressed in dusty-rose silk trimmed in cream lace. Her hat was a reasonable size but smothered in pink and cream roses. She straightened and put her frilly parasol down like a cane, then looked around like she was adding up the value of the place in her head.

Our Mr. Winters stepped forward and greeted his cousin first. I couldn't hear what they was saying from where I sat. They didn't yell like that nasty little boy, whose food I planned to spit in. The two shook hands—awful formal for family, but you know white people—then he greeted the lady. He leaned over, his lower half not moving but bent forward like the letter K and pecked her on one cheek, then the other. She kissed the air next to his cheek. I swear.

Then the cousin introduced the two ladies, and Mr. Winters kissed the green glove of the old lady. The younger lady straightened up even more, if it was possible, and posed while she was being introduced. Mr. Winters leaned down and kissed her hand through the glove and said something that made her tilt her head and smile.

"Shall we go in?" he asked loud enough for me to hear. The others all started toward the house, and I'll be if that little hussy didn't take my daddy's arm and get herself escorted inside. My stomach knotted up, but then she outclassed Miss Grayson by a mile. Maybe she'd be better.

Gladolia and I sprinted to the top of the stairway, scrunching up against the wall to avoid everybody hauling up trunks, leather suitcases, and hat boxes all piled up so's you couldn't see the person's face, and watched the white folks all come in. I pushed down a step until Daddy caught me gaping and shot me a look that made me jump back and hide behind Gladolia, who tried to get behind me again.

"Welcome to Salem Spring," Simon intoned. He stood in the entryway, ramrod straight, gloved hands folded in front of him, looking just over their heads. "Would the ladies prefer to freshen up before tea is served in the parlor?"

"Where's Ruth?" Mrs. Winters asked, her voice peevish.

"Here, ma'am."

"Take me to my room. I simply must lie down. The Carolina roads are not well kept. Not like Virginia."

"Yes, ma'am."

"Is there hot water?"

"Yes, ma'am." Ruth picked up her mistress's small bag from Jedidiah and started up the stairs.

"Freddy. Lucille. Come along now." I reckoned these was the children's names. "We'll find your rooms," Mrs. Winters called.

Ruth reached the top of the stairs, where me and Gladolia stood gaping. "You best get outta here," she hissed.

We took off down the hall and ran down the servants' stairs, ending up near Momma's room. Weren't nobody free enough to find us and put us to work, so Gladolia grabbed some clean towels so we'd look like we was doing something, and we carried them with us. We spent a couple of hours snooping at doors and listening from the nooks and crannies I knew about. We didn't learn much 'cept the Virginia Winters was more full of themselves than the Graysons would ever be. They barked out orders to their coloreds, and while we was hiding behind the grandfather clock at the top of the stairs near Mrs. Winters's room, we heard the sound of a slap ring out. Pretty soon Ruth come out, her face red with a hand print.

"Whatchu doin' here?" she whispered.

"You all right?" I asked, reaching up to touch her cheek.

She pulled my hand away. "It's just how white folks is. Now you git afore worse happens to you."

She looked at the towels we carried, all in knots by now. "Take those down to the laundry."

"Yes, ma'am," we both said.

Momma found us on the way. "I been lookin' all over for you. Get cleaned up and ready to serve tea." Then she noticed Gladolia. "You go help Ellie. Lord knows we got enough to do around here without you two up to the Lord knows what. Now scat."

Suzie served tea in the parlor that Mr. Winters kept locked up most of the time. "No need to keep it open just for me," he'd said. It looked out on the formal rose garden backed by large magnolia trees. Weren't much to see this time of year, though, 'cept for the maples, oaks, and sweet gums bordering the woods, all red and rust in the sunlight. The gardener had planted a couple of them Japanese trees called gingkos with leaves like fans that were the first to turn bright yellow in the fall.

Ellie handed me a tray of German wedding cookies sprinkled with powdered sugar. "Walk slow and act like you got some dignity. You representin' our house." She grabbed the tray. "Don't tilt it like that. You drop one of them cookies, I'll take it out of your hide."

I knew she wouldn't, but I said, "Yes, ma'am," just the same.

Simon lectured me before I went in. "Don't look anybody in the eye. Don't speak unless asked a direct question. Keep your answer short and polite. Always call them ma'am or sir. Serve from the left. Don't hover. Circulate. When your tray is empty, go back to the kitchen."

"Yes, sir," I said.

Simon frowned his doubt. "When you come up to somebody, give a little curtsey. Try it."

I dipped down, and Ellie squealed 'cause my tray tilted and the cookies started to slide.

Simon grabbed it. "Better leave that part out."

"Yes, sir."

This time he snorted but pushed me inside.

Mrs. Winters had ensconced herself on the blue silk sofa with the new lady next to her. Mrs. Winters wore bright orange satin and the other one a magenta brocade with a lighter red silk shawl. Both had they skirts all spread out for us to see. The clash made my eyes water. I offered cookies to the ladies first, but the two brats came up and took half the tray. I walked up to Mrs. Winters, who pursed her lips, then took four of them, the greedy thing. There wouldn't be any left for me. The young lady didn't even look at me, so I went over to the two Mr. Winters standing by the mantel sipping from their cups.

My Mr. Winters reached down and took two cookies. "Why, thank you, Pearl." The buzz of low conversation in the room paused, and all eyes turned to me. I flushed all dusky red, and, realizing his mistake, he asked in a sonorous voice, "Frederick, you're closer to DC. What do you hear about the new territories we've gained from Spain in the Caribbean?"

I stared at the tray. Mr. Frederick Winters grabbed up all six of the remaining cookies, and I almost let out a sigh of relief. I headed for the door but made the mistake of turning around and looking when I reached it. Mrs. Winters and that high-nosed lady was both staring at me. The young one snapped out her silk fan and leaned over to Mrs. Winters and commenced to whispering. Mrs. Winters's eyes narrowed, still looking at me. The lady straightened up and fluttered her fan, her attention on my daddy. I got to the kitchen as fast as I could.

Momma was right behind me. "I swear, that man ain't got the sense God give a donkey."

"What he say?" Ellie asked.

"Drew too much attention to Maggie, that's what."

"Oh, Lord. Want me to keep her here?"

"Naw, they'd notice."

Ellie filled my plate with jam cookies next, raspberry and strawberry. I reached a finger out to touch one and got it slapped.

"Go serve to that big aunt. Then the children. Stay away from the men. I'll take care of them," Momma said.

I reckoned she would, too, once she got him alone. Daddy—now there was two Mr. Winters, so it was easier to think of him that way—ignored me for the rest of the tea serving like he was supposed to, and I started to relax. I stood near the fireplace, right up next to the window near the curtains, and tried to blend in. The men talked about Teddy Roosevelt and how he was buildin' some canal down south in Panama. I wondered if it was as far as Georgia. Then they talked about the governor of Virginia, who turned out to be a distant relation. I'd pretty much forgotten about my tray, although I held it out straight as the top of the letter T, but figured I could stay 'cause I still had some cookies on it.

"Now see here, Henry," Frederick said. My ears perked up. "Rosalie comes from a fine family, the Jacksons."

"Stonewall Jackson?"

"He was an uncle. This branch of the family had a passel of daughters, and she's close to the youngest. Their lands are still producing quite a bit, and the one son is involved in politics. Might be a senator someday. You could help him there."

Mr. Winters looked over at the young lady. So her name was Rosalie, and she was here to marry my daddy. I knew it. I glanced around for Momma but didn't see her.

"I suppose so," Daddy said, not sounding very enthusiastic. "I'm quite a bit older than she is."

"Evelyn was a dear woman, and we all were sorry for your loss, but you've been unmarried for too long now given your holdings. It was a tragedy about Henry Junior, of course." He paused, maybe out of respect. "Spend a little time with the lady. Get to know her."

"I'll take her for a stroll," Daddy said. Sounded like he was talking 'bout a horse.

"The cotton and tobacco families don't have any daughters?" Mr. Frederick asked.

"They look down their noses at me."

"Have you given them reason?"

"I married into the German settlers. I guess that was enough for them."

Mr. Frederick sniffed. "Still too lenient with the colored."

I glanced up and found him looking at me. I walked over to the children, my back firmly to the men, and offered the children the rest of my cookies. The little boy hit my tray, and the jam cookies flew off, some landing upside down on the carpet.

"You stupid nigger," the little boy shouted. "Look what you did."

I started picking up cookies, hot tears burning my eyes.

"Aren't you going to apologize?" He stood next to me, little fists clenched.

"Freddy," his mother said mildly, "come over here and let the nigger clean up her mess."

Momma appeared with a damp cloth. She put her hand on my arm. Gratitude surged through me. She wiped up the jam from the rug, put it on the tray, and stood. "Go on and take that to the kitchen," she said, her tone firm for the benefit of the white folks. I was glad the boy wasn't related to that Rosalie, but I was still dreamin' up my revenge.

Momma appeared in the kitchen soon after I'd told Ellie all about that little brat and how I was gonna spit in his soup.

"Mm, mm, mm." Ellie just shook her head. "I knowed it was too good to last. Now some real white people done showed up."

"I hate him," I said.

"Now don't you be ruining my soup neither. Like to get me whupped."

"But—"

Momma came rushing in. "Looks like they finishing up."

"He hit the tray, I swear," I started, but Momma shushed me.

"I know. I saw."

"I'm gonna get him back."

"You'll do no such thing," Momma said. "Less'n you want one of them white people to beat you."

I looked from Momma to Ellie. They both nodded.

"Time you get outta the house for a while. Go change clothes and then see if Mick can help you cool that hot head of yours."

I opened my mouth to protest, but Momma cut me off. "Looks like Maggie's done been spoiled by Mr. Winters. He's the easiest-going white man there is."

"Uh-huh," Ellie said. "I'll just be glad when they's gone."

"They ain't goin' nowhere," I said, my chest burning with the news.

"Whatchu mean?" Ellie asked.

"They brought that woman down here for Da—Mr. Winters to marry."

"What woman?" Ellie asked.

"That Rosalie—the young one in the second carriage."

"Why you say that?" Momma asked.

"Mr. Frederick said so—" I glanced at Ellie, then just blurted out "—to Daddy."

A big clatter came from the sink, where Ellie had carried over some dishes.

I ignored it. "Said she come from a fine family and it was high time he had someone to inherit."

Momma's face flushed the color of the apples in the orchard this time of year. Her eyes took on a gleam like the fire in the heart of the woodstove. After a minute, she unclenched her hands. "Go get changed. You can go see Mick or—wherever." She flapped her hands in the air. "Just be back to help serve dinner."

"I'm sorry, Momma."

"A new woman in the house will change the way we're treated," was all she said.

Turned out Momma wouldn't let me help in the dining room. She made me watch from the edge of the service entrance. I scrunched up there, hidden from view but able to watch the ballet as each course was carried from the kitchen to opposite sides of the table. After a moment's hesitation to gather the eyes of the diners, the silver lids were lifted in synchrony, then the trays carried around to each person, starting with the older ladies, then the young one, and finally the two men facing each other at the ends of that long, gleaming table. The nasty little brat and his sister were already in the nursery being put to bed by two beleaguered servants. I knew 'cause I'd heard the boy bossing Charlise around. He'd better be careful. She might haul off and belt him given her past, but when I listened at the door, she sounded calm as Mick with a scared horse.

Momma came to stand beside me when she could, talking all about which direction to serve from, how the people standing against the wall was to fill the glasses with water, then different types of wine depending on what they was eating. Which utensil they'd use with what food. How to clear and when. It made my head hurt.

"Why they got to—"

"Hush, keep your voice down."

"But—"

Her fingers pinched my upper arm.

"Momma—"

She pinched harder. I didn't say a word for a whole minute, so she whispered. "Best you know all this just in case."

I wanted to know just in case what, but I was afraid to open my mouth.

"In case this schooling idea don't work out and you have to fall back on serving in a big house," she said, like she could read my mind.

First they had oysters, then some kind of soup. Next came the fish course, then the fowl, and then beef and vegetables. Lord help me, you coulda fed the whole town for a week on just this one meal, and they weren't done yet. Ellie made something called a *chaud-froid*. She lit up like a church window over it, proud as could be, but it looked nasty to me. I wouldn't have eaten it even if they paid me a whole dollar, but those white folks gobbled it up like it was chocolate cake, which came last, by the way. But this was no ordinary chocolate cake. It had five layers, each one smaller than the other, and was decorated all over with purple and blue flowers made from frosting. Then they dolloped fresh cream on each slice. I swayed from side to side waiting for our turn.

Once the meal was cleared, my Mr. Winters stood up and announced he and his cousin would retire to the library for cigars and port. Mrs. Jackson took Miss Rosalie's hand, and they went to the front parlor along with Mrs. Winters. I don't reckon they smoked any cigars, but they did have sherry. Too sweet, is what I say. I stole a taste behind Momma's back while we was setting it up before they came in.

What they called the ladies' maids had eaten the same time as they white folks, so Momma let me go in the next shift. I ain't afraid to say I stuffed myself on that fresh trout and steak, potatoes cut up all fine, what Ellie called French string beans, but I saved room for cake. It tasted just like her ordinary chocolate cake, which is really fine, don't get me wrong, but it was almost too pretty to eat. I was so full I could hardly keep my eyes open, so Momma took pity on me and let me go on up to bed. Ellie was still ordering everybody around, telling them how to clean up, letting some of the men take food out to the cabins. She'd have to be up again way before dawn. Looked like she wouldn't get a wink of sleep. I didn't envy her one bit.

The next day, the weather turned warm like it do in November sometime, and Miss Rosalie took it into her head to have a picnic by the lake, which for her meant just getting dressed and sashaying down there. But for us it meant finding the right utensils, the right plates, tablecloths that looked "country," as she said, laying out tables, packing up all the food, and hauling it all down there, then standing around acting like our toes wasn't gettin' cold.

She did her sashaying with her arm tucked in Daddy's arm, her little head cocked up, laughing at his jokes, looking at what he pointed out on the plantation. She sat next to him at lunch and let him help her with her plate. Then they took a stroll along the garden path and into the woods, hidden from view. The two visiting cousins gave each other a significant look.

"Looks like our plans have worked out," Mrs. Jackson said.

A big horsefly landed right on her forehead, and I had to bite my cheek hard to stop from laughing.

After they ate, we had to drag everything back up to the house and barn. Once we'd done that, Momma told me to go up and help the maids clean the bedrooms.

"I'm tired. When do I get to study? I ain't done no writing in a whole week."

"Child, you don't know nothing about working."

"I ain't seen Mick or Duke in ages."

Momma let me sit out back with her for a minute.

"I'm tired of working day and night."

Momma just laughed at me. She told me this was how life was back in slave times when the white people had to be catered to night and day and the field hands had to sow and plant and weed and harvest while the owners of the plantations said they did all the work.

"The house was full in those days, Maggie, full of folks to help."

"Sounds hard."

She tsked at me. "You children is spoiled nowadays. Don't know how to work anymore."

I didn't answer back. She'd gotten hard on me arguing with her. Said these new white folks would smack me around if I opened my mouth to them. Then she started to reminisce. "Our Mrs. Winters was a grand lady. Refined, always soft-spoken and kind. If anybody needed discipline, she handed us over to the overseer. She couldn't stand to watch any whipping."

"But she let you get whipped?"

Momma looked flustered. "You got to keep some order. Nobody wanted that Bobby Joe to get ahold of them, so we all behaved."

I grunted.

Momma put her chin up in the air. "We had it all right. She was a fine lady. Too bad she died."

"How old was you when she died?"

"Just a child."

"When did you and Mr. Winters—you know."

"Oh, it was about ten years later. After he came back home from Washington. I always thought he was such a good man. I couldn't believe he sent for me that night."

"You didn't have no choice?"

"You don't understand how it was back in those times."

"Not so different now."

"He was more headstrong in the early days. I thought because he was an important man that he'd treat me right." She brushed a tear away.

"Did he?"

"I suppose, but I've learned to handle him. Like to think I've mellowed him over the years."

"Do you love him?"

She shrugged. "He's like a job sometimes. Something I ain't got no choice about. I always thought it was better than taking to the road. Never had no man to go with me. But then he'll surprise me with a kindness. He loves you, you know. Always been proud."

"I think he loves you too, Momma."

She ruffled my hair but didn't say anything.

"How come he didn't marry nobody again?"

"I prayed for that the first couple of years, even though it might not have made any difference." Momma squared her shoulders. "Looks like that about to change."

7

After the Virginia Winters had been at Salem Spring for a couple of weeks, a whirlwind of dinner parties with the upper crust of our county started up, none of which included the Graysons, culminating in a ball in honor of the Jacksons, "who fought so hard for the Confederacy," it said in the invitations. I know. I had to write them.

"Now, Pearl, haven't you been telling your mother you miss your lessons?"

"Yes, sir."

"I could use your help. You can practice your penmanship."

I must have looked skeptical 'cause then he said the magic words. "I think you've advanced enough in your skills to use my fountain pen."

He made me practice with it on scrap paper until I had all the curlicues and flourishes just right. Then he gave me the fine paper that looked like a weave off Lottie's loom. If you held it up in front of a candle, you could see what he called a watermark. It was his family crest. Mine, too, I reckon. Looked like a shield with a knight's helmet above it. I sat for ten minutes, afraid to blot it.

He looked up from his newspaper where he sat by the fire. "You can do it, Pearl."

So I dipped his pen in the ink and started in, slow and careful. Took most of the afternoon. Momma popped in once and asked him when I'd be finished.

He looked at the invitations I'd inked and sanded, then piled neatly on one side of the desk. "She looks about half done."

"Henry, I could use her help. We don't have the staff we had in the old days."

"I need her, Jenny. You'll just have to make do."

Momma took a breath to answer him but changed her mind and turned to leave. She thought he was gettin' uppity these days what with the Winters visiting and how they treated us.

"Jenny," he called after her, his voice softer now. "I'm sorry it has to be this way. There's been talk, well, threats against Salem Spring. With no one to take it over. With the unrest and violence coming up again." His shrug was elegant.

He looked over at me and sat straighter in his chair. Took a deep breath like somebody about to leap into cold water. "I'm sorry you can't inherit, Pearl."

I jumped so hard I almost knocked over the ink well.

"Your momma told me you heard us talking. I love you more than I can say. I'll always do right by you."

A big tear plopped right down on the invitation I was writing. The ink ran, making a washed out circle. "I messed this one up," I said.

"Come here, child."

I ran to his arms, and he pulled me into his lap like he used to when I was little. "I'm so proud of you."

Momma put a hand on each of our shoulders, then leaned down and kissed him. Right there in front of me. "Rosalie's a little hard on us, Henry."

He grabbed her hand. "She's used to her mother's ways. I'll talk to her." He took a deep breath and squared his shoulders. "Better get those invitations finished."

So, like I say, after all them parties and dinners and such, Daddy had to travel up to her people's place in Virginia and do the same thing all over again with the upper crust of her county. It took a lot of cleaning and washing and ironing and packing, but finally I stood along the drive and watched as the carriages all pulled out. Mick was driving. Said he didn't hold with no strangers takin' care of his horses. The two teams had been in his stable long enough for him to claim them as his own.

Finally, we was on our own.

At first it was heaven. No mean little brat to torment me. No rushing around stringing beans, peeling potatoes, washing sheets, helping to serve. No meeting all those new people from town who looked through me like I was a windowpane, but who I studied real good.

I wandered out in the woods sometimes. The trees was bare now, and the owls came out early, hootin' from their perches. The barn felt empty, but I dropped in to help feed the horses every evening. Old Joe had a new boy helping out.

Daddy had made Momma promise that she'd make me work on my studies for at least an hour a day, so late mornings I had the run of his library. I had to show Momma some writing and figures every day, but she couldn't read it, so I'd copy out something quick, then do some figures from the shopping, adding and subtracting what George had already done. It kept her satisfied. I drug down books I'd longed to explore and read them next to the fire. I started on *Little Women,* then tried out *The Scarlet Letter,* but that one reminded me of the white preacher at the Baptist Church. I tried me some poetry—Mr. Wordsworth and Longfellow. More Shakespeare. It was slow going at first, but the Bible ain't easy, so I was able to make out the story. I coulda spent the whole day in there if Momma had let me, but she always made me help Ellie with dinner or Suzie with cleaning.

"Now's a good time to polish the silver. Done used every dish in the house. Plus there's new holes in the sheets. We've got to repair the curtains in the front parlor afore Miss Rosalie comes back home." Suzie had a new project every day it seemed like.

"You think her family will approve?"

Suzie snorted. "Of course they will. She'll be back here come spring. We want the house to look real fine for our new mistress."

"I hope she ain't mean like those other folks was."

"Mr. Winters will teach her our ways."

"Things'll be different, though."

"Things always change, Maggie. It's the way of the world."

Speaking of, near about Christmas, I came into my blood, and the women of the house had a little celebration for me.

"Now you can produce life," Momma said.

"You a woman now," Suzie added.

Charlise watched me from the back of the kitchen. "You be careful, you hear?"

"Yes, ma'am. I sure will." She hesitated, about to say more, but I didn't want to hear no stories, so I said, "I know," and she left it.

They broke out some red wine from Mr. Winters's cellar, and I got to drink a small glass. Since there was no white folks to take care of, the women stayed celebrating for a good while, finishing off a few bottles. Momma said he never kept track of all of it and we might as well enjoy it while we could. They got downright tipsy and started telling stories regardless of whether I wanted to hear them or not.

"Lord, I used to have the worst cramps when I was your age. Tried to stay in bed, but that family I was with made me work all through it," Suzie told me.

"Cramps?"

"Child, you lucky. I hurt till I had my second baby." Nettie looked out the window at the bare branches tossing in the winter storm. "Wonder if he's still alive."

Momma patted her shoulder.

"I had three. All sold off," Flossie said. Momma had added her to the staff when we was so busy, and it looked like she was gonna stay.

"Uh-huh." The wine had loosened Ellie's tongue a bit.

"Two was like this one." Flossie pointed at me. "No offense. Mr. Winters is a sight better than that one was."

"What happened to your children, Flossie?" But Flossie just shook her head, started rocking in her seat, staring at the floor. Momma changed the subject right quick.

After a while, they got to talking about sex, which fascinated and terrified me.

"I was so scared my first time, but Jimmy was good to me. Took it slow."

"Wish my first time had been nice. Frank didn't care nothing 'bout how I felt. He just stuck it in and went to pumping."

"Now old Butch, he was a good man, uh-huh," Ellie said. "He knew how to use what God give him."

Everybody went off into peals of laughter, knocking each other on the shoulders, pounding on the table. My face flushed bright red like I was sittin' in front of a big fire. I'd never thought about Ellie having no man.

"Mick used to do pretty good hisself," Nettie said. "Afore his arthritis got so bad. His knees, you know."

For some reason, this made them laugh even more. I believe they'd done forgot I was there. For some reason, I didn't want to hear about Mick, so I snuck out.

Charlise joined me. "I don't want to talk about no mens neither."

I didn't blame her one bit. We wrapped up in some quilts and went outside once the storm passed off, sitting in the rocking chairs, staring at the stars. You know how they so clear and sharp after a good rain. We laughed about the Winters and they ways, wondered how Rosalie would treat us.

Charlise's head snapped up. "You hear that?"

"I didn't hear nothin'," I said. "Now when—"

"Shh." She stared out at the woods closest to the house. Leaned forward to listen. She got up outta the rocker and walked down the steps. An owl hooted and flew off on silent wings, its silhouette shadowing the round moon for a moment.

She wrapped her arms around herself. "I reckon it was just the bird."

For some reason, it give me the shivers. "Let's go back in."

Another week passed by in a sort of heaven with just us at the house. Christmas came and we put up a small little tree. Didn't decorate like we did when Mr. Winters was around. Had a good long service at our church. Visited with everybody. Folks was jealous we was on our own. I reckon word had got out.

The next week, we cleaned, mended, and sewed—worked hard, but at our own pace with nobody bossin' us around. We shook off the shadow of the Virginia Winters. We had ourselves a feast on New Year's Day. I started in on *Oliver Twist*. Seemed like some of them white people in England had it hard, too. Took down the world atlas and tried to imagine what other countries was like.

After dinner close to New Year's, the womenfolk gathered in the kitchen gossipin'. The men had gone off to the cabins. Charlise said they was probably gonna open up some moonshine and get snookered, whatever that meant. Only Simon was in the house.

That's when it happened.

A big crash came from the front porch. The front door bust open, and a bunch of men all dressed up in white sheets ran in. Everybody froze for a split second 'cept Charlise. She let out a scream that scraped the inside of my bones raw and ran out the back door.

"Where's that nigger bitch thinks she's better than my sister?" one of the white-sheeted men yelled out.

Must be Billy Grayson.

Momma grabbed a butter knife from the table. There was nothing sharp closer. She held it in front of her, trying to back away toward the door.

Billy lunged at her.

She swiped at him with the knife. Missed.

She danced behind the kitchen chairs.

Two other men knocked them over and grabbed her arms. Another one blocked the doorway, laughing.

Ellie snatched a big knife out of the dish drainer and buried it in the side of one of the men holding Momma.

He squealed like a pig being butchered. Blood spurted all over Ellie's clean tablecloth.

The man guarding the door pulled Ellie away and slugged her in the face. I heard a bone snap.

Momma pulled the hood off the man in front of her. It was John Miller. He owned one of the stores in town. He grabbed Momma and pulled her arms tight behind her. She looked at me, her face desperate, hopeless, like a cat hanging from the jaws of a mastiff. "Run," she mouthed.

I ducked under the arm of the man near the door and lit out the back door. But there was more of them outside. I ran toward the woods, thinkin' I could hide down in the hollow near the creek.

Poundin' footsteps followed me. "I'm gonna git you, little nigger. I'm gonna play with you all night long."

Fire burst in my belly, and somehow I ran faster. Just before I reached the first line of trees, he grabbed my arm and jerked me to the ground.

I kicked and screamed, hit and bit. All I could see was blue eyes, but then his hood come loose and I was staring at Leo Carlson. I snorted in surprise—a memory of him helping my mother with a bag of potatoes flashed through my mind in a split second. I got my legs up and pushed into his stomach. He grunted, but another man ran up. He grabbed my arms and pulled them above my head. Leo ripped my dress right off me.

"Think you're so high and mighty. We're gonna take you down a peg or two."

He fumbled with his pants, and I aimed a kick at his knee, but he stepped on my ankle. The bone let out a sickening pop. Anguish tore up my leg. I screamed.

Leo didn't pay that no mind. "Hold her," he screamed, but none other than Billy Grayson elbowed him aside. "This one's mine." He dropped on top of me, pulled my legs apart, and a sudden searing pain split me in half.

I bucked and squirmed as best I could, but Billy seemed to like that. The other man, this one younger, I could see from his eyes, half-ashamed, half-delighted, held me tight.

Billy thrust and grunted till I thought my insides would fall out. Then his face screwed up and he groaned and went slack.

He stood up and said to Leo, "Tie her hands so's you can have a turn."

I screamed, but they stuffed something in my mouth, tied my hands together, and staked me out on the ground, the rope pulling my broken ankle.

"Think you're too good for us, little Miss Winters? Huh?" He pulled my face to look at him. "Like I said, we're gonna play with you all night long." He kicked me in the ribs, and pain shot up my left side. I heard a roar and looked over my shoulder to see Salem Spring, my old home, burning bright against the moonless night.

After a while, I passed out from the agony, which is a mercy, I reckon. Musta been around dawn, I felt wet on my face, like water, different from before. It woke me up. I tried to open my eyes, but they was crusted shut. I recognized Charlise's voice.

"I'm here now, Miss Maggie. I'm gonna take care of you. Just like you took care of me."

I never saw my Momma again.

8

C aroline—1950s
My father always told me it snowed the morning I was born. Unusual for early November in the Carolinas. Maybe that's why the doctor never showed up. Mother said they kept calling her—the doctor, that is—and whoever answered the phone said the same thing each time. "She's out."

"Passed out is more like it," Mother said years later, twirling the end of her cigarette on the ashtray in front of her. "They pushed my legs together, then put me in a chair and one nurse sat in my lap to stop you from coming." She fixed me with her lake-blue eyes. "They hurt me so bad. Finally they gave me a shot to stop labor."

Years later, I tried to recapture the memory, squeezed down into the birth canal, waiting for the next contraction to shoot me out, lungs poised to take their first breath. And then—nothing. Everything ground to a halt, and me stuck there, head crushed against my right shoulder. So close to life, then barred just short of the door. Maybe I panicked in that tight, hot wet, poised between the water world, the steady drumbeat above me, the long rope of placenta filling me still with red, oxygen-rich blood with each beat, like the waves of an ocean. Poised there wondering if they'd changed their minds, decided they didn't want me after all.

It's too late now, I tried to tell them.

Then a sudden contraction of those walls, and I was pushed into the air world. The ragged first breath let out in a loud objection to gravity and lights and rough hands.

"Six hours," Mother said. "I lay there six hours before they gave up on that doctor. The first female obstetrician. You'd think she'd do right by other women, but your father signed for a new doctor, and they gave me another shot. When the nurse leaned over to lift me up, I grabbed at her shoulder but latched on to her dress instead and pulled it right off her. You should have seen her face, but I didn't mean to. I just hurt so bad I didn't know what I was doing."

Whenever my mother recited this story in front of Aunt Rose, my father's favorite sister, Rose's mouth would purse up at this last bit and she'd set her shoulders. When I was older, she finally voiced her disapproval. "Your mother is too dramatic. She shouldn't have done it."

"But she didn't mean to."

"I don't care. You just don't lose control of yourself like that. And you certainly don't brag about it."

This from the German side of the family. Caught up in the chaos that started with the Thirty Years' War and dragged on, my grandfather's ancestors fled Upper Alsace in 1727 and cut a farm from the Cherokee nation, then a small town with a green square surrounded by colonial houses a few blocks deep next to the brown water of Salem Creek, a stream big enough to be called a river out west, a creek that flooded regularly. Daddy used to drive me down the hill to see it, those iron-colored waters spreading over the streets, filling the parking lot of the local businesses. Our own little Nile.

I wasn't told many family stories from the early settlement days. Just shown pictures from subsequent generations, everyone stiff—the men dressed in starched white collars, the women in dark dresses with white lace collars, ramrod straight and no smiles. They must have been used to those old cameras, where you have to sit dead still or the image would come out blurred. There's another picture of my grandparents holding me on the couch, dressed in their Sunday best for my christening, black suit and starched white shirt on my grandfather, Swiss dot dress and brooch on my grandmother, poker faces with round wire-rims, and me, a confection of lace, blond curls, pink receiving blanket, and periwinkle eyes smiling at whoever held the camera.

That picture was taken at the house on Broad Street, a white clapboard two bedroom, my first home. I think it had green shutters and a front porch with rocking chairs painted to match. I loved those chairs. My first memory is of my pudgy toddler hands pushing on the screen door. It was always latched, but this time it opened. Delighted, I looked to see that mother was busy washing dishes in the kitchen, then I pushed open the door and climbed into one of those chairs. I rocked back and forth, harder and harder, in ecstatic abandon until the chair flipped back and flung me into the bushes. I screamed bloody murder.

Mother came flying and took me on her lap. "Stop crying. I need to know if you're hurt." She squeezed each arm and leg, gently poked me all over, asking, "Does this hurt?" I shook my head *no* each time. Satisfied, she held me close. "Now you can cry." And I did.

Next to those bushes I landed in was a sidewalk. I was lucky I didn't crack my head open. The sidewalk was lined with flowers. There's a picture of me inhaling them, face down in those white blossoms, bottom stuck up in the air, the bulky white diaper the face of some sudden strange species carrying on the theme of white. I remember this and my brother's rabbits, the intense delight of stroking soft white fur, the quivering bodies, pink noses, and liquid eyes. And the smell of hair spray and permanent solution from the beauty parlor next door where mother sat in an empty chair, smoked cigarettes, and gossiped in the afternoons while I learned to walk going back and forth between the outstretched arms of beauticians, all their hands ending in the lust-red fingernail polish of the early 1950s.

The nights cooled, and my brother started school again. Mother grew restless and talked my father into letting her go back to work. Weekdays, she went to sell children's clothes at a department store downtown and I went to my grandparents. They already took care of my cousin Tommy, Aunt Rose's youngest son, so my father had argued two kids would entertain each other and not be too hard on my grandmother. We visited often, so I knew the place. There's a picture of me in the arms of my older cousin, reaching for the chickens over the wire fence, white diaper bright beneath my darker dress, an intent look on my face.

Each morning Grandmother fed us toast and jam at the well-scrubbed wooden table tucked in the corner next to the potbellied black stove, as if our mothers hadn't fed us already. We munched our toast and watched her clean up the dishes, cut up vegetables for canning, whatever she was up to. Every time she added wood to the fire in the stove, I'd jump up out of my seat and run to her side, watch her reach for the silver coiled handle and pull open the round door where the glowing embers lay. She'd place the wood carefully inside, take up the long black poker and stir up the fire. Then she'd start making a meal and, soon enough, chase us out. "What are you children doing sitting indoors on a day like this?" And we'd run out to the dirt backyard pecked by the hens or play in the grass of the front yard, but never were we to venture past the boxed hedges where cars had replaced the sedate horse and buggies.

My father had been born in this house, and every one of his twelve brothers and sisters. For those blessed events, the children were shooed out of the house, and they'd cross the dirt road past the boxed hedge and sit on the triangle of land that Acadia Avenue curved to avoid. "We sat in a circle holding hands, waiting for the news," he told me. They'd speculate on whether they'd get a brother or a sister this time. Eleven children in all. Only one carried off by the flu epidemic in 1919. Daddy said they laid her on the ironing board in the living room because the undertaker had been too busy to come right away. The triangle still exists to this day, but the large farm and woodlands Granddaddy had inherited were sold off, parcel by parcel. Those couple acres were all he had left. That's why Daddy would always say his poppa worked in real estate, then laugh. I never figured out what that meant until much later.

Tommy and I had our regular routine. We played all morning, making up games, climbing the spreading evergreen in the corner of the front yard until Grandma came looking for us and made us climb down. "You kids need to play where I can see you," she said, so we watched Granddaddy in the fields behind the house.

Spring had come again, and he worked his couple acres himself. He was out there behind the mule, borrowed from somewhere because I don't remember that mule otherwise, who trudged along pulling the plow, turning the red soil over. The birds followed, madly pecking for worms. Granddaddy looped the long reins over one shoulder, encouraging the animal with clicks of the tongue and an occasional touch of the whip, hands on the worn wood of the plow. Every few rows, he stopped, bent over to catch his breath, and cursed. Reached in his back pocket and took out his big blue handkerchief. Wiped his face.

We wanted to pet the mule, of course, so when he stopped, we ventured out across the mounds of now moist, dark dirt. He waved us away from his fresh-turned rows.

"Please let us pet him," I said. Tommy stood beside me, hopeful.

"Oh, you want to pet him, do you? You want to help?"

I nodded eagerly.

"It ain't no fun, you know. Niggers won't even hire out to do it no more."

"I'll help." I thought following that mule around would be the best fun.

"You think you're strong enough, Missy?"

"I can do it." I was tall now.

"Come here, then." Granddaddy took off the harness that went around his shoulders and waist and lifted it over my head.

Grandmother flew out the back, screen door slamming like she told us never to do. "What are you doing with that child?"

"She said it looked like fun. I'll show her how much fun it is. Backbreaking work is what it is."

"John, she's too small." Grandma took a hold of my shoulder and dragged me away, protesting.

"You children go play in the front."

"Why is he mad?" I asked as we went around the side of the house. "Why can't we play with the mule?"

"'Cause he's got to do it himself." She gave me a gentle shove and steered Tommy toward the front yard. "No telling what he's liable to do when he's like this. Stay away from him."

Once he planted, he'd hoe between the rows, always fighting weeds, but again refused our help. "Y'all will trample my beans. Now git away from here."

Feeding the chickens was something we were allowed, and I considered it a regular entertainment. I took huge handfuls of grain out of the brown sack and threw them to the laughter of any adults who were present.

"Easy now," Granddaddy yelled. "We don't want them to get that fat."

I threw another big handful.

"That's too much. I can't afford for you to waste all that."

I tried to scoop it back up.

"Now you got dirt all in it."

I hid behind my grandmother but soon came back to watch the chickens. The birds, some golden, others reddish brown, ran to the grain, chased each other away with flutters of wings and outstretched necks, pecking at the heads of the smaller birds. This offended my childish sense of justice. I took pity on the smaller hens and threw them a few grains, but the queens of the yard would just run over and chase them away from the new food. Then the small ones would run back to the abandoned grain and the larger ones would come defend that. But the rooster ate first, to the approval of my grandfather. Then the bird stalked up and down, cocking his grand head, his red comb flopping back and forth, watching me with his beady eyes.

After lunch, Grandma put us in the tub together, where we floated boats, a grand fleet. What wars we had. After we'd soaked a good, long time, she came in, soaped each of us, and gave us a scrub, hard, too, leaving each complaining in turn. Then we stood while she scooped up water in a cup and rinsed us off, then dried us in her rough-edged towels. We'd put on our pajamas, then be sent to nap upstairs in one of the attic dormers. When we woke, we always found our clothes hanging clean and stiff on the line, waiting for the afternoon's adventures.

With the garden planted and the weeds controlled, Granddaddy took to wandering the house, ignoring all suggestions from Grandma that started with, "Why don't you—"

One day he was standing out in the hallway while we splashed. "Why don't you make them take separate baths?" we heard him say.

"It's easier for me if they're together, John. They entertain each other so I can wash up the dishes." Her soft voice barely reached us. "There's no harm in it."

"They're getting too old," he said.

We looked at each other, eyes round.

"A boy and a girl," Granddaddy said. "They'll figure it out soon enough."

Grandma's head popped in. Tommy looked up at her, and I took advantage of this lapse of attention to grab the new tugboat his mother had bought him. Grandma turned back around. "They're playing with their toys."

"It ain't right, I tell you."

Tommy and I ran our eyes over each other, searching for the source of the controversy. "What's he talking about?" I whispered.

"They're just innocent children," Grandma's voice continued in the hallway.

"Maybe it's this," Tommy said, pointing between his legs, but there were too many bubbles for me to see clearly.

"What?" I looked down between my own legs and shrugged.

"This, you don't have one." He picked up a small scrap of flesh. "See?"

"You see." Granddaddy's voice rose in triumph. "I told you."

Recognizing that voice, I grabbed a boat and tried to start a new game.

"Well, you don't," Tommy said, mysteriously offended.

"If you hadn't said anything, John," Grandma said.

"I don't want those kids taking a bath together anymore," he commanded.

We sent up a wail. Not take a bath together? But what about the boats? How could we live without our daily naval battles, where the blue boat rammed the red one? Or when we piled slivers of soap on the tug and hauled our load around the tub? Or the time I'd brought a dead sparrow in and staged a funeral? Grandma had screeched when she'd seen it—emptied the tub, refilled it, grumbling all the time about having to heat water, having to get more wood for the stove, and scrubbed us red that day.

"That's my final word," he said.

Grandma recognized that voice, too, because she just answered, "Whatever you say, John, but it's twice the work for me."

"Why aren't their mothers taking care of them is what I'd like to know," he grumbled, then the screen door slammed.

Grandma came in and scrubbed us, halfheartedly this time, then sent us upstairs for our nap in the steep-sloped attic room that my father had shared with all his brothers—long and narrow, the south wall wainscoted in dark pine, the top a faded floral wallpaper. Daddy said there'd been two double beds and two twins stuck in the various corners, most gone now to the children as they married. The boys slept in the one long room, the girls across the hallway in a smaller version of the same room. Grandma and Grandpa had a bedroom downstairs, and the eldest son took the other one across the hall. When he'd leave home, the next eldest would get it and so on.

Grandma had set up a fan in the long attic room, and we slept in the heat and humidity, hot and uncomfortable, but gradually lulled by the white noise and our exhaustion. Granddaddy took to looking in on us, jerking the door open and clomping to the side of the bed where he'd stand for a while, breathing heavy as a horse. Then he'd clomp back out, more like as not slamming the door shut, finishing the job of waking us up.

The next day started the new routine. Baths alone were boring. I floated a few boats, but they no longer held my interest. I yelled for Grandma to come wash me.

"In a minute. Just let me finish up in here," she yelled from the kitchen. Then she hit on a new strategy. "You're old enough to do it yourself."

As much as I protested Grandma's rough handling with her wash rag, doing it myself was no fun at all. I was to wash and tell her when I was finished, then she'd come for inspection. No matter how I tried, she was never satisfied with the area behind my ears. I hated that part. She'd hold my head in a vicelike grip at just the right angle for water to run into my ear. I would shake like a sheep dog, and she'd grip me tighter and scrub, leaving my ears red and ringing. Then I was sent to lie in bed and wait for Tommy to arrive, but by the time he did, I was already asleep.

Then one day Granddaddy issued another of his edicts. "Why are you letting those children sleep in the same bed?" he asked over a lunch of fresh-picked butter beans, corn, and sliced tomatoes.

Grandma heaved a sigh and put down the ear of corn she'd been working on with her small, even teeth. "Why in Sam Hill not?"

"You know," he said, giving us both a mysterious look from under his shaggy brows.

"John, for heaven's sake. All they do is sleep."

I snuck a look at Tommy across the table from me. He shrugged.

"Well, sooner or later they'll start exploring, and I won't have it, I tell you."

"John—" Grandma put both hands firmly on the table "—there is nothing to worry about."

But soon he got his way. Tommy stayed in the boys' room. Grandma had her special room where the girls used to sleep, now reduced to one double bed and a vanity table in the corner, so she put me in there. Really, really boring. Granddaddy came in a few times, just to see that we were not sneaking across the hall to play a little, I guess.

He stood up close to the bed and asked me to sit up. "Let's play a game," he said and unzipped his pants. He fumbled around and brought out some pale mushroom-looking appendage. "See, it gets bigger." He squinted up his eyes and rubbed his hand along it. "Want to try?"

I shook my head.

"Here."

Suddenly the thing was in my face.

"Come on. Let me put it in your mouth."

I shook my head no.

He pushed against my lips. "Come on. It won't hurt."

It smelled loamy, like his sweat. He seemed to really want to play, but I didn't like his game much. He pushed a little harder, and I opened my mouth. He pushed farther into my mouth, and I gagged. I pulled away.

"Oh, come on. Just a little longer." He seemed out of breath.

I shook my head again.

"For your granddaddy?"

I felt a twinge of guilt.

Grandma burst into the room and chased him downstairs. She came back to see if I was all right. Made me open my mouth to inspect. Satisfied, she told me to lie down again and settled on the other side of the bed. Then she took to napping with me. She said all that work wore her out.

One day, Grandmother sat in the low seat before the dressing table and pulled pins from her bun. Each one made a click when she dropped it into a small ceramic dish next to her. After she pulled the last one out, she gave her head a shake, and her hair fell in a rope down her back. She tilted her head and ran a brush through the river of silver.

I watched from the bed. Our eyes met in the mirror.

"You're supposed to be asleep," she said in a soft voice.

I closed my eyes for a minute, holding my small frame rigid in an imitation of slumber, then peeked again. Grandmother still sat in front of the mirror. She put the brush down, gathered her hair and twisted it like twine, then rolled it all into a bun and repeated the process in reverse. I pushed myself up to see better.

"Caroline."

I jerked my head back on the pillow and giggled.

"Can't sleep?" Grandma got up and walked over to the bed. "Do you want me to lie down with you?"

I nodded.

"Scoot over."

Grandma unlaced her shoes, toed them off, and stretched out on top of the covers. "Now close your eyes."

I cuddled up against her and must have drifted off because the creak of the door woke me. I didn't move. Grandma's weight shifted, then a sharp whisper, "What are you doing here?"

"I just came to see if she was asleep." Granddaddy's voice drifted over my head. I pressed my lips together.

"I told you to leave this child alone," she said in a low voice.

"I didn't—"

"I'll not have it."

"Woman," Granddaddy's voice rose, "don't take that tone with me."

"Careful, you'll wake her."

I lay perfectly still, almost holding my breath, desperately feigning sleep. The door slammed shut.

"Go back to sleep. I told you I'd be here."

Granddaddy stopped coming to visit me when I was napping, and soon Grandma's chores took her away as well. A week later, Granddaddy's steps outside the door woke me, but this time he opened Tommy's door. I heard muffled voices, then silence. I slept again. The next day, the same thing happened, and the next, but this time Grandma came up to my room, got me out of bed, and sat me in front of the vanity and started brushing my hair, hard, like when she scrubbed behind my ears.

"Ow," I complained, but she wasn't really paying attention to me. Her eyes kept straying to the closed door. "Grandma," I protested again.

Then I heard Tommy yell. His voice rose into a scream, like he had that time when he'd fallen out of the evergreen and really hurt his ankle. I tried to jump up, but Grandma pushed me back down in the chair.

"You stay right where you're sitting."

I stared, incredulous. "But, Grandma, Tommy's hurt."

"If you run in there, he'll do to you what he's doing to him."

My mouth flapped, wordless.

"You're a girl. It'll ruin you. Tommy will heal."

I stared at her in the mirror. She stood rigid, her hands clamped on my shoulders. Then the door burst open, and she grabbed the brush and started talking in this fake girly voice, primping my hair, spreading it over my shoulders. "See?" she said. "See how pretty?"

Then in a low voice pitched for my ears, "Play along."

I jerked my eyes back to my reflection but didn't really see. Granddaddy came up beside me, his breath rough, his stance challenging. Tommy's sobs filtered in from the open door.

"Isn't that nice, now?" Grandma picked up one of her ribbons at random and draped it over my shoulder. "It matches your eyes."

I giggled, right on the edge of hysteria.

"What are you doing?" Granddaddy asked, his voice harsh and defiant.

"I'm fixing Caroline's hair."

He looked down at me, and my eyes strayed to his face. Beneath the fall of my hair, Grandma's fingers on my neck pressed and pushed my face back around, away from Granddaddy's gaze.

"Look straight now. Do you like this ribbon?"

I nodded like one of those dolls with a spring head.

"What you got to say?" he asked her.

"We're doing girl things, aren't we?"

"It's so pretty, Grandma," I said, sick to my stomach, a betrayer, a liar, a mouse cornered by a huge tomcat.

Granddaddy reeled around and left, slamming the door, the sound of his footsteps heavy on the steps as he went down. The front door slammed shut. Seconds later, the car engine roared to life. I heard the sound of gravel scattering in the driveway even up in the attic.

"Now you stay in this room," Grandma said, her breath quick and shallow now that all need for pretense was over, "and don't you come out no matter what."

"Yes, ma'am."

"And lock the door behind me. He might come back."

I nodded, eyes wide.

"I've got to clean Tommy up."

"Will he be all right?" I gulped for breath, tears starting to flow.

"He'll be fine. Now be a big girl and don't you cry. Your cousin needs me."

She left in a flurry. I locked the door and sat on the bed, listening. I heard her open the door and her soft voice, soothing. Then Tommy's weeping growing louder as she led him down the stairs. I sat on the bed listening to Grandma heating water on the woodstove, her voice reaching up the stairs, but not her words. I stood by the window and watched the occasional car drive by, stood by the other window and watched the birds in the limbs of the evergreen. Then I sat at the vanity table and opened the jars, smelling the perfume, fingering her hair clips. I opened the closet, but nothing hung there. At long last, a knock came on the door. "It's me," Grandma said. "You can come out now."

I turned the lock to find Grandma standing in the hallway, apron damp. She tucked a strand of silver hair up into her now messy bun. "Come on."

I stepped forward and she took a firm grasp of my shoulder, answering the question I was afraid to voice. "Tommy's okay. I called his mother, and she's coming to get him."

I made my hesitant way down the steps, expecting Granddaddy to come charging through the door any minute, but he didn't. I walked to the back door, pushed it open, and sat down on the back steps. Soon I found a stick and started drawing in the dirt. The side gate opened. I held my breath, but Granddaddy didn't walk through. Tommy did. I ran to him and tried to put my arms around him, but he just stood, hands in his pockets, huddled into himself. He kept looking over his shoulder, back to where Granddaddy usually parked the car.

"Are you all right?" I asked.

He shrugged.

"What happened?"

He shook his head, staring at the dirt beneath his feet.

"What did he do to you?"

"The worst thing in the world," he said, his breath hot.

"What?"

He shook his head. After a silence, he looked up at me through red-rimmed eyes. "Where were you? Why didn't you come help me?" He studied the ground again.

"Grandma wouldn't let me."

His head snapped up. "What?"

"She made me stay. She said it was because I was a girl."

Tommy shook his head, his face white. "She said she didn't hear me."

I stared.

"Why didn't she come? She's big. She could have stopped him."

"I don't know, Tommy." My voice took on a pleading whine. "What happened?"

"I'll never tell you," he said. "You should have helped me."

"Grandma said that if it happened to me, it would ruin my whole life, but that you'd be okay."

Tommy jerked in disbelief.

"Honest. I swear."

Tommy stared at me through slitted eyes. "I hate you. I'll never forgive you."

I wailed, but just then a car pulled up. Aunt Rose jumped out and ran to us. Tommy had already started toward her. "I want to go home. I want to go home."

She frowned down at him. "Get in the car, then. I'll go get your stuff."

Tommy ran to the car, me following, and slammed the door against me.

"I'm sorry, Tommy. I'm sorry." I tried to open his door, but he locked it and all the other doors and sat, huddled and miserable, refusing to look at me.

I ran back to the house to find Grandma and Aunt Rose talking. They stopped dead when I arrived. I burst into tears. "Tommy says he'll never forgive me."

"He'll get over it," Grandma said.

Aunt Rose turned to the door, the bag with Tommy's stuff in her hand, not saying a word to me. "I'll call you later," she said to Grandma, then left.

"You go on outside and play," Grandma said. "I've had enough for one day."

9

The next morning, I arrived at Grandma's house only to hear that Tommy was sick and had to stay home. "But is he all by himself?" I asked.

"No." Grandma smoothed down her faded apron. "Your Aunt Rose stayed home to take care of him."

"Maybe we could go visit him," I suggested.

"We don't want you getting sick, now do we?" Grandma turned back to washing up the dishes.

I wandered around the house aimlessly for a little while, trying to figure it all out, then Grandma called me to help her check for eggs. Specks of dust floated in the air, gilded by the sunbeams that managed to push through the spaces between the slats of the henhouse. The golden space filled with the soft clucking of chickens and Grandma's meaningless, soothing sounds. She stood on her tiptoes checking for eggs, made a little exclamation of discovery, and lifted a white globe from the straw nest. Then farther down, another. A reddish-gold hen watched her hands, cocking her head this way and that, pecking at Grandma whenever she tried to reach beneath her spread feathers.

"This one's broody," she said. "We could use some new chicks, don't you think?"

I nodded.

"We'll let her sit."

The next day, Grandma told me the same thing about Tommy, and soon it was taken for granted that he wasn't coming back.

After that, I had to entertain myself. I was bored and a little tempted to test the boundaries Granddaddy had set. He'd stood, hands on his narrow hips, his suspenders an endless source of envy, eyes glinting beneath his busy gray brows. "Do not go past these hedges, you hear?"

We'd easily agreed then. With two of us, there'd been endless games inside and out. No need to stray beyond the yard. But some mysterious rebelliousness grew in me now, and I wanted to break the rules for the first time, to test the limits, to be a part of that big world outside where the cars whizzed by. Before, I'd always thought of myself as a good girl, obedient, neat and clean, smart and pretty. Now the hedge sang to me. I would stand at a thin spot and watch. Did I dare step through?

Then one day I walked through the front entrance that nobody used anymore—they all parked their cars on the side of the house—and I crossed the small dirt road in front of the house to the little triangle of land that used to be a part of the yard. It was hardly breaking the rules after all. But the big world was calling. This little patch didn't satisfy me for long.

One day I stood at the side of the house and screwed up the courage to push through, but Granddaddy caught me when he was coming up from weeding the field. He grabbed my arm and twisted it. "What did I tell you, huh?" He gave my arm a painful jerk. "Where you think you're going?"

Grandma appeared on the porch, her mild presence a check. "What is it, John?"

"I caught this little minx trying to slip out."

"Grandma," I called plaintively, depending on her rescue.

"Your Granddaddy told you not to go past the hedge. You'll have to deal with him." She turned and went back into the house.

"You see, girly. She won't save you this time."

A chill deep as snow in winter ran through me.

Granddaddy gave my arm another twist and said, "Now you mind me."

Soon Grandma called us in for lunch and fed us tomato sandwiches picked from the garden, heavy, fleshy and a deep red. After I was excused from the table, I banged open the screen door and plopped down on the swing attached with rope to the apple tree. I twirled around, twisting the rope as tight as I could. Scrunched up my legs and elbows, letting the swing unwind, relishing the speed. I pushed off in a puff of red dust, and after a few more pushes, got going as high as that swing could go, leaning all the way back to gaze up at the little globes of green swelling in the heat. But this little piece of board suspended by rope couldn't compete with the shiny swings hung by chains between tall metal poles that were popping up in playgrounds all over. Even the poor kids just two yards down from my daddy's new house, the ones who had to share a bedroom, had one.

I tried to push higher. Bees buzzed among the fruit as if it were still filled with the white blossoms of spring. One took a dislike to me and buzzed around my head. Then another took up the cause. More hung in the air, their golden segmented bodies suspended by gauze fairy wings, their huge black eyes surrounded by golden fuzz. The air was thick with them. Something was wrong. I dragged my legs on the ground to slow down. One bee lit on the trunk and crawled down. Another followed, then another. Then the hum reached me, a strong, steady buzz, alive and urgent. I looked at the trunk beside me. It was black with bees, hundreds of them, a mass of writhing bodies.

I screamed and jumped from the swing.

Dishes clattered in the kitchen. "What's wrong?" Grandma ran out, wiping her hands on her flowered apron. I met her halfway. "Are you hurt?"

"Bees." I pointed. "There's bees everywhere." I started crying.

She took hold of my arm and pushed me behind her, then took a few steps toward the swing. The tension in her slacked. "John," she called, "the bees have swarmed."

The screen door slammed, and Granddaddy appeared, pulling up his suspenders. Then he stuffed his hands in his pockets, nonchalant. "It's about time. I got a new box waiting."

I stared back and forth between these two placid faces. "But . . ."

"Never seen a swarm before, have you?" Granddaddy asked me.

I shook my head.

"Wait here." He turned and went back into the house.

I took a tentative step toward the buzzing tree, but Grandma called me back. "Careful, now." She reached a hand out to me. "Bees are jumpy when they're swarming. Might take out after you to protect the queen."

Before I could ask what she was talking about, the screen door banged again and Granddaddy came out dressed in some kind of spaceman suit straight out of *The Day the Earth Stood Still*. I gaped.

"Help me with this hat, Sarah." He bent down, and Grandma put the silver contraption on his head, then pulled down veils of black mesh. She straightened them, draping the gauze over his shoulders, making sure they fell just so, like the mother of the bride. Once she was done fussing, he straightened up. "Wanna help?" he asked me.

I eyed his suit.

"You don't need one of these. Just stay behind me." He headed toward the tree, but I ran to Grandma.

He looked back. "Come on, now," he coaxed. "They won't hurt you."

A mad, writhing mass of buzzing bees and him dressed up like an alien?

"These bees are looking for a new home. They won't bother you if you don't bother them."

"It's all right," Grandma whispered, handing me around to her front.

"I got something special to show you," he called.

My eyes flickered to his pants zipper before I caught myself.

"Well, I reckon you're not interested." He walked over to the undulating tree trunk and bent down. A few bees launched themselves at this intrusive object, but the thin net hanging from the hat defeated them.

I was drawn forward, hypnotized by the hum.

"Wanna see the queen?" Granddaddy asked in a quiet voice.

"What's a queen?" I whispered.

Granddaddy grunted, a satisfied sound. "She's right there." He pointed to the middle of the swarm, but I only saw black legs and segmented bodies, all vying to occupy the same space, maddened by some inexplicable force. "Come close. They ain't gonna sting you."

I took another cautious step.

"Once a hive gets too full," he continued in his quiet voice, "another queen is born. When she gets big enough, she flies off. And all these ones follow her."

"Why?"

"She's the only female in all these bees." At his wide gesture, at least a hundred bees took flight.

I broke and ran, several bees following, me flapping my hands, knowing better. Grandma waved them away with her apron.

Granddaddy stifled a curse. "Now didn't I teach you never to make sudden moves around bees? You're supposed to hold still." He stood in his black-and-silver suit waiting for the bees to settle. Then he gestured for me, slowly this time.

I crept back, revolted but compelled by the roiling mass of bodies, a passenger watching a wreck on the side of the road, unable to look away, not wanting to see.

"Come next to me."

I slipped in beside him.

"Here's the queen." He pointed to a place on the trunk where bees climbed all over each other, three and four deep.

"How can you tell?"

"She's bigger than the rest. See?" Granddaddy gently brushed a few bees aside.

And there she was—majestic and terrifying—huge, her long body gangly, cumbersome, a burden to her. "Can she fly?"

"The young one can. Now I'm gonna pick her up and the rest of the bees will follow."

"Why?"

"'Cause she's their queen—she's the only one who can have babies." He looked down at me. "See how important girls are?"

I stared at this gangly insect, hampered by her long, heavy body, the recipient of such fanatic devotion.

"You remember that," Granddaddy said. "Now you two go back in the house.

Some of these fellas might take offense to me messing with their royalty."

I retraced reluctant steps to my waiting grandma, who pulled me in to the screened-in porch. I ran into the kitchen, climbed up on the counter, and pushed my nose to the window over the sink.

Granddaddy leaned down and picked up the queen. An angry buzz rose from the swarm, but he took a step forward. Hundreds of bees blacked the air, their incensed voices vibrating. They started to settle on his hand and arm. I whined with anxiety, but he took another step. Then another. The bees flew around him, a storm cloud as he made his ponderous way to the edge of the field where a tall wooden box stood. He opened a hatch and stuck his hand inside.

Fascination carried me out to the backyard.

"Stay back, now. This here's the tricky part." He stood still as a fence post, and the black swarm on his arm slowly dripped into the box. After what seemed a long time, he pulled his arm out, the silver of his suit visible again. He untangled a few bees from his sleeve, then shook his arm. A few more specks flew out.

He walked away a few paces, pulled off his hat, and surveyed his work. Then he turned to me. "We'll have us some fine honey come fall."

The next afternoon, Grandma told me to go outside, that she and Granddaddy had something to talk about. In the backyard, I threw a pebble into the next square of the hopscotch game I'd sketched into the dirt. A hen ran over to investigate, pecked at the rock, cocked her head to study it, then wandered off. I hopped down the first three squares and leaned over to pick up the pebble. Just then, my father's Ford pulled into the drive. I ran to the fence. "Daddy," I shouted, arms stretched up.

"There's my girl." He strode through the gate, picked me up, and swung me through the air.

"Son, I need to speak with you."

I looked up to see my grandfather, his overalls stained at the knees with red soil. Daddy put me down, and I stood behind his leg.

Granddaddy studied the ground for a minute.

"How're things going?"

"Fine," Daddy said.

"And that job your wife has?"

My father stiffened. "Going good."

"How much money does she make at that anyway?"

"Not that much, but it helps, and it keeps her happy. That's the main thing."

"And why isn't she happy looking after her own children and husband?"

"I know you don't approve—" he began.

"Your mother's getting too old to babysit. You're going to have to make other arrangements."

"Has something happened? Is Mother all right?"

"She'd never say anything. You know your mother." Granddaddy prodded the ground with the toe of his boot. "But she gets tired. That wife of yours doesn't need to work. Can't you support your own family?"

My father's face blanched. "I see."

"How soon can you take care of this?"

Now it was my father's turn to study the ground. He took a deep breath and then faced his father. "I'll take care of it tonight, sir."

At dinner, I sculpted a wide hole in the middle of her mashed potatoes, and Mother spooned gravy in. "More."

Mother poured in another spoonful.

"More."

Mother laughed. "Eat that first, then we'll see."

My father ate steadily.

"We got in the fall shoes today. Some real nice ones," Mother said.

"Early for fall," he said.

"They come the season before," Mother explained, pride evident in her voice.

Daddy cleared his throat, and something in the sound made her look up. "I think it's time you quit that job. You should take care of your own child, not gallivant around with those friends of yours from work."

"We talked about this already." Mother's voice sounded thin, like ice on a Carolina pond.

I put down my fork.

Daddy continued as if making a prepared speech. "It's not right, a woman working. I make enough to support this family."

"I bought that furniture." Mother pointed in the direction of the living room.

"I don't like it, that's all. I wear the pants in this family, and I say you stop working."

"What's got into you?" Mother's brow furrowed.

I turned wide eyes to my father's face.

"It's time you stop working. Take care of Caroline and Jimmy."

"But Jimmy's in school and—" Mother began.

"There's no use arguing. I've made up my mind."

"Did your mother complain?"

"Don't blame this on her."

Mother opened her mouth, then closed it again. She looked at me, but I looked down, shoulders hunched. "Do you know something about this?" she asked.

"Leave her out of it," Daddy shouted. "She's got nothing to do with it."

So Mother quit her job, and we were left to entertain each other at home. She fixed me Campbell's chicken soup for lunch, canned pears with cottage cheese, sometimes grilled cheese sandwiches. One day after my father had driven off to work in his green Ford with the fins on the back, Mother came into my room early one morning asking if I knew anything about what had happened. I told her solemnly that I'd promised Daddy not to say anything, that it was a secret.

"Secrets that hurt other people are wrong, Caroline," Mother said.

I was sitting on the side of my bed. I kicked my feet back and forth, trying to reason it out.

"You can tell me. I'll never let him know."

I squinted up at her through my bangs.

"I'll just go crazy cooped up in this house," she said, her voice high and trembling now. "Please, Caroline, tell me. I'll handle it all. You don't have to say a thing."

Never one to be defeated, she extracted the whole story out of me, like a wisdom tooth.

After that, she started in on him every night during supper. Her skill amazed me. She appealed to his vanity, his sense of fairness, his enjoyment of what she could buy with the money she earned.

"But you quit," he said the third night.

"They'll take me back. They were sorry to see me go."

"What are you going to do with Caroline?" Daddy asked the next night. "My parents won't take her."

"We'll find day care."

"How you going to afford putting her in some day care?" he asked, a little scandalized at doing something so modern.

I could tell by the way she wiped the quick smile off her face that she had won. "I'll pay for it all myself."

"I don't hardly see how you'll be able to afford it."

"Just let me worry about that," she answered smooth and sweet, but I could see her hands clasped together in her lap under the table, her knuckles white.

Thus began the search for a day-care center for me. After a day in the first one, I streaked out to the car when Daddy arrived and cried all the way home. The second one produced the same results. The third one took. I liked being at the Salem Baptist Church, just up the hill from Old Salem and close to home. We sang every day in a huge room before a grand black piano. Musical instruments filled the side near the windows. The playground was enormous, complete with huge seesaws and big swings, the kind that would fly so high they scared even me. There was a kindergarten and school, so the place was filled with kids.

Life settled down.

I never saw Tommy again all that long, hot summer. We went over for a family visit sometime after Christmas. Once the adults were ensconced in their family room, I called to Aunt Rose from the hallway. "Where's Tommy?"

She walked out of the room and beckoned me toward the bed-rooms. "Down in the basement playing."

"Can I see him?"

"Sure, why not?"

I stared at the carpet, twisting my toe into the deep pile. "Because he said he hated me after . . . you know."

"He doesn't remember that now," she said in a quiet voice.

"But," I looked up at her, my forehead wrinkling, "how could he forget?"

"He just did." She watched me carefully. "So you can go play with him, but don't talk about it."

I did want to play with my favorite cousin again. I missed him.

"Promise?" she asked.

I nodded solemnly. "Promise."

She opened the door, but I balked at the steep wooden steps.

"Go on, now. I'm right behind you."

We climbed down together. I stood at the bottom on the concrete floor and looked up at Aunt Rose, lost.

"Tommy, your cousin Caroline is here to play with you."

He popped out from behind a big table. "Hey." He had the same freckled nose, the same guileless brown eyes, the same eager smile ready for anything. "Come see my train."

"You're not mad at me?"

Aunt Rose took in a loud breath, partly for my benefit.

"No, why should I be? Come on."

He took me over and showed me his marvelous trains with two tracks, a whole town in the middle, bridges, tight curves, and little evergreens. After I derailed one twice in a row, he wouldn't let me play with it. I had to watch because I couldn't resist the speed even if it sent the miniature red engine and various cars spinning off into space. He told me when we were adults, reconnecting after many years, that he'd sold that train set for half a million dollars. I never asked him if he remembered that day with our grandfather.

But I'm ahead of myself again, maybe trying to forget to tell you how my mother and Maggie became such good friends.

10

M aggie—1950s
She sat at the counter of the soda fountain in the drugstore, head bent, studying her Coke like she could discover the secrets
to the universe in there if she looked hard enough. Maybe she was
searching for a way to straighten out her life, get back on the track she
dreamed of as a child. Don't none of us ever do, but she was too
young to know that yet. I figured that was it since I knew who she'd
married. The family must still be practicing their old ways 'cause this
woman looked about wore out.

She'd come to our church last Sunday. Only white woman there.
Brunette, those blue eyes, trim figure, dressed up with a hat with
sparkles that sent little dancin' lights all over the walls when she
turned her head. Sat in the back row and clapped a little. She had a
strong voice. Paula greeted her after the service. Invited her to come
back. Asked if we could help out.

"That woman's full of trouble," Paula said later.

"Married a Grayson."

"Said her name was Hauser."

"Married Miss Grayson's great-nephew."

"Vera Grayson? That woman?"

"The very one."

We made our way back to the cabin, ate our Sunday dinner, and
forgot all about her. But here she was again. I must have paused too
long resting my bad ankle 'cause her head came up and those lake-
blue eyes hooked me like a brown trout on a line. Something taut
pulled between us. A ghost of a smile passed over her face, but it
didn't do nothing to lift the well of sadness in her eyes. She lifted
a hand and waved for me to come in. She could see me real good
through those big plate-glass windows they'd just installed. Couldn't

pretend I didn't notice. I pointed to myself, and she nodded. I don't know why, but I stepped inside and stood beside her. "Yes, ma'am?"

"Didn't I see you at church last Sunday?"

"I go to the Church of the Merciful Savior. That little white wooden one down by Main Street." I don't know why I didn't fess up right away.

"I talked to a lady there. She was real nice. I thought I saw you with her."

The man who worked behind the counter planted both his meaty hands with their red knuckles on the Formica and snarled, "May I help you?"

The white lady gave a little jump and grabbed up her drink. "We can sit in a booth, right?"

"You can sit in that booth," he said, pointing to the sign that read "Coloreds Only."

"Thank you." She moved over to the booth, sat down, then looked at her soda and asked me, "Can I get you something to drink? Or a sundae?"

I was so surprised that I said yes.

She went back over to the counter and ordered a banana split. "You like nuts?" she asked over her shoulder.

"Whatever you like," I said.

"Two spoons," she told the man.

He glared at her, shook his head, then turned around and started making it, mumbling the whole time.

She winked at me. I had to bite my lip to keep from laughing, but I kept an eye on him in case he decided to spit in our food. She paid the man, nice as could be, carried the treat over to us, plopped down the two spoons, but made no move to pick hers up.

Another customer came in, and as soon as he started talking to the man working the counter, my benefactor whispered, "I can't stand these rude men."

I caught myself right before I said, "Yes, ma'am." Instead, I said, "I reckon I'm used to 'em by now."

She picked up her spoon, dug out some walnuts covered with hot fudge, and stuck them in her mouth. "I love nuts in ice cream," she said, still chewing.

I still ain't touched my spoon. The sundae sat there, vanilla ice cream pure as porcelain skin, hot fudge dripping over the sides like mink draped over white shoulders, whipped cream like my momma's pearl necklace, some unexpected jewel offered up to me suddenly. I ain't never had one before.

"Aren't you going to eat any?"

"You don't mind?"

"Mind what?"

"Sharing your food with me?" I whispered.

"Why should I?"

I decided I liked this woman right then and there. I picked up the spoon and scooped up a bite with every ingredient in it—'cept I left that cherry for her.

We demolished it. It reminded me of Ellie's chocolate cake back when I was a girl. Only this was cold. She handed me a napkin and pointed to the corner of my mouth. "You've got a little bit of sauce right there."

"Oh, thank you."

She gave a long sigh and sat back. People walked by us, some with their noses up in the air, others giving us the evil eye. She didn't pay them no never mind.

"I needed that." She reached up and touched her eye. I could see it was swoll up and she'd tried to cover the bruise on her cheek with makeup. Them Graysons was definitely up to they old ways. I pushed my own memories way down in a dark hole somewhere.

"I'm Lily, by the way, Lily Hauser."

"Maggie," I said.

"Good to meet you."

"Likewise."

"You live around here?"

"A few blocks east. Down in the hollow."

"We just moved from Broad to Cascade."

I kept my eyes off her injuries, but she touched her cheek again and winced. "Men," she said, as if in explanation.

I nodded. "I know. You want some ice for that?"

"No, don't want to advertise it, you know?"

"Husband?"

Her eyes hooded over. "How'd you know?"

"That's who it usually is, is all."

"Yeah, he hits me when he doesn't get his way." She studied me a minute, then blurted out, "First time was when I came home from the grocery store just after we were married. I was so proud. My own house. Got to fill up my own pantry. And he beat me 'cause I spent so much money." Her eyes filled, but she blinked the tears away.

"I'm sorry." I didn't know what else to say.

"I don't know why I'm telling you this." But I could see she had to tell somebody or she'd split open like an overripe watermelon laying in the sun too long.

"Mr. Nathaniel George Hauser. Big man."

"Nate's your husband?" I acted surprised.

She gave a little start. "You know him?"

I nodded. "Knew his great-aunt, too." I didn't mention his grand-father.

"How'd you know her?"

"She taught me my letters."

"No kidding?" Lily leaned her elbows on the table.

"I reckon I owe her since I made a living teachin' children for a good while."

"Well, I'll be. How long ago was that?"

"Oh, way back. Almost sixty years now."

"What was it like back then? What was she like?"

I picked up the spoon and wiped it off with my napkin. "That's a long story."

She sat back. "Tell me."

"It's not all that interesting."

"I've got all day. The kids are at their grandparents' house, and Nate won't be back until around four." Then her face sharpened, like she remembered me. So she was a little bit white after all. They all was, but none of 'em had ever bought a banana split and shared it with me.

"You've got to be somewhere," she said, gathering her purse.

Paula would be working for another few hours, and I only did half days at the Jones's house. "Not really."

She noticed the big man behind the counter glaring at us. "Let's get out of here."

So we walked toward the park. I still ain't figured out what it was about her made me go along. We found a bench down near the creek and sat, listenin' to the water running through the rocks, lettin' it tell us its little story.

"I always tried to figure out how to please him—Nate," she said. "To make him stop, you know."

"Runs in the family. He probably got beat, too, when he was little. It ain't just him neither. Some men's just mean."

"What was his family like?"

"Well, I never went to they house."

She sat back and stretched out her legs. "Tell me everything."

I laughed. "Miss Grayson had her hat set for Mr. Winters. Family was countin' on her marrying him and saving them from bein' poor. Leastwise, what they though of as poor."

"But he never asked her?"

"Nah, his Virginia family came down and brought some high-falutin society woman. I reckon he married her when they went up there to meet her family."

"You reckon?"

"Plantation burned down. We all scattered. Da—Mr. Winters never came back."

Those lake-blue eyes sharpened. "So he was your daddy? A white man?"

I couldn't say what got into me. I was startled how fast she figured it out and just nodded.

"That must have been hard," was all she said.

"Yes, ma'am."

She put her hand over mine. "Please, call me Lily."

"Lily," I repeated.

"Thank you." She gave my hand a little squeeze, then let go.

"But don't many people know that, leastwise white people. The coloreds in town all know who my daddy was."

"I won't tell anybody." She stretched like a cat.

"It's getting late."

"I guess I got to get back. It's getting close to when Nate gets home from work, and I've got to pick up the kids and start dinner."

"I reckon I need to get back, too."

"Can we talk again?" she asked. "I get so lonely, just me in that house."

"That'd be all right," I said. Truth be told, I enjoyed talking to her.

"What's your phone number?"

"We ain't got no phone, ma'am."

"Lily," she said, kinda firm. "You got Tuesday afternoons off?"

"I do."

"I'll meet you at the drugstore."

"Here's better," I said. So we had ourselves a kind of date.

11

C aroline
     The day my father disappeared, a cop picked me up from day care. A teacher came to find me on the playground, explaining that my father had been in an accident and a police officer was coming to take me to the hospital. She said they were all right and I'd be with them soon. I sat huddled in a corner of the front office, waiting.

When the cop arrived, he took off his hat and kneeled down in front of me. "Don't be scared. Your parents are not hurt. I'm taking you to them."

I'd gone to the hospital once before from day care when I'd turned my head and the edge of the huge swing had smacked into me and cut me above my eye. I'd ridden up front with the teacher, who kept handing me tissues to hold against my eyebrow and talking gently to me the whole way. At the hospital, I got four stitches, and it left a very satisfying scar I showed to all my friends.

I got to ride up front with the policeman this time, too, where a handset hung from the dash and the scanner kept crackling and broadcasting announcements from time to time. Once, he picked it up and talked into it, glancing at me out of the corner of his eye.

In the emergency waiting room, a big black woman sat clutching her purse and rocking. Her family surrounded her, a few children and adults, tense and silent. My parents sat in the corner. Mother grabbed me to her when I walked in. "Thank God. Your father had a wreck, but he didn't get hurt." She pushed me down into the chair next to her.

Daddy sat in a penitent huddle in the corner, his hands clasped together in his lap, eyes down.

"Your father and I have to talk, so just sit here quiet." She patted me absently and turned back to him.

The cop was bending down in front of the black woman toward the front of the room, talking to her in a low, soothing voice, almost reverent. The woman kept shaking her head, shooting looks over at my father, an aching, lost look in her eyes.

"What's going on, Mother? What happened?"

"Hush, Caroline. We've got a lot to figure out." She glanced over at the big woman, who'd gone back to rocking, and shook her head. "Just be quiet."

After a while, I walked up to the woman and stood in front of her, challenging her with my stiff little body. I knew I shouldn't. I knew I should leave her alone, but she was clearly the source of the threat, and no adults came to stop me. Maybe she would go away.

The woman noticed me, and our eyes met. "You leave my daddy alone," I said.

She looked at me, then glanced over at my parents, who didn't even know I'd moved. She stared at me, jaw muscles working. Her struggle to stay still was monumental.

"My daddy didn't do anything to you. You leave—"

She lunged at me but stopped herself with a deep groan. The cop grabbed me and hauled me back over to my parents, whose heads were together, buzzing like bees, oblivious.

"You need to explain to her what is going on," he said to them.

"Sit down and be quiet, Caroline," my mother shouted.

"But—"

"Oh, just be quiet."

A skinny redneck and his rotund wife sitting near my father watched the proceedings with open delight.

The cop threw his arms up in disgust and pulled me out into the hallway. He bent down, took a deep breath, willing himself to gentleness. "Your father hit a young boy, driving home from a—" He shook his head, mouth tight.

Now I know he stopped himself from saying "bar."

"—driving home. The child is hurt bad. That woman," he pointed back to the door of the waiting room, "is waiting to hear if her child is going to live."

Hot shame flooded me. My eyes filled with tears. "I'm sorry."

A small sigh escaped him. "Your parents should have explained this. I'm sorry they aren't taking proper care of you."

I stood, legs squeezed tight together, uncertain what to say. It was the first time a grown-up had put into words something I'd only felt intuitively up until now.

He studied me a moment longer and held out his hand. I wrapped my own small hand around two of his fingers, and we walked back into the waiting room. I stopped in front of the black woman and whispered, "I'm sorry."

She nodded her head.

I took a breath to say more, but the cop tugged at me. "Come on. She doesn't want to talk now."

I sat next to my mother and assumed the same huddled position my father had been in when I first arrived.

A man clad in a white coat rushed into the room and stopped in front of the black woman and her family. They all leaned toward him, like sunflowers eager for light. He shook his head. "I'm sorry."

The woman wailed and reached for the person sitting next to her. My father groaned and put his face in his hands.

"Do you want to see him?" the doctor asked the woman.

She nodded. They all stood and left the room, two adults supporting the grieving mother, her other children following, some crying, others with pale faces and large, shocked eyes.

The cop came over to my father. "Let's go."

My father stood, and the cop took his arm. They walked toward the door.

"No." I jumped to stop him.

"Caroline," my mother said. "He has to go with the policeman now."

I turned and stared at her.

"You come with me." Mother clutched her purse tightly to her side and grabbed my arm, dragging me along. We got into my father's white Chevrolet, and she started it up, then leaned her head against the steering wheel, breathing heavily.

"Mother, what's happening?" I asked, but she just shook her head. "Where's Daddy?" I reached out to touch her arm, but she straightened up and put the car in gear. "Is the policeman bringing Daddy home?"

She looked over at me. "I need you to just be quiet for a while. Mommy needs to think. I'll explain it when we get home."

I don't remember if she ever did explain it, though. She probably said something, but I don't recall it. I do remember her reading the newspaper in the morning to Jimmy, my brother, who was going on fourteen, nine years older than me. She shook her head after every other sentence, picked up her china cup we got from the laundry detergent boxes, one coupon in each box, a whole set eventually. My aunt collected them, too, only she got brown flowers, my mother green.

Mother sipped her coffee, squared her shoulders, and read the next two sentences. I don't remember what the newspaper said. I don't remember the trial. I'm sure I wasn't allowed to go. I asked when Daddy was coming home from time to time, but she would always just shake her head. I remember her telling my aunt as they huddled around the kitchen table, smoke rising from two cigarettes, sipping more coffee, that she just couldn't handle both me and my brother. "Caroline is so young," she said.

I crept back to my room.

One Sunday my mother told me I'd be going to church with my grandparents. She was going to see Daddy.

"I want to go with you," I said.

"Your father doesn't want you to see him in that place. He's ashamed. He says he doesn't want you to remember him like this."

I frowned in confusion. "But I love Daddy. I'm not ashamed of him."

She dabbed at her eyes so her mascara wouldn't run. "I'll tell him that."

She pulled on her Sunday white gloves, straightened her hat, and walked me to the end of the driveway. Granddaddy's big car rumbled down the tar-topped road and stopped. He jerked his head toward the back, where my two cousins and brother waited. Jimmy had moved in with my grandparents a few days before. I hopped in, and we drove off.

Maggie

So it became a part of my routine, dropping by the park on Tuesday afternoons, just to talk mostly. About a month into it, she was already sittin' on our bench waiting, dressed in what they call pedal-pushers and a matching checkered blouse. She had sandals on, and her toenails was painted red to match her nails and lips. Looked like she could be on the cover of *Good Housekeeping*.

I'd told Paula about her. "Sounds like she needs somebody," she'd said.

"I reckon. I kinda like her." It was nice to have a friend, even though she was white. Her people come from up north, New York State, so I reckoned that's what made her different.

"We can all use friends. 'Long as the white folks don't get up in arms over it."

"I can always pretend I'm her maid," I'd joked.

After our hellos, Lily pulled a paper sack from her purse. It put me in mind of those bums laying in the doorways of abandoned buildings downtown, but to my relief, she took out two Cokes instead of some Jim Beam.

"Talking is thirsty work," she said, forcing a smile. She braced each bottle in the bend of the metal on the bench, and they opened up, easy as could be. She took out a bag of peanuts. "I like nuts in mine. You want some?"

I ain't never tried that, so I handed over my bottle. She had a way of getting me to try things out. She poured some in, and they floated toward the top. She took a big swig, leaving a red lipstick kiss on the bottle, and leaned back. "Lord, Lord, Lord, it's good to get away."

I didn't say nothin' about her taking the Lord's name in vain. Paula would've, though. She stretched out her legs and sighed heavy like.

"Tough week?" I asked.

She shook her head, but a tear crept out. She wiped it away and straightened out her back.

"Nate?"

She sputtered. "No, Caroline. That child, I swear."

"What she do?"

She studied me a minute. "Can a young child be crazy?"

"More like she could drive you crazy." I laughed. "What she do?"

She sat silent for a long while, watchin' the creek, lettin' the shade cool us off in the August heat. "I always liked this place."

"It's nice," I said, letting her decide if she wanted to talk about it, like Mick woulda done.

"She talks to people who aren't there," she whispered.

"Most kids got imaginary playmates. Nothin' to worry about."

"You think?"

"I do."

"I hope that's all it is."

"You could bring her to church one Sunday. We could see how she is."

She kicked off a sandal and dug one of her toes into the dirt. She was a beautiful woman, but there was something about her that had never quite growed up. Maybe that's why she was willin' to confide in me. "Have to go to her father's church. I don't much like it. Too stiff."

I chuckled. I knew just what she meant. No spirit of the Lord in them straight backs and all that shushing. "Bring her by. Let the reverend talk to her."

Caroline

The next Sunday, mother leaned down in front of me, hands on her knees. "Want to go to a new church this morning? I don't get nothing out of that one your daddy goes to."

I nodded, bemused by her last statement. Mother chattered away in the car about some new friend she'd met, how I was going to like the singing, how this was a church like she'd gone to as a child. She pulled the car over in front of a small white building. A dark man dressed in a darker suit shook the hands of the stream of people coming in. Mother got out, walked around to my side of the car, and opened the door.

I sat rigid.

"Come on, Caroline."

I shook my head.

Mother let out an exasperated sigh. "Oh, for heaven's sake. We're going to be late." She took hold of my arm and started to pull.

"Do we have a shy one?" The man who'd been greeting people at the door had snuck up behind Mother. His voice boomed deep bass notes.

I shrank back against my seat. White people weren't supposed to go to colored people's churches.

"She's just used to going to another church, is all."

"Why, look at you all dressed up for Sunday meetin'." He leaned down, imitating Mother's stance earlier, hands on his knees. His starched white collar threatened to cut into his fleshy neck. "We'd be right honored to have such a pretty girl in our church today."

My eyes traveled up to the roof of the old storefront. Their eyes followed.

"You're looking for a steeple?"

I nodded.

"We're usin' this here old store for our church. Jesus said (he added a syllable, pouncing on the second one so it came out Jah-EEE-sus), 'For where two or three are gathered together in my name, there am I in the midst of them.'" He stretched out his hand and beamed at me. "Come on, little lady."

I took his hand, and we walked in together.

"Thank you, Reverend," Mother whispered as she slipped into a back pew. At least they had the right kind of seats.

A sea of sepia, rose-beige, and mahogany faces watched us settle, then turned and followed the reverend as he mounted the pulpit and took his place behind the lectern. They had that part right, too, so I settled back.

But as soon as the reverend greeted everyone and started to talk, people shouted back at him.

"Praise the Lord for this beautiful day."

"Hallelujah."

"It does my heart good to see all you fine folk here today to worship the Lord," the preacher said.

"Praise Jesus." That person didn't add a syllable.

"Let's start our service today with song." The piano played a short introduction, and the congregation took in a collective breath and opened their mouths,

> "I shall not be moved
> Like a tree planted by the water
> I shall not be moved."

A large woman dressed all in purple let out a holler and moved to the aisle, where she commenced to dance. The feather on top of her hat shivered and swayed as she moved back and forth, moaning out, "Jesus saved me." I waited for somebody to grab her, but everybody nodded, and some shouted, "Hallelujah" or "Praise the Lord."

They started on the next verse. I didn't know this hymn, but Momma seemed to. She sang in her perfect soprano,

> "When my cross is heavy
> I shall not be moved."

"Oh, Lord," the purple woman shouted, then started talking in a sort of gibberish.

I hid behind Mother's skirt. She bent down and said, "It's all right. She's got the spirit, is all."

I peeked around Mother and looked in the air. I didn't see any spirits, but I was glad to be somewhere where other people saw them, too. People joined her in the aisles, and the hymn lost its words and became a humming, a moaning. Some people shouted, raising their arms in the air and shaking. Mother even gave a few shouts herself. I started jumping up and down.

Soon the hymn was over and the preacher prayed over everyone, asking for mercy, for forgiveness, for healing. He called out a name once in a while and seemed to know everything that person needed. Some he admonished for drinking. Others he comforted because they seemed to have lost somebody. He called out "Agnes," and the purple woman fell down on the floor and started to roll. Two men came and knelt by her, praying up a storm. I grabbed Mother's hand and watched, my eyes wide. The preacher asked for healing to come down on this woman, for help of all kinds. She quieted and opened her eyes, catching my gaze in hers. Something passed between us, and I shuddered.

When the preacher was done, people found their seats again. Then he cleared his throat. The piano struck a chord, and I jumped out in the aisle and started hollering and dancing. The preacher sucked in his breath and frowned at me, dark as a thunderstorm. Pointing at me, he shook his head. "Sister Lily?"

Mother grabbed me by the arm and dragged me out the door, down the three steps, and threw me into the car. She got in and fumbled for her keys, muttering all the while. "I swear I don't know what I'm going to do with this child. She'll be the death of me. Oh, Lord, you've got to help me. Please help me."

She started the engine, drove a block, then looked over at me. "I've never been so embarrassed in my life. What got into you?"

"But, Momma—"

"Don't you 'but, Momma' me, young lady. Doing all that yelling and carrying on. Interrupting the preacher. Just wait till your daddy gets—" Big tears welled up in her eyes. She pulled over to the curb and stopped the car. We both knew Daddy wasn't coming home. Not for a long time.

She cried for so long it scared me. Finally she pulled out a tissue and wiped her eyes. She put the tissue in her pocketbook, and we drove the rest of the way in silence.

The next Sunday, Mother announced she was going to drop me off at my grandparents' so I could go to church with them from now on, but she was going back to the shouting-and-rolling-in-the-aisles place. Of course she didn't say it that way. I never figured out what I'd done wrong, and when I asked, all she'd say was, "Never mind, Caroline, just never mind."

So on Sundays Mother took me to my grandparents' house, where my brother was staying now because she said I was too much for her without my father around. My two cousins were living there, too, along with Aunt Rose, who had left her good-for-nothing, rotten, philandering husband, as my mother explained it to me. She told me I couldn't repeat that, which was fine since I didn't know what that last word meant. Aunt Rose's bruises had healed, and her wrist was coming out of the cast next week. I wanted a cast, too, so me and Tommy wrapped our limbs in newspaper and limped around the house. This made Aunt Rose madder than a half-drowned cat, so we only did it when she couldn't see.

Mother got to leaving me there longer and longer. At first, she'd come for Sunday dinner, but soon she started showing up later and later until one day she drove the car into the driveway after dark. Granddaddy was waiting for her, hands on his hips. He shooed me inside and commenced to yelling at her, but I couldn't make out the words. After that, Mother showed up for Sunday dinner and sat on the front porch in those dark green rocking chairs with Aunt Rose and Grandmother, watching us kids playing whatever game we came up with, her face a stone mask.

As it turned out, though, this wasn't a good thing. Not at all, because she went back to her old ways worse than when Daddy first left. Worse than when I'd been a baby. These memories are all a jumble. I can't say how I remember them at all. Even how old I was. Seems I'd be too young to recall them at all, but they stand out clear as day. The red-hot cigarette burning me. Her red fingers pushing the diaper pin through flesh. Her red lipstick close to me.

But this time must have been worse because Daddy, my savior and safe shoulder, was gone. My brother was living with my grandparents. I was all alone with her except for my crowd of friends that nobody else could see, except maybe the purple woman at mother's new church. Mother started muttering sometimes, in that dark, choked kind of way, and when she did, fear ran through me like an icy, killing river. To this day, I still can't remember what she did to me this time.

I got help, though, from somewhere I could never have imagined.

12

M aggie

Midmorning there come a poundin' on our cabin door. Out the window, I could see Lily all in a state. Her hair was messed up and she weren't wearin' no lipstick or nothing. Her eyes was all red. I opened the door.

"Oh, thank God." She started to rush in, then stopped short when she saw Paula. "I'm sorry."

"Come on in," Paula said. "Looks like you need some help."

"I do." She looked around with that lost look of hers.

"Please have a seat," Paula said. "Can I get you anything?"

"No, thank you." She shook her head, then one fat tear rolled down her cheek, followed by another.

I sat down beside her. "What's the matter?"

"She's bad."

"Who?"

"Caroline."

"What happened?"

"She won't talk to me anymore, only those spirits. And she talks in tongues."

Paula handed her a tissue, and she wiped her eyes.

"Only not the kind they talk in church. More like growling and groaning." She squeezed her eyes shut and whispered, "Sounds like demons."

"Where she at now?"

"With her grandmother. She don't act like that around them."

Paula gave me a look over Lily's head.

"You?" I mouthed.

Paula shook her head and pointed at me.

"You want me to come see about her?"

She grabbed my hand like it was a rope thrown out to save her from drownin'. "Would you please? I'm at my wit's end. I just don't know what to do."

"I can come round tomorrow. That okay?"

So the next morning I walked down her street. I expected she'd live in one of them little row houses, all white and pretty much the same, based on how she talked and acted with me. But when I went past what used to be the Winters plantation house, my old home, I started to wonder just how rich her husband was. I knew it wasn't her family had the money. No siree. Not the way she talked and acted.

I walked down the tar-topped road, the edges hardened now in the fall weather, to the next street and turned down the hill. The house I was looking for sat up on its own hill, just below the Winters house, like it was trying to compete, to say to the world, "Look at me. I'm here too." But it didn't have no chance. All eyes turned to that golden mansion. This lady's house was what they call a ranch style, long and all on one floor, made of redwood all the way from California, she told me later.

I retraced my steps back up the road to the driveway and walked past a border of some kinda flowers I didn't know—looked like tiny roses—to the back screened-in porch. While I was trying to decide whether to knock here or go through the porch to the back door, it opened, and Lily came running out.

"Oh, thank heavens. I thought you weren't coming," she said in a rush, a half-smoked cigarette held between her fingers, her nails polished a perfect red.

"I said I'd come. I keep my word."

She gestured for me to follow.

"How's the child this morning?"

"About the same." She stopped, her hand on the doorknob, and turned to me, her blue eyes tinged red. "I just at my wit's end, I tell you."

I nodded. She stood looking at me like a child waitin' to be told what to do. "Let's go see, then," I said to get her attention.

She dropped her cigarette on the concrete walkway and stepped on the still burning end, crushing it with her shoe.

The kitchen looked new, with a big white stove and a wringer washer tucked in the corner next to the refrigerator. It had a freezer underneath. The walls were honey-pine paneling.

"She's right next to the table."

I walked over and saw the child, blond and blue-eyed, her face smeared with some kind of food. She cocked her head to an angle and studied me. The little devil.

"Have you ever done anything like this before?" Lily asked.

"I've helped Paula, but she thought I should come today." I didn't tell her Paula was working in somebody's house. Did that every day.

"She's acting like a baby. Too young for her age. Sucking her thumb. Talking to—" Lily waved her hand vaguely.

"Demons?"

"Can you help her?"

"I think so." I looked at that beautiful, chiseled face with the lost eyes. "You ready? It might be hard at first, but it's for the best."

Lily nodded.

Caroline

I sat at the table, peas scattered on the placemat, picking one up occasionally and eating it. I was talking to a group of people in the corner between the refrigerator and the door to the back porch. Nobody else could see them. We made noises together—growling, guttural sounds—and I screwed up my face and rocked back and forth. They came when things got bad, but lately they'd been staying all the time.

"You see, you see," my mother said to her new friend.

The new lady stood with one hand leaning on the counter, the other on her cocked hip, studying me. She was small and lean, her dress buttoned all down the front, her sparrow-brown skin dotted all over with tiny moles.

This new lady told my mother to leave. I ostentatiously took no notice as she glanced at me, wringing her hands, then went to leave, stopped, and walked back as if to object.

"Go on, now. It's got to be done."

My mother left, and the new lady—I later learned her name was Maggie—watched. Soon I forgot she was there and I threw peas and chattered like some demented parrot at the gaggle in the corner.

"Who you talking to?"

I stopped and looked at her, then went back to piling peas in one corner of my plate.

"Who you talking to?" she asked again.

I pointed to the group in the corner.

"There's nobody there."

"Uh-huh."

"I don't see anybody."

"Friends," I said and looked back at them.

"Who are your friends?"

"Mine." I banged my hands down on the table.

"You have to stop talking to them."

"No."

"Look at me."

I peered up at her, head lowered, fists tight.

"Do you want to go to hell?"

Puzzled, I lifted my face to look at her square.

"You have to stop talking to them."

My friends in the corner muttered, and I joined in. We made terrible growling sounds. I shook my head and—

"You have to stop talking to them, or you're going to hell. Do you want to be damned for all eternity? Do you want to burn in a lake of fire?" Now she was hissing, too.

I watched her carefully.

"Because if you keep talking to those demons, that's what's going to happen. They'll lead you astray, and you'll burn in a lake of fire forever."

I started shaking my head *no*.

"Yes, because you're bad. And bad little girls who talk to demons go to hell."

"No." I banged my hands down again. Peas jumped.

"Yes." She leaned closer to me. "If you keep talking to demons, you'll burn forever. Do you want that? Do you want to go to hell and be damned?"

I looked over at my only friends. Hot tears stung my eyes.

"Stop looking at them. Look at me."

I wailed and reached out to the corner.

"Look at me."

I shook my head.

"You can either stop talking to those demons and go to God or keep it up and you'll go to hell forever. It's your choice right now."

I balled up my little hands. If I couldn't talk to my friends, I wouldn't have anybody. I'd be left all alone. But I didn't want to go to hell either. She'd left me no choice. I'd have to die. I didn't want to die, but this skinny woman had blocked all other paths. I squeezed my eyes closed and screamed from the bottom of my tiny, vital body. How would I make myself die? I sobbed.

"You're a good girl, aren't you?" Her now soothing voice cut through my hot misery.

I nodded vigorously.

"You want to be a good girl," she cooed at me. "You want to come to me?"

I reached out both arms to be picked up, to be saved from dying, to be safe again.

My mother burst through the kitchen door. "What's wrong?"

I turned to my friends in the corner, and together we started growling.

Maggie held up a hand, like a cop directing traffic. "Wait."

Mother took a step toward me.

I shook my head and started spewing nonsense words in a low, gravelly voice.

Light dawned in Maggie's eyes. "You have to leave," she said to my mother.

"But—"

"It's all right. Go back out into the hall." My mother took a breath to object, but Maggie waved her away. "Just let me see something."

Mother walked out and shut the hallway door. I started to cry again.

"Caroline," Maggie said in her gentle voice. "Look at me, sweetie."

I continued to cry, kicking my legs against the chair.

"Come in again," she called to my mother.

My mother opened the door, and hot anger filled me. I screamed.

"Okay, go back into the hall," Maggie said to my mother. She watched me sob. "You're a good girl, aren't you?"

I nodded again.

"You talk to them when your mother's around, don't you?"

Long, shuddering sobs shook me. Finally somebody understood.

"Then come to me."

I reached out my arms, and she picked me up. "You're safe now. You don't ever have to talk to those demons again."

I snuggled against her. My friends weren't demons, but I could never explain that to her.

"You want to come home with me?"

I nodded, head still tucked under her chin.

"Okay, you just let me talk to your mother."

I tightened my grip.

"It's okay now."

She called my mother back in. When she entered, I turned my face away and held on tight. "I'm going to need to take her home for a few days. Let her live with me and Paula."

"But—"

"Just for a few days."

They talked, Maggie explaining why I had to go home with her. She asked Mother about how she was coping now that Daddy had disappeared.

"It's just too much with Nate being gone. I need to work to pay the bills. Jimmy's with his grandparents."

I stopped listening. I think I might have fallen asleep. The next thing I remember is being in their little cabin and standing in front of a woodstove, watching the fire. Maggie and the tall woman named Paula talked in soft voices. The fire crackled. Then came the smell of food, and Maggie spooned some into my mouth. Afterward, I sat quiet in the same spot, eyes closing.

"Come on, now." Maggie picked me up. "Let's get you cleaned up." She sat me by the sink in the kitchen and pumped the handle for water. Wet a wash rag and cleaned me off gently, humming under her voice. Paula stood in the doorway and watched. Once I was clean, she put me in a nightie and carried me into a small room just off the main area with the stove. She sat me down on a low cot. "This is where you're going to sleep."

I grabbed her around the neck. There were no more words. I was wrung out.

"It's all right. I'll just be in there." She pointed to a door between the stove and the kitchen. "With Paula."

I looked up at her. She pulled my arms away from her neck.

"If you need anything, you just come get me."

I tried to grab her again, but she held my arms by my sides.

"We're going to sit up for a while. You let us know if you need anything." She patted the pillow. "You lay down now." She tucked me in, kissed me on the forehead, and prayed for a moment for God to protect me. I fell asleep before she finished.

13

Maggie

The next morning, Paula and me washed up quick and drank our coffee next to the stove, creepin' in to check on her from time to time. That child slept like an animal that had run from some predator and finally found a hole to curl up in and rest. When she stirred, I sat next to her and reminded her where she was. She wrapped her little arms around my neck, and I carried her to the outhouse and held her over the seat, then brought her in and cleaned her up. Paula put on the grits while I dressed Caroline, then put her in the middle of the living room rug where I could keep an eye on her. Paula fried up a bit of bacon she'd gotten from the people she worked for. We had three eggs left and a dab of butter for the grits. We had ourselves a little feast.

The child ate quietly, watching each of us with those indigo-blue eyes. Paula had the day off, so we made a fire and sat. Our cabin was down in a hollow. A fire felt good down here deep in the shade. I gave Caroline the doll her momma had packed with a few clothes the day before. She sat on the rug clutching it to her, staring into the fire. Reminded me a little of Charlise when she first came to us.

We got to talking and let her sit there. Suddenly Caroline crawled up into my lap. "Can I stay here?" she asked.

"Why you want to stay here?"

She lowered her head, mouth quivering.

I rocked her a minute. "You scared to go home?

She nodded.

"What you scared of?" I asked in a low voice.

She struggled against tears.

"It's okay to tell me."

"Mommy pinches me."

I had to put my ear right up next to her mouth to hear her.

"She hits."

I tightened my arms around her.

"Sometimes she burns me."

"Burns, did you say?"

She pointed to the hand-rolled cigarette lying on the table. "She's mean."

I rocked her until she snuggled in and closed her eyes. Once she was asleep again, I looked up. Paula was watching us. "What we done got ourselves into?"

"That woman married into a mean bunch," I said. "Nate's grand-daddy. He was the one—you know."

"I remember," Paula said. She reached out and squeezed my shoulder. "The Good Lord will show us the way."

"He gonna have to," I said, trying to square my shoulders for what might come.

Paula had half a day off on Saturday. She watched Caroline while I went over to visit with Lily. With Nate behind bars, we didn't have to hide out in the park, so we sat at her kitchen table. She'd bought a sugar cake from the bakery down in Old Salem, one of the original settlement towns from over two hundred years ago. She pulled the treat out of the oven when I arrived and served me a fresh slice with a cup of coffee with cream. Lily ate a bite, then lit up a cigarette. I could see the ashtray was spilling over. She saw me glance at it.

"If I don't smoke, I bite my nails." She held out her perfectly man-icured hands, nails the color of candied apples at Halloween. "I've got to go back to work. Di Stefano's is picky about how the girls look."

"How you holding up?" I asked.

"How's Caroline?"

"Seems a little better now."

"You figured out what's wrong with her?"

"Maybe." I studied her, trying to figure out how to say what I'd come to say. Paula thought the best way was to come right out with it, but I remembered Mick. What would he do?

"Demons?" she whispered. "Was she talking to demons?"

"Whatever it was, we got her to stop. They'll go away if we can keep her attention off them. She seems to do it more when she's with you."

Lily ran her hand through her hair, the permanent wave bouncing right back into place. "I can't tell you how much I appreciate it. I'll get Old Man Hauser to pay you."

"We don't need no money," I said. A normal mother would have asked me why she thought her child talked to spirits or whatever when she was around her, but she hadn't asked me that.

"Still." She shook her head, picked up her cigarette, and took a long draw. "Take whatever you want out of the refrigerator. I got cans over there." She gestured vaguely.

"Thank you."

She took another long drag off her cigarette, blew out the smoke, and rolled the edge against the ashtray to keep the end short and glowing. "Don't know how long Nate's going to be gone. No telling what he'll be like when he gets out. I can't tell you how glad I am the Hausers took Jimmy for a while." She gazed off across the street at the stone of that golden mansion, rebuilt just like it had looked all them years ago.

"You see, this here is my chance, and here I am saddled with two kids to take care of. Thank God Old Man Hauser coughed up some of his renters' money to help out, which makes me beholden to him." She frowned.

After the Graysons had run Daddy away, they built little row houses on their old fields. They was landlords now—at least the Hauser branch of the family.

She went on. "I gotta go over there every Sunday. Listen to that redneck run on about things he doesn't know nothin' about. Pretend to be happy with his son, who's tried to beat the life outta me."

She ground out her half-smoked cigarette. "But this here's my chance finally, for once in my life, to live."

I didn't say nothin'. Just like Mick, I sat quiet. Gave her her head, so to speak. She lit another cigarette. Smoked them Salem menthols. I don't care for 'em. Like to roll my own. I just sipped my coffee and waited.

"I was born at the height of summer. I came right in the middle of a bunch of brothers and sisters, some who'd been there before I came and were fighting for their place. More just kept coming. That was the way of it back in those days. It was a welter of chaos and confusion. Women didn't have no choice in the matter. Still don't, if you come right down to it. Maybe I shouldn't have had any children at all. One's crazy and the other an ungrateful brat."

I didn't answer that. Seemed like crazy run in the family, but sometimes circumstances can drive you to it. "Where was you born?" I asked.

"We were in New York at the time. I was born in the Onondaga Hospital near the reservation." She paused. "My momma's what Old Man Hauser would call a squaw. She's Indian. Makes me a half-breed."

"No kidding?" I said. "I'd never have guessed it." I noticed she was soundin' more like her childhood background the more she talked. She'd learned to cover it up, just like I had.

"My daddy was white, though. Just like yours." She smiled at me like we'd just joined some kind of secret sorority. "But Nate don't know. You're the only one I've told. Besides the kids."

I reached out and squeezed her hand. That would have been a rough row to hoe.

She teared up a little. "My daddy was a railroad man. Moved around a lot until he opened a grocery store in Gastonia. Went bankrupt during the depression." She stubbed out her cigarette and took a sip of coffee. Made a face. "It's gone cold. You want some more?"

"Sure." I did want to hear her story. The answer lay somewhere in it.

She got the pot and poured, steam rolling up. Good, hot coffee was what you needed sometimes.

She sat back down and added a teaspoon of sugar to her own cup, then some cream. Took another bite of her sugar cake, which had also gone cold, but it was good either way. "Lord, if I never eat another pinto bean, it will be too soon for me. That's all we had was beans. No meat for weeks on end. And no pork to flavor them."

"Us, too. It was tough times."

"All I got to wear was hand-me-downs, stuck in the middle like that. No money for school. I dropped out in eighth grade." She eyed me, but her eyes was a little glassy. She didn't really see me. She was seeing the past.

"We had to pay for textbooks, but Daddy didn't have any money. Everybody owed him. He didn't have the heart to starve people. But that didn't matter to those teachers. So I stole a book. They caught me and kicked me out of school. All I wanted to do was learn, and they kicked me out." She searched my face for the answer to why they'd do something like that to her.

"So you never went back?"

"Too embarrassed. I graduated, though." Then she laughed. It had the edge of hysteria. "I graduated from the School of Hard Knocks."

I chuckled.

"How long you reckon Caroline needs to stay with you?"

"Depends."

"I just need some time," she whispered. "I ain't never had no time to myself. I always shared a room. Hell, I never had a bed to myself. Never had my own clothes. Nothin'." She stared into her cup, her shoulders hunched up, halfway between guilty and defiant. "I thought Nate was my ticket out. His daddy had all those houses. He worked at the mill. A good, solid job. But he takes after his daddy with that temper."

"You not worried about Jimmy?"

"He's got his cousins to play with. Rose is staying there, Nate's sister. She left her husband finally. Got tired of gettin' beat up. Braver than me, I guess." She gazed out the window, then gave herself a little shake. "With two adult women there to keep an eye on him, Old Man Hauser will behave better. At least for a while."

I watched her steady. How a woman could leave her child in a situation like that was beyond me, but I didn't have no room to judge, not after what I'd done. I could see she'd about run out of rope. People got trapped by life.

"So how we gonna keep an eye on you when Caroline comes back?"

She winced like I'd struck her. I'd said it in a quiet voice. No blame. Like I'd asked her about her flower garden.

When Mick would put a saddle on a horse for the first time, it would stiffen up like this. He would just stand there, not moving, let it get the feel of it for a minute. I could see her struggling to deny it, but she shook her head against the temptation to prevaricate.

"I don't know why I do it," she said in a whisper, not looking up from the tablecloth. "Something just comes over me."

I made a little encouraging sound.

She folded her arms around her stomach like she was tryin' to keep her guts from spillin' out all over her shiny linoleum. Big tears stood in her eyes.

I sat still as a cat waitin' for the mouse to show itself. 'Cept I wasn't gonna pounce.

"Nate wanted another child. I was pregnant before we got married. He took me down to some man who got rid of unborn babies." She screwed her eyes up tight. "He hurt me so bad. Scraped that baby right out of me. Sent me home. But Momma didn't notice nothin'. Told her I had the flu. After Jimmy, I had trouble getting pregnant. But Nate wouldn't leave it alone. Called me all sorts of names when he beat me."

She looked up, eyes flaring angry. "Like he didn't have nothin' to do with it."

"They always blame the woman," I said.

She nodded, getting her feet back under her. "So the doctor thought my tubes was blocked. They did something to clear them. I was only in the hospital overnight. After that, I got pregnant again. I thought another baby would save us. That he'd be happy. And he was, but . . ."

"Uh-huh," I said softly.

"She's just so damned perfect. All blond and blue-eyed. Smart, too. Nate worships her. Forgot all about me as soon as she was born."

So there it was. She was jealous of her own daughter. I didn't say nothing, though. Just let her sit there and hear what she'd just said.

She reached for a paper napkin and blew her nose. "But he still hits me. And now here I am stuck with another baby. Can't leave until she's grown." A tear escaped, then two more. She squeezed her eyes shut, but the dam had broken. She rocked back and forth, sobbing like a lost child.

Best to let her cry it out. I didn't move. Didn't want to distract her.

Her crying slowed after a few minutes, and she blew her nose again. Went to the kitchen sink and washed off her face. Dried it on a kitchen towel.

"You stuck with a man who hits you."

"Yes, but now he's gone for a while, and I have a chance."

"What do you want to do?"

"Wish I could move away. Go to New York or somewhere like that. Start all over." She straightened the silverware next to her square of sugar cake, like this would straighten out her life. "But I can't abandon the children."

"So all that's bottled up and comes out sometimes? You lash out at Caroline?"

She looked up at me like she ain't never thought of it that way before. "I guess so."

She sat back down at the table and rubbed her hands up and down her arms like she was trying to get warm. "I really don't want to do it. It's like I can't help myself." She looked at me sideways, like a dog that had made a mess on the living room rug.

I wasn't goin' to feed that excuse, though. So I said, "You don't want to leave the two kids with they grandmother? Just up and disappear?"

"Some days I wish I could. I reckon I'm not brave enough."

"You're plenty brave, Lily," I said.

"I figure Nate's so mean because of how he was treated when he was little. How can I leave my children to the same fate?"

"You love them." I said it like there was no question.

She looked a little surprised. "I guess I do."

"You want to protect them."

She nodded.

"So how can you do that?"

But this was too much, too soon. She started rockin' back and forth again. I reached out and touched her shoulder. "We can keep Caroline a little longer."

"Would you?"

"Say a week?"

She grabbed my hand like I'd just given her a million dollars. "I can't tell you what that would mean to me."

"I'll see you tomorrow. Tell you how she's coming along."

"Thank you. I just can't tell you how grateful I am." She walked me to the door. "Same time?" she asked.

"I got a job tomorrow, so around six o'clock?"

"I'll feed you dinner," she said. "I'll cook something."

I would rather eat with Paula, but I reckoned I'd contradicted her enough already. "That's mighty kind of you."

"Oh, it's nothing. Believe me."

Back home, I found Paula sitting on the porch, the child sitting in the middle of the yard holding on to her doll, staring up into the trees. That lost look was fading, but she was still actin' like a baby. I sat close to Paula and told her about my visit.

"What we done got ourselves into?" she asked again.

"Seems like it's always something."

"Colored folks is one thing, but a white woman?"

"Says she's part Indian."

"Still." She watched the child, who'd started drawing pictures in the red dirt. "I reckon we can keep her for a while longer. Poor little thing."

I leaned in and kissed her ear.

"Watch out, now. No telling who's around."

"Want me to cook or watch Caroline?"

"I already got a pot of beans on."

"I can mix up some corn bread."

"That sounds real fine." She turned and gave me that slow smile I loved.

"Got any collards?"

We walked to the back where our little vegetable patch fought for its life every day, vying with the kudzu. The leaf vegetables was still doing good. And the broccoli. "Looks like we could pick some kale."

"Sounds like supper." I looked around, then pecked her cheek quick and ran for the house before she could react.

Paula followed me, calling to Caroline over her shoulder to bring her doll inside. Paula unfolded the newspaper Mrs. Prichard gave her and read me the headlines. I cracked an egg and beat it a little with my fork, then stirred in water and milk. We didn't have much sugar left, so I skipped that.

"Looks like that Thurgood Marshall is still getting threats against his life," she reported.

"That is one brave man. I hope the Lord protects him."

"You reckon they'll follow the law and desegregate the schools?"

"Ain't likely." I finished greasing the pan and poured in the batter. Then checked the fire in the stove and put the pan on the rack. I sat down at the table and rubbed my bad ankle. Too much walkin' today.

Caroline watched us from the rug in our living room, hugging her doll to her chest, her face as serious as any lawyer arguing before the Supreme Court. Suddenly she got up and walked over to Paula. Stood in front of her, all serious. "Will you be my mommy?"

Paula exhaled like someone had kicked her in the stomach. "What? But you already got a momma."

Caroline shook her head and repeated her question.

"Why me?" Paula pointed at me. "Why not Maggie?"

"Because you're the leader."

Paula sputtered out a laugh, and I just shook my head. No wonder she spooked her mother.

"Why you want me? Just look at you." She picked up a lock of her blond hair. "You're beautiful. I'm . . ." She pointed to her mass of frizz.

"Please."

Paula pulled the little girl into her lap and cuddled her. "Don't you worry now, child. Everything is gonna work out just fine. You'll see."

We lazed the day away, Paula preparing her Sunday school class for tomorrow's church service, me watching Caroline to make sure she didn't start up with that crazy talk again. But she napped. Slept a good long time, like she was recovering from some illness. I reckon she was in a way. Then she watched me make up the fire when the sun settled down for the night. Caroline loved watching the flames, and I had to keep an eye on her. We had a little supper, then I got out the child's nightie, but she clutched her doll to her chest and shook her head.

"You ain't sleepy yet?" I asked her.

She shook her head, those blond silk tresses wisping around her face.

"You want to hear a story?"

Her eyes brightened.

"Got to put on your nightie first."

"You think she needs a bath?" Paula asked.

"I reckon we can put her in the sink."

"Tub," Caroline demanded.

"The sink is better," I said. "Keeps the water hotter."

She wrinkled up her nose.

"You'll see." I put the kettle on the woodstove in the living room. She stood up to watch.

"Want to add some wood?"

She nodded, her face still earnest. She clutched the small branch I handed her in her chubby hand and carried it over to the stove. Paula opened the glass door, and she carefully laid the branch on top of the glowing log. It flamed up right away. Caroline jumped back just a little.

"Let me put this big one on."

Paula pulled the child onto her lap, and I laid a bigger log on the fire, then started to close the door.

"No." Caroline jumped down.

"It gets hotter if it's closed," I said.

"We can leave it open a minute," Paula said, "but stand back in case it pops." She kept a hand on Caroline's arm.

The child watched, hypnotized, until the kettle boiled. I took it into the kitchen and filled the sink, adding a little cold to get the right temperature. We was lucky to have sweet water in our well. I went back into the living room. "You ready?"

Caroline shook her head. Paula closed the door on the woodstove, then walked into the kitchen. Caroline hesitated, so we started laughing together. The child showed up right quick.

"Hold your arms up," Paula said, holding her own straight up over her head.

Caroline copied her, and I pulled off her dress, then her undies, and bent down, holding my arms out. She walked into them, and I put her in the sink. We scrubbed her up good, then dried her off and put her in front of the fire again to let the heat finish off the job. After she'd turned a deeper pink, Paula slipped on her nightie, pulled her up between us, and started telling her the story of Noah building his ark. The child snuggled between us, happy as a kitten in a litter. Paula named all the animals that Noah took on the ark, her voice getting softer and softer until Caroline's eyes closed and her breathing evened out. We waited a little while, then carried her to the cot. We was just as tuckered out, so we followed to bed soon enough and lay talking in the close dark.

"Can I sleep with you?" came a little voice behind me.

Startled, I turned away from Paula. "You got your own bed. Go on back to sleep."

"Please?"

"We're just talkin'. I'm going to my own bed soon."

"Where?" she asked, like she some kind of policeman.

I pointed into the other bedroom. "The bed's made," she said. I did keep my clothes in there, but this little detective was not convinced. Looked like she was growing back into her real age.

Paula raised up on one arm. "You want to sleep between us?" She sounded a bit incredulous.

Caroline didn't wait for an invitation. She clambered over me, nestled down between us, and smiled. Paula hummed a little tune, and the child's eyes closed. Soon she was back asleep. In the middle of the night, I carried her back to her cot. She woke halfway there, but I stood stock-still and she fell back asleep. I didn't want her to see me still in our bed in the morning. I mussed the covers of the other one before going back to sleep.

14

Maggie

We put Caroline in the nursery at church on Sunday, where she retreated to sleep, pro'bly 'cause she was in an unfamiliar place. That was her way of coping. But when I came to get her for lunch, she was playing with a much younger child on the rug, showing him how to pile blocks to make an elaborate building. During the community meal, she huddled between me and Paula, but ate a prodigious amount, so we knew she was on the mend. Caroline started acting more her age the next day. For that, I was grateful. But later in the week, Paula caught my attention and pointed over to the child, who sat in the doorway of her little room talking to the air.

"Do you want some tea?" she asked an invisible presence.

"Yes, thank you," she answered herself in a slightly different voice.

She poured from an imaginary pot. "Do you want cream?"

"Yes," she answered herself.

I crouched next to her. "Who you talkin' to?"

She startled, then put the pretend pot down on the ground. "I'm just playing. There's nobody really here." She sounded a little put out that she had to explain this to me.

"Whatchu playing?" Paula asked.

"We're having a tea party," she said.

"Who?"

"Just me, but you can't have a tea party by yourself."

"Why don't you play with me?"

Caroline frowned. "You don't like playing tea party."

"Of course I do." Paula patted the sofa next to her.

Caroline got up rather begrudgingly and sat next to Paula. The child picked up something invisible and handed it to her.

"What's this?"

"It's a cup."

Paula held it by the pretend handle.

"No, it's in a saucer."

"Oh." Paula adjusted her grip.

Caroline pretended to pour into Paula's cup and one of her own. "Do you want sugar?"

"Yes, please."

She made all the motions of spooning sugar. "Cream?"

"I do believe I'll have some cream."

Caroline giggled while making the motions to pour cream. Then she stirred the air above Paula's hand, picked up her own cup, and drank.

Paula mimicked her.

"Hold your little finger out like this," Caroline instructed.

Paula stuck her pinkie out in the air.

"Do you want a cookie?"

They went on like this for about fifteen minutes, sipping tea, eating cookies, and patting their mouths with imaginary napkins. I mended my blouse and watched. Paula kept looking at me and making faces. She ain't never played tea party before, I reckoned. After a while, Caroline got bored and picked up her doll. "Can I talk to my dolly?" she asked.

I snorted, then caught myself and answered yes.

"Thank you," she said, like a prissy little lady.

When the child was engrossed in her game, Paula whispered, "When you think we can bring her mother over?"

"Tomorrow?"

"We're busy with church all day. Let's give it a couple more days. Just let her come in casual. Chat with you while I play with Caroline."

"I'll go talk with her," I said. "See how she is."

I paid Lily a visit during our regular time on Tuesday. We sat around her kitchen table, and she served me coffee just like her daughter had served Paula tea. I caught myself watching her pinkie finger and looked up at her face.

"You think I can see Caroline soon?" she asked me.

"That's what I've come to talk about. We think you should come tomorrow. Sit and chat with me and let Caroline play."

"I can't talk to my own daughter?" She was fixin' to get huffy.

"Caroline's still a little skittish. Let's do this slow. We want what's best for her."

"If you think that's necessary." She sounded skeptical. She poured me a cup of coffee in her green-flowered china cup.

"Sugar?" she asked. She pushed the sugar bowl and creamer over toward me, not waitin' on me like her daughter did Paula. "You hungry?"

"This is good."

She watched me fix my cup and take a sip, then put both palms on the table like she was bracing herself. "I have an idea."

"I thought we decided."

"Not that. I'll do whatever you say about Caroline as long as she doesn't start that awful jabbering again."

"She hasn't talked to any spirits at all since she's been with us."

"That's good, then."

"And she's acting more her age."

She nodded, but I could tell there was something else on her mind. "I've decided to tell Old Man Hauser that I'm going back to work. He doesn't want to pay for this house. Support me and the kids. I think he'll agree," she took a deep breath, "as long as I have somebody to look after the children."

"You said you'd like to go back to work."

"I would. I feel so much better when I have my own friends and can get out." She paused, watching me carefully. "I want to hire you full-time to take care of the house and Caroline while I'm at work."

I tried not to clatter my cup when I set it down. "Me?"

"I like you, and so does Caroline. At least you said Caroline is doing better with you and . . ."

"Paula."

"Right. That is, if you'd want to do it. I could get you good money. Old Man Hauser's got it, you know, but you'd have to go meet him," she said all in a rush.

I bit my cheek to keep from making a sound. She had no way of knowing what she was asking of me.

"I'll do all the talking," she continued. "I can't tell you what it would mean to me to have you around. A friend."

"Well, now, that sure is an idea." Things was tight with me only working a few half-days. Plus I could keep an eye out, see that Lily acted right with her child. See how to help her if there was another problem. She was a bit of a child herself, this woman, but she tickled me with her unorthodox ways. She didn't seem to be prejudiced, leastwise not so much as other white folk. Still, I'd have to face John Hauser, who had no idea in the whole wide world who I really was to him.

"I'll have to give notice," I said.

"Oh, you got another job?"

"Part-time is all."

"Good, then. Can you come talk to the Hausers next Sunday afternoon?"

"Let's just see if we can get Caroline back to normal first."

I waited until we'd gone to bed to tell Paula. I didn't want the child to hear and get excited afore it was all decided. Paula liked the idea right away.

"But it's the Graysons," I said. "Lily don't know my full relationship to them."

Paula reached across the pillow and stroked my cheek. "That family owes you."

I drew my legs up to my chest. "I swore I wouldn't have nothin' to do with them ever again. I always watched him from a distance. His parents never did tell him."

"'Give unto them beauty for ashes, the oil of joy for mourning.' So it says in Isaiah."

"Maybe." Paula knew the Good Book upside down and sideways, but I'd copied a good bit of it out for Miss Grayson, so sometimes I could give her a run for her money. Not this time, though.

"You only have to see . . . the grandfather once. All you have to do is stand there and let Lily do the talkin'. You can still say, 'Yes, sir' and 'No, sir,' can't you?" She said this with an exaggerated accent, real country like. Made me laugh.

"Would it help if you told Lily about—you know?" She flipped over onto her back.

All of a sudden, Caroline jumped up my side, almost knocking the breath outta me. She crawled between us, brazen as could be. "Is it story time?"

"Goodness gracious, child—" I ain't even heard her comin'. "—we just talkin'."

"Uncle Remus," she crowed and settled down, ready to listen.

We just laughed.

"Br'er Rabbit."

"It's your turn," Paula said. "I reckon you'll have to know a bunch of stories soon." She winked at me.

"All right, but we got to turn the lights out."

Caroline snuggled deeper, only her quick breath betraying her excitement.

"Once upon a time," I began, and then I told the story right to the end. I was quiet for a while. Both Paula's and Caroline's breath was steady and even. I slipped out of bed, picked Caroline up real slow, and carried her back to her cot. I mussed up the other bed on my way back, then curled up behind Paula, stealing warmth and courage.

The first thing on the agenda was Lily's visit. I cooked up some pinto beans with a touch of pork rind for supper. Paula picked a mess of spinach from the garden. We told Caroline her mother was coming to visit after we ate. She looked back and forth between us for a minute, but we changed the subject, Paula telling some funny story about the dog where she worked. Soon Caroline was laughing.

She and Paula was on the couch together when the knock came. Caroline jumped up to see, but when she heard her mother's voice, she ran back and tried to hide under Paula's arm.

At the door, I whispered to Lily, "Just come sit by me at the fire. Act like you don't see her."

Lily started to huff, so I said right quick, "Treat her like she's a wild cat. Let her come to you."

I don't think she liked me calling her daughter feral, but she'd almost been when we'd taken her in. I sat between the couch and the other chair I'd put out. She waffled, but finally settled down. Her perfume filled up the room, not in a cloying way, but rich, recalling the deep greens and voluptuous flowers of summer. "What's your scent?"

"I use Jungle Gardenia." She held up her wrist. "Do you like it?"

I took a whiff. "It's nice."

"Maybe I can get you some with my store discount." She kept looking over at Caroline, who was hiding behind a pillow.

"It's a little too bold for me, but it suits you. I think. I like rose water."

Paula started to tell an Uncle Remus story real soft so Caroline had to come closer to hear.

"They may have that." Lily looked back at me, her eyes wide with confusion.

I shook my head to tell her not to pay any attention to her child. "You got your job back yet?"

"I've got an appointment to talk to them tomorrow. I'd like to know something before we—" Her eyes strayed to Caroline, who had firmly turned her back on her mother and was listening to Paula, who had added voices and gestures to engross the child.

"Talk to Mr. Hauser?" I finished her sentence for her.

She looked back at me. "Don't worry," I whispered. "You're her mother. She'll come back to you."

Her eyes teared up, so I asked right fast, "What do you do at—where you interviewing again?"

"Di Stefano's. I'd only been there six months before Nate made me quit."

At the mention of her father's name, Caroline risked a look at us, but Lily didn't notice.

"I was selling shoes there."

"What's that like? You got to touch everybody's feet?"

She chuckled. "You don't want to hear about that."

I tilted my head toward Caroline. "It's best if we just keep talking."

"Oh," she stretched out her legs. "Well, it's a nice store. Got a lot of Italian shoes."

So I kept asking her questions, pulling out more about the store, about other jobs she'd had.

"But I really wanted to be a singer," she said after a while. "That's how I met Nate."

"No kidding."

"I'd always sung in church."

"You do have a good voice. I've heard you."

"Thank you. When I was about seventeen, I entered a singing contest. I was helping Daddy out in the grocery store, but this came along, and we needed the extra money. Plus it was my dream, you know?"

"Sure."

"I won the local contest in Gastonia. The regional was in Greensboro. Nate and his two brothers came to listen. I won that one, too. I sang 'Summertime,' you know, by Billie Holiday."

I was a bit surprised she knew that singer.

"Anyway, he walked up to me afterward, all shy, holding his hat in his hands. He said, 'You have a mighty fine voice, Miss.' I could see his brothers were egging him on, sort of laughing behind his back, but he blushed like he'd never talked to a woman. But those two were older than him, so I figured they had girlfriends. Wives, even. Nate's six years older than me."

Caroline was hunkered down behind the pillow listening to her mother's story. Lily looked over at her. "Act like you don't notice her," I whispered right quick.

"Anyway," she said, a little flustered. "He asked me out. Said he had a car and Gastonia wasn't too far to come see a beautiful woman like me. That's how we met. Asked me to marry him six months later."

Lily looked over at Caroline. As soon as the child saw her mother had noticed her attention, she dove behind Paula.

"It's all right," I said, standing up to indicate it was time to leave. "It was a good start."

"It was nice visiting with you." She raised her voice a little. "Nice seeing you, Paula."

"You, too, Mrs. Hauser."

"Please, call me Lily."

Paula hesitated. "All right."

She turned back to me. "Sunday afternoon at two o'clock."

Come Sunday, I left Caroline with Paula after church lunch and walked down to the Hauser place. I steeled myself to talking to this family that I had such a complicated relationship with. Lily had promised to do all the talkin'. She still didn't know what she was askin' of me. I ain't told her the story yet. But this was good money she was offerin'. Besides, I liked her and the child. And I'd get a chance to study John up close.

When I arrived, there was trouble. Lily weren't on the porch like she'd promised. Mrs. Hauser was waitin' on me. I lifted my foot to the step, but she said, "You that nigger taking care of our grandchild?"

I put my foot back down on the gravel. "Yes, ma'am."

"How come you got our child at your house and nobody told us?" She stood at the top of the steps to the porch, hands on her hips, eyes narrowed.

"You'd have to ask Li—Miss Lily, ma'am, how it come to be."

"Her father-in-law is talking to her now. I'm asking you."

"Miss Lily asked for my help. She was real upset by her husband going to—uh, being on her own, you know."

"We took Jimmy. I raised eleven myself." She shook her head, put out with Lily.

The old lady was right. Our generation was used to hard work. "Yes, ma'am. Miss Lily seemed real shook up by the turn of events, and Caroline can be a handful."

"She's a lively child. Very imaginative."

So that's how they were going to spin it. Maybe they didn't know about her talkin' to spirits. I done forgot what Lily had told me, so I played it safe. "Yes, ma'am. Smart, too."

The old lady studied me another minute. "I reckon you can come in, then."

We walked across the porch that stretched the whole front of the house with a row of big rocking chairs and a swing at the end. The front entrance had a table tucked in under the stairwell. Big black telephone sittin' there for everybody to see. I could hear Mr. Hauser yelling from the living room.

"What in the Sam Hill you thinking, girl? Here I am taking care of your son, but that's not good enough for you? Who you think you are anyway?"

Took after his father all right.

"Your people ain't nothing but white trash, I tell you, but you act like you married to N.T. Richardson instead of N.T. Hauser."

Richardson owned one of the cigarette companies in town.

Lily stood in front of him, her head hanging down, her cheeks scarlet. John Hauser sat in an overstuffed chair next to a tiled fireplace. I studied him from the doorway. Same piercing blue eyes his daddy had. Bushy eyebrows. High forehead, and his blond hair had turned that silver-gray. I pushed down a rush of grief.

He was still yellin'. "You need to get off your high horse and come back down to earth. You act like you too good to cook and clean for your husband. Now you too high and mighty to take care of your own children?"

Lily let the silence draw out. "I wasn't my right self, sir, after Nate was arrested. Caroline was acting all crazy—"

"There ain't nothing wrong with my grandchild."

"No, sir. It's just that—I was thinking that you've already raised a big family, sir, and you've got Rose with you now and her two children. It hardly seems fair to ask you to take care of us."

"I'm a man. I meet my responsibilities."

"Yes, sir. It's just that—" Her eyes raised up a little toward that unyielding face. I swear you could cut rocks with that chin of his. "I could earn some money. If you'd let me."

"I don't need no woman working in this family."

"No, sir. I'm just trying to help, is all. That store would take me back, and you could pay Maggie here less than it's taking to take care of us."

The old man started to interrupt, but she added, "I know you have enough money, sir."

"I ain't made out of gold, you know."

"No, sir. It's just that she could look after the children while I'm at work. Caroline likes her."

"Is that right, Missy? Does Caroline like you?"

It took me a few seconds to realize he was talking to me. I studied the Persian rug under my feet, not really seeing it. I was trying hard not to shake.

"Well, does she?"

"Yes, sir. She's happy with us."

"Us? You living in sin with some nigger down in that holler?"

I looked up, scared he might know where our house was.

"That's right. I know about your little cabin down there almost swallowed up with kudzu." He pointed out the window with a gnarled finger. "I'm the one building these houses. It's my business to know the neighborhood."

"Yes, sir," I said. Best to fill him up with as many "yes, sirs" as we could get down his mean old gullet. "I live with a church woman, sir. She teaches Sunday school. Neither one of us is married."

He glared.

"We don't allow no men in the house, sir. 'Cept the reverend."

He sat back and studied the two of us standing in front of him like we was criminals answering to a judge.

"You taken care of children before—what's your name?"

"Maggie, sir."

God only knew if I'd taken care of my own child, things woulda turned out different. He woulda been nicer. But I never had a chance.

"Well?"

"Yes, sir. I taught school for near on thirty years." My back straightened with some residual pride.

"School? I ain't never heard of no nigger teaching school."

"It was a colored school, sir. But now they requirin' a college degree, so I been working for the Wilson family."

"The tobacco people?"

"Yes, sir." I tightened my mouth so as not to smile.

"Well, now. I reckon I could talk to them about you."

I thought I'd better warn them I'd been offered something full-time. I didn't think Mrs. Wilson would mind. I knew a girl at church could replace me there.

"You think that store would take you back?" he asked Lily.

"Yes, sir. They were happy with my work. Hated to see me go."

"Let me talk to Mr. Wilson, then."

The old man looked mighty pleased to have a reason to call a rich family. He nodded, dismissing us, but I was studying his hands, just looking for any resemblance, so he barked, "You can go now."

I went home and wept while Paula tried her best to console me. She sang to me, listened to me rant and rave, rocked me, finally made me drink a shot of whiskey we kept for medicinal purposes. In the end, though, weren't nothin' to be done about it. What was past was past. He'd been ripped from me—body, then soul.

By the end of the next week, it was all settled. Lily would start back to work at Di Stefano's the next Monday, Jimmy would move back home, and I'd be taking care of the both of them when he got home from school in the afternoon. We had Lily drop by the house again midweek. Caroline didn't seem as scared of her. Even talked to her a little. The next day, we told Caroline that I was going to be taking care of her at her old house, that her mother was coming on Sunday, and that she'd have to go home with her, but that I'd be there the next morning bright and early.

"You promise?" she asked, grave as a bishop this time.

"I do," I said.

"Every day?"

"Monday through Friday."

She stared at me for a long while, then nodded. When Lily came Sunday afternoon, Paula had to tell Caroline to leave with her. The little girl stared at her for a minute. "Will you come take care of me, too?"

Paula reached down and hugged her. "You can come visit me any-time."

And so we started a new phase. Things worked out pretty smooth for a good, long time.

15

C aroline
Maggie took care of me during the day, and Mother

seemed happy now that she was working again. Things settled back to normal. Time melted into a golden haze, almost eternal, like it does when you're happy and nothing much interrupts the flow of events. Children forget the bad times. At least I did.

One morning Maggie declared that I was ready to learn to write. She'd been a schoolteacher when she was younger. How she ever became a maid is a testament to the Old South—not many black women avoided that fate. Teaching me must have been a welcomed respite from cooking and cleaning. First came the alphabet. Then while she ironed, I sat and copied out of the Bible. Then she'd read me what I'd written, careful to point out my mistakes. Soon I graduated to writing on my lamp shade, but Mother put a stop to that right quick. I thought about the wall once but remembered her hand on my behind.

Next came learning to read what I'd written. For this, she sat beside me, sipping her afternoon coffee, and sounded out the words. Soon enough I'd read to her while she washed up the dishes after lunch or did the laundry. If I stumbled, she'd come over and look, but oftentimes she seemed to already know what I'd copied out, just like she'd written it all herself. We got along good, Maggie and me. We spent the rest of the summer together, all fall, and she and Paula even came over for Christmas. By the next year, it seemed Maggie had always been with us.

Come spring, Mother told me she had a surprise for me. She parked the car and climbed up three concrete stairs to a small white bungalow that sat next to the drugstore. She knocked on the door, then put her hand on my shoulder as if to reassure herself I was still there. It opened to reveal a woman with flyaway dark hair wearing a faded house dress. She nodded at Mother like she'd been expecting us.

"Caroline, this is Miss Miller. She's going to teach you to play the piano."

I clutched at Mother's hand.

"We talked about this, remember?"

I didn't. I had a gift for forgetting.

She gave my hand an encouraging squeeze. "After you're done, you walk on down to Maggie's house. She'll be looking for you."

I squinted up at her.

"You get to spend the night there."

"Really?" I asked.

"Yes, if you listen to Miss Miller."

I would have cleaned out the whole bathroom to get to spend the night with Maggie and Paula or stood on my stool and washed all the dishes, so I stepped inside.

Thus began my weekly lessons with my new piano teacher. First I found middle *C* and from there learned to play scales. "Like this," she said, and easy as pie pressed down three ivory keys, then tucked her thumb under and played the last five, ending on another *C*.

I tried, my tongue stuck between my lips in concentration, but I just couldn't reach.

"Your hand is too small to do it properly, so just let go of *E* and jump ahead."

I punched the keys, Miss Miller showing me every time I faltered.

Soon she played a song for me. She had elegant hands—long, slender fingers topped with smooth nails trimmed into half-moons. They didn't match the rest of her at all—rounded shoulders, drab clothes, and slightly turned-down mouth.

"Now it's your turn."

I just stared at her.

"See, this is what I played." She pointed to the sheet music propped up on the piano. "This is the song I played, written out."

"You can't write down music," I said.

"Sure you can." She taught me how to read the musical notes, which one matched *C* and up the scale.

About halfway through our lesson, another woman came in. She took off her hat and gloves, then kicked off her shoes just like Mother did when she came home from work. She gave Miss Miller a shy little wave and walked down the hall. I heard a door close. Miss Miller and I went back to matching notes on the page with keys on the piano. Soon the new lady came back out dressed in a somewhat less faded house dress than what Miss Miller wore, still shaking out her hair from the tight bun it had been in.

I stopped looking down at the ivory and ebony keys and stared at her.

"This is Agnes. She lives here, too," Miss Miller said.

Agnes went into the kitchen and came out with a glass of iced tea and took a seat behind us, listening to Miss Miller's instruction. I'd almost learned all the notes by the time the hour finished, although I still couldn't make out why the scale started with *C* instead of *A*.

So began my new Tuesday routine, which was Mother's day off. I stayed with her until lunch, and then I'd go to Miss Miller for my music lesson. After that, I walked down to Maggie and Paula's house all by myself. I felt all grown up and never dallied. I passed by our old white house on Broad with the beauty parlor next door, but didn't stop. A new family lived there now. They didn't have any rabbits with little pink noses. Maggie would be waiting, and we played the most wonderful games. Then we made supper.

"Do you want to feel grit in your teeth when you eat those greens?"

I shook my head.

"Then you got to rinse them three times," Maggie said.

"But—"

"Three times. Now lift them all out of there, fill up the sink again."

I reached for the kettle.

"Cold water. You don't want to cook them in the sink."

"Why?"

Paula looked over her shoulder as she was frying up some chicken. "Because you got to get the sand out of them first," she answered, like Maggie hadn't said it already.

I turned on the faucet and ran cold water.

"You got to rinse the sink. See that dirt that came off the greens the first time? Honestly, child."

I threw handfuls of water on the sides.

"Try not to get it all over the floor, please."

I sighed.

"You want to eat, don't you?"

"Yes, ma'am."

"Good, 'cause the way you carryin' on, I thought you didn't care about supper."

I filled the sink and dunked the greens, swishing them around like Maggie had shown me. Then I lifted the curling, dripping leaves onto the dish tray, cleaned out the sink again, and repeated the process.

Once I was done, Maggie ran her fingers along the bottom of the sink, lips pursed. "Hmm, looks like you got it all this time. Now take that pot there and throw them greens in it. Put in some water."

"Wish we had some pork rind," Paula said.

"Momma has some," I offered.

"We ain't at your house," Maggie said. "Not too much water. Now carry it over to the stove. Paula will light the burner for you. Cook it until it steams. No longer. We don't want to eat mush."

"Yes, ma'am."

Close to Paula, I could smell her lilac scent beneath the tantalizing smell of cornmeal-dusted chicken. I leaned in closer.

"Watch out, now. The fat might splatter on you."

So my life orbited around these women except on Sundays when Mother, Jimmy, and I had to go over to our grandparents' for Sunday dinner. Granddaddy used to grab me and rub his stubbled cheek against mine. I hated it. Jimmy escaped with the older cousins and played near the big evergreen in the front yard, its skirt of branches low, creating a secret place. They climbed and I gravitated over, fascinated, but Mother always pulled me back, telling me not to muss my dress. My brother lived with us then, but he was in school and then out playing with his friends, so we hardly saw each other. It seemed I lived in a world of women, a solid, safe, predictable world. So the winter months passed, and early spring green braved the cold evenings and crept out on the limbs of trees.

Then one day after my music lesson ended, a seedy-looking man walked in the door. "Hey, doll."

Miss Miller jumped up and kissed him. Right in front of me.

I stared at the intruder. He wore a blue plaid suit coat with navy trousers. His tie was pulled loose, and his white shirt opened at the collar. On his feet were two-toned Oxfords. "Well, hello, little lady. Who do we have here?"

I just stared. He leaned against the doorjamb, one foot propped over the other, making himself at home. He smiled at me all friendly while his sharp, hawk eyes searched me out. He took off his fedora and twirled it on one finger. He looked like some hustler in a gangster movie. I turned and stared at my sheet music.

"This is Joe," Miss Miller said. "Joe, meet Caroline."

"Hello," I said, not looking up.

"Hi, Caroline. Whatchu playing?" he asked.

I shrugged. I really didn't know the name of the piece.

"Joe and I are going to be married," Miss Miller announced.

"That's right, doll." He grabbed her around the waist.

Miss Miller ducked when he went to kiss her again.

"But you can't marry him. You've got Agnes," I blurted out.

"Agnes?" Miss Miller asked. "What do you mean, I've got her?"

"But what's she going to do?"

Joe slapped his knee and guffawed.

Miss Miller shook her head at him. "Agnes can live with us. It will be the three of us. There's enough room."

Everything in me rebelled. This was a big mistake. This man wasn't to be trusted. I could tell just by the way he slouched and watched me like I was a mouse to be snatched up and eaten. Why couldn't Miss Miller see it? Besides, he messed up the symmetry. Here there was Miss Miller and Agnes, and at Maggie's house there was her and Paula. He didn't fit.

"But I thought it was you and Agnes," I blurted out, not really knowing how to say what I was feeling.

Miss Miller stared at me, hands on her hips. "She's my sister, Caroline. We ain't lesbians."

I didn't know what that word meant, but I knew it was bad the way she spat it out like a taste of something rotten.

Just in time, Mother's car pulled up to the curb. I'd forgotten she was picking me up today. I ran toward the door, eager to escape the gangster and his girlfriend, sorry for poor abandoned Agnes, but Mother was already on the porch, calling out in her loud, cheerful voice, "Can I come in?"

Miss Miller introduced Joe, repeating her intention to marry him. "Your daughter's worried about Agnes. Seems like she thought I was in love with her or something." Her face was red.

"What?" Mother looked from Miss Miller to me.

I hung by the door, trying to hid behind Mother's big purse.

"She thinks we're lesbians."

Mother sucked in her breath. "What did you say?"

"Lesbians, your daughter thinks we're lezzies." She laughed, harsh and mean.

Mother's spine straightened like an umbrella going up in a sudden storm. "Caroline," she said, her voice imperious, "go to the car."

I didn't need any further encouragement. I ran, but something made me linger by the gate behind a gangly forsythia bush.

"I have a maid who takes care of Caroline sometimes at her home. She lives with another woman. She's just thinking about them."

"Are they lesbians?" the woman spat.

"No, Caroline just doesn't understand. She's just thinking you were like them—two women living in a house together. She doesn't know what a lesbian is."

"We ain't like no niggers, if that's what you're saying."

Mother stared at her for a minute. "Do you realize who you're talking to?"

Miss Miller eyed her right back.

"My last name is Hauser. Ring a bell?"

Miss Miller took a step back.

"That's right. Hauser, as in your landlord, Mr. John Hauser—" Mother pointed toward the car "—that child's grandfather. So if I were you, I'd be a little more respectful." Mother turned on her heel like a star ballerina. I ran for the car and slipped into the front seat. Mother got in and drove away fast, like the storm was about to break and the lightning would strike Joe and Miss Miller down. I sat hunched over.

She turned down a side street that ran down to the park and pulled the car over. "Tell me what happened."

I stared at my lap, afraid to look at her.

"It's all right. I just need to understand," she coaxed.

I hazarded a glance at her. She was smiling, but her mouth was tight. "It's important that you tell me. You're not in trouble."

"She said she was going to get married."

"And?"

"But what about Agnes?"

"What about her?"

I fidgeted, trying to find words for what I was feeling.

"Have you ever met this man before?" Mother asked.

I shook my head *no*, then screwed up my face and whispered, "I don't like him."

Mother matched my conspiratorial tone. "Why not?"

"He's mean."

Mother sat in silence for a minute, studying me. After a while, she said in a normal tone of voice, "You know, I don't like him either."

Relief filled me.

"Do you want to go back there?"

"No."

"Do you want to keep taking piano lessons?"

I shrugged.

"All right, then. I'll tell her."

So my piano lessons stopped, but that wasn't the end of Miss Miller. Her little house still stood next to the drugstore. As spring advanced, my group of friends moved from paper dolls and board games to playing outside. Sometimes we went to the drugstore in the afternoons for candy.

Roxie was my best friend of all the gang. I'd met her first. It had been maybe three years earlier, the day we moved into the new house, back before Daddy disappeared. I emerged from the car that late summer day and looked at my new house, then behind me at the stately golden stones of the mansion across the street, and saw a girl staring out at us from behind a row of boxwood hedges. She stood behind her cover poised like a deer, or a hunter of one, imaginary bow and arrow suspended over one shoulder, moccasins silent on the pine needle floor, and I knew that if I didn't capture her now, she would be gone. So I walked straight toward her, reaching after her with my name when I saw her start to shy away. "I'm Caroline. I just moved here."

"My name's Roxie." Slightly older and a little taller than me, her olive face was set with liquid brown eyes beneath brown bangs, and her hair hung to her shoulders.

"Do you live here?"

She nodded.

"That's my new house," I said, pointing across the tar-topped road.

We contemplated each other.

"Can I play with you?" I asked.

"Sure," she said. "What do you want to do?"

I shrugged. We walked around her yard, and she introduced me to the rose bower, the vegetable garden, the compost pile, apple and pear trees, and chicken coop. Just when we'd finally managed to slide through a hatch in the empty chicken house floor and crawl around beneath it, my mother called.

"Coming," I yelled at the top of my voice. "I've got to go. Will you play with me again?"

She nodded her head, her smudged cheeks rounding in a smile.

"Good." I wiggled out and ran home.

It was in this way that the daughter of a mill hand and the daughter of the vice president of Swan Textiles became best friends.

I don't remember exploring my new house that day. I do remember my mother asking me if I wanted to see my new room, prodding me to get excited about it as we explored. We'd moved only six blocks or so, about three from my grandfather's, to a neighborhood that had started as country mansions about a hundred and fifty years earlier. Gradually the town grew out to them, so that succeeding generations either moved to more fashionable neighborhoods or slowly sold off tracts of land to enlarge the family coffers. Up the hill past Washington Park, the houses were grand like my friend's mansion, but down the hill in my direction they shrank to the size of cardboard boxes, each with the same floor plan.

My father felt he'd arrived at the pinnacle of his success, being able to have a house built to his own specifications. Ours wasn't one of the cookie-cutter bungalows. He'd hunted rabbits in the woods surrounding these mansions, sneaking off to wander and play in the muddy creek at the very bottom of the hill. Now he'd built his house among them. He belonged. But the day we moved in, I went straight to Roxie's house instead of crossing the threshold of his pride and joy. He declared allegiance with me to my mother. "I liked that house when I was a boy, too."

After Roxie and I got to be friends, she included me in her circle. There was Joan from next door, whose father was nicknamed King Kong by my mother because of his loud voice. Joan's mother dressed like a man, trousers, white button-down shirt, the whole nine yards. I wondered if she was really their mother. How could she be, considering how mannish she was? Yet there were five children stuffed into two bedrooms in her white-clapped bungalow.

Across the street was Polly in another bungalow. Her mother taught her about sex before all the rest of us. Polly shared what she learned, but we didn't believe a word of it. Across from Roxie's huge house was Judy, whose brick ranch house bridged the gap between the richest and poorest of us. We were a girl gang, ranging in age over about four years, spending summers in a tight circle but school days in different classes.

That summer day after my music lessons had stopped and I'd forgotten all about having a daddy, the gang went for candy at the drugstore. Polly always got those wax lips and thought they made her look funny. She spent the whole afternoon chewing on them and making funny eyes to go with her clown mouth. Those fake lips tasted awful. Just like those wax bottles. They weren't worth chewing through to get to the liquid inside. Judy liked M&M's and Sugar Daddies, which were a second to anything chocolate in my book.

We'd take our candy to somebody's house and lay it all out like discovered treasure. I'd open the M&M's and separate them by color. Then the trading began. Chocolate ones were worth the most, of course, with red coming a close second. Green ones were okay, and orange and yellow ones worth the least. "I'll give you four yellows for one chocolate," Judy said.

"Nuh-uh."

"The yellows are chocolate inside," Roxie said, two years older and wiser than me. "You'll get more chocolate to eat."

After candy, we'd take our jacks outside on the sidewalk and bounce the little red rubber ball to see how many we could pick up. Or ride our wooden horses around pretending to be the Lone Ranger and Tonto, only there were too many of us, so we had to make up names. We fought over who could be the Lone Ranger.

One day soon after I quit my piano lessons, we walked by Miss Miller's house after our raid on the drugstore candy shelves, our pockets stuffed with treasure. Miss Miller and Joe rushed out onto the porch, and she hollered out, "Are these your lesbian friends?"

I jumped in surprise.

"What did she say?" Roxie asked.

"Lezzies, lezzies," Miss Miller taunted.

Judy stopped in the middle of the sidewalk, gaping. "Who is that?"

Fervently wishing the ground would open up and take me, I managed to whisper, "She used to be my music teacher."

"Music teacher?"

"Let's go." I tugged at Roxie's arm.

"Lesbians, lesbians." The accusation had become a chant.

"What are lesbians?" Joan whispered.

I didn't know, so I made something up. "They're mean ladies."

Roxie put her hands on her hips, looking grown up. "It's women who like other women—you know, they marry them."

"Women can't marry other women," Polly said. She turned and glared at the two adults on the porch like they were idiots. "We're not lesbians," she shouted.

"Yes, you are," Miss Miller shouted.

"Are not. Are not." Judy and Joan took up a chant.

Joe walked down the steps with Miss Miller on his heels. "Get out of here, you little lesbian tramps."

"Well, I never," Roxie said, a perfect imitation of her high-class mother. "I'm going to tell on you."

The two adults burst out laughing.

Roxie stuck her nose high in the air and said to us, "Let's go."

We stopped yelling and followed Roxie to her house, where she went in search of her mother, candy forgotten. Mrs. Jameson's frown deepened as she listened. "Now who is this woman?"

"I used to take piano lessons from her," I admitted, my face burning.

"And why is she shouting at you when you go by?"

"She's getting married, but I asked her what would happen to Agnes."

"Who is this Agnes?"

"She says she's her sister."

Mrs. Jameson stared at me, hands on her hips. "When your mother gets home from work, would you ask her to call me?"

"Yes, ma'am."

We were dismissed. We remembered our candy, and soon things were back to normal. Mrs. Jameson reminded me to ask Mother to call her as I was heading out the back door.

"Our maid lives with another woman—roommate, you know," Mother said into the black mouthpiece of the telephone. "I guess she just got confused when this man showed up at the music teacher's house. She's used to just women with Nate . . . away on this job."

She listened for a minute.

"I can't believe she shouted at the girls. I'll tell you what I'm going to do. I'm going to get Mr. Hauser to kick them out. He owns that house."

She listened again.

"Well, if they don't have any better sense than to rush out on their porch and yell at the children, I don't think they should be staying there. The girls need to be able to go to the drugstore and not be embarrassed."

After she hung up, Mother turned to me. "I want you to stop walking past that house. Whenever you go to the drugstore, go the other way down Banner. Stay off Acadia."

"Yes, ma'am."

"Good girl. I'll let you know when it's safe again."

I forgot about Miss Miller in the rush of spring and my older friends getting out of school. We climbed trees, fished for crayfish in the park, and rode our wooden horses around Roxie's one-acre yard. But one day, Mother put me in the car and drove off. "I want you to see this."

She parked next to the drugstore near Miss Miller's house. There was a truck in front of the house and the three of them were loading boxes into it. Mother got out of the car and marched up to them. I slunk behind her. The three stopped and stared at her.

"So Old Man Hauser kicked you out, did he? Couldn't find another of his houses to move into? Serves you right, treating my daughter like you did. Calling her and her friends names. They couldn't even walk down this street. Now you ain't got a place to live." Mother talked more like Maggie when she was mad.

Miss Miller opened her mouth to say something, but Mother marched right over her. "I hope he's worth it. He don't look like it to me." She turned her back and said to me, "Tomorrow you and your friends can walk by this house again, no problem."

I stuck my tongue out at Miss Miller and jumped into the car.

16

Caroline

One afternoon late that next fall, Maggie sat with me in my room watching me color. This was unusual in itself, but she kept lifting her head and listening, like she was expecting something to happen. When she heard a car pull up, she grabbed her handbag, kissed me good-bye, and went out the front door. Just like that. I'd never seen her do that before, use the front door and sneak out, but I was coloring a page from Cinderella and didn't spent a lot of time thinking about it.

I heard the noise of the back door opening, but I was putting the stars in Cinderella's crown, so I stayed in my room. Soon my mother called me to come into the kitchen. She was wearing her navy suit with a fancy hat, which she'd forgotten to take off, and a strange man sat in the chair at the table that was usually empty. When I came in, he drew in a sharp breath.

"Caroline," Mother said, "do you know who this is?"

I studied the man sitting a bit huddled up, his eyes darting from my face back to his hands folded in his lap. He wore a blue shirt and black pants, and his hair was cut real short.

I shook my head. "No."

The man winced and closed his eyes like somebody had slapped him.

"This is your daddy," Mother said.

"I don't have a daddy."

The man shook his head back and forth, then put his face in his hands.

"You do have a daddy. He's just been gone a while." Then she reached out and pulled his hand away from his face. "Don't worry. Just give her time. She'll remember."

She stood up. "Come on, Nate, let's get you unpacked."

He scraped his chair back, wincing at the sound.

"You can go play now," Mother told me.

I shrugged and went back to my coloring book.

My brother remembered him, though, and told me stories about him. I got used to him sitting quietly in the extra spot at the table, meekly eating what was put before him, asking us about what we'd been doing while he was gone. Shaking his head and saying, "I've missed so much." Pretty soon I even started to remember him carrying me around looking at the lights in the house.

One day he took me out for an ice cream cone. We drove up Cascade Avenue, aptly named for the series of small hills that flowed down to one final descent that swooped down past my house and dead-ended at the woods. He stopped at the sign on Broad and said in a hushed voice, "I have something to tell you."

"What?" I stopped kicking my legs on the bottom of the seat and turned my head toward him.

He took a breath and looked down at the floor mat. He drove through the intersection and pulled over in front of one of my favorite houses, a white Colonial with big columns and an expansive front porch. I couldn't decide which of these old mansions would be the best one to live in if we couldn't have Roxie's.

Daddy took another deep breath, then shook his head. "This is hard for me."

I looked over at him. He studied me, his forehead wrinkled. I reached out my hand to touch his arm. "What's the matter?"

"I'm afraid you won't respect me anymore."

"I will."

He took a deep breath. "I'm a felon."

"No, Daddy, you're a Moravian," I said. That was the church we went to.

He laughed, enormously relieved.

I never did figure out what that word meant. Not until a long time later.

Roxie and I did everything together. Every Saturday morning we watched cartoons in her family library, a room I loved. Books covered one wall and filled a nook next to the stone fireplace. Pictures of fox hunts hung above the desk—horses, their manes braided in neat rows, men in red coats, and dogs milling around the horses' legs. We spent the night at each other's houses, explored her mother's walk-in closet and tried on clothes. We even got matching boxer dogs. We played with the gang, too, but I remember being with Roxie more.

Jimmy's school ended soon after Daddy came back home. I had gone all the way to second grade already. Public school wouldn't take me yet. They said I was too young. "But she's reading and writing already," Mother argued. "Maggie taught her."

This was lost on the system. "Rules are rules," they said. "Besides, there's just too many kids to make an exception for her." So I stayed at Salem Baptist and went to third grade there.

The school year went by in a flash, and Roxie and I spent the summer in a haze of heat and flowers, pushing our feet into the melting tar road between our houses, and watching the black-eyed Susan that grew in the ditch between our houses bloom.

One hot July day, we sat on Roxie's screened-in porch off the kitchen eating sandwiches. Roxie ate lunch here in the summers. Her house had three places to eat—a formal dining room complete with chandelier, a heavy, long table and matching chairs, stiff drapes hanging in the window. The breakfast nook off the kitchen was my favorite, narrow and rectangular, flanked on two sides with leaded glass windows that looked out on an ivy border and large, spreading trees. Shelves and drawers were built into the other wall, and crammed with blue china, linen, and silverware. The family sat at a long parson's table with a bench built into the wall and large chairs on the other side. The screened-in porch was almost run down, holding an old kitchen table with metal legs and an odd collection of chairs. The maids ate here in summer when a family meal was progressing in the breakfast nook, interrupted by rings of a bell kept by Roxie's mother's hand. The children sometimes ate on the screened-in porch when the family was spread far and wide.

We ate our sandwiches, legs swinging from our too-high chairs, and watched Bessie and Jeanne washing dishes and cutting up vegetables while Madeline ironed from the board built into the wall. The smell of hot cement permeated the air, and we were bored. Madeline had her hair up in braids and, intrigued with the change, we kept staring at her. I'd never seen braids like them before. Mother gathered up my long straw-blond hair, divided it into three sections at the neck, and simply braided the strands together. The other variation was to part my hair in the middle from crown to nape and make two plaits, one on each side. I'd lean over and brush my hair so that it hung straight from the top of my head to the floor. There was always something joyous about hanging upside down and brushing my hair in the wrong direction.

But Madeline's braids were magical. They started right at the part on top of her head and worked their way down the side right where the hair grew. How could she have separated out three strands to braid together from the middle of her head when new hair grew all the time and constantly had to be picked up into the strand?

Our afternoon project presented itself. Getting instructions from Madeline first, we ran upstairs to Roxie's room, took out comb, brush, rubber bands, bobby pins, even metal hairclips, and started in. We brushed, parted, pulled up little wisps of hair to begin a braid. But I ended up with short, stubby little braids that stuck out all over, not those majestic, neatly tucked rows Madeline had.

I threw the brush down. "I can't do it."

Roxie looked at my bristling head and tried to be kind. Adopting the manner of a beautician who has to salvage someone whose head was run over by a lawn mower, she said, "Oh, it's not all that bad. Here, let me try to smooth it out." She patiently patted my stalks, joining them together with bobby pins. Each plait was progressively longer than the previous one, and all pinned together, I looked helmeted, ready for battle. Halfway through the back, Roxie ran out of silver metal clips and resorted to brown bobby pins, so even the helmeted look was flawed. We both surveyed the wreck. Even my beautician couldn't think of anything to say.

We trooped downstairs to the kitchen and silently confronted Madeline, who smiled at the ironing board and bit her lip, trying not to laugh at the two solemn-faced little girls, I suppose, one with hair sticking out all over her head. "Been trying to braid your hair?" she observed casually.

"Yes, but we can't get it to look like yours," I said, staring in wonder at the neat rows on her head.

"You've got to keep picking up the hair," she explained again, "and blend it in with what you've got in your hand."

We nodded like we understood, but her explanation was incomprehensible to me. We ran upstairs again and repeated the same operation with the same results. In a temper, I tore all the pins out of my hair, pulled out all the rubber bands, and undid the braids. I stood staring at my witch self in the mirror and started to cry.

At a loss, Roxie said, "Come on. Let's go outside. We can climb the tree." She waited.

"No, I want to braid my hair."

"But we've tried and tried, and we can't do it. Let's go outside."

"No."

Roxie had never seen me so stubbornly set on something. Being naturally even natured, she certainly didn't understand it. She tried again. "Let's go ride our bikes to the store and get some candy. I've got a whole quarter."

"No, I want my hair braided."

"But we can't do it."

"Let's ask Madeline."

This had never occurred to Roxie, but she was sure there was something wrong with the idea. "But she's working. We're not supposed to bother them."

"Come on," I said.

Down the stairs we went one more time with comb, brush, pins, and rubber bands. We inched into the kitchen, bumping into each other, trying to look meek and deserving of special favors. "Madeline," I said after Roxie refused to open her mouth, "we just can't do it. We tried and tried, but it never comes out right. Would you please, please, please braid our hair? Please?" Roxie stood back, shamefaced over my fervor yet a little hopeful.

"Now, child, I've got to do all this ironing this afternoon." She pointed to two baskets full of clothes.

"Please," I pleaded with all my might. "Please, your hair is so beautiful."

She looked at me, then at Roxie, who had edged closer, and smiled at us.

"Oh, go on," Bessie said, looking over her shoulder at us from her place at the sink. "Go on." She was the live-in maid at Roxie's house, older than the rest, the authority under Mrs. Jameson.

"All right, now, but no squirming. I ain't got all day to be combing other children's hair."

"Me first, me first," I squealed.

"Well, all right." She lifted me onto the kitchen stool that stood between the stove and the ironing board and started combing out my hair, dividing it into sections, pinning each section. I closed my eyes, enjoying her touch. She divided the first few strands to start. I opened my eyes, trying to look around and see.

"Now hold still, you hear?" Madeline started her braid, pulling my hair tight in her fingers, braiding it in very tight rows. It hurt, but I was afraid to move. It was such an honor to have this magic being performed on me that I couldn't complain. She pulled my hair even tighter and I let out a squeal. "Ouch."

"Hold still. You're worse than my children."

I tried to hold still, but my hair stung at the roots. My hand strayed up to poke at the braid.

"Keep your hands down."

"But," I hesitated, "but it hurts. It's too tight."

"It's gotta be tight, elsen it won't straighten your hair," Madeline explained.

"Her hair's already straight, Maddie. You ain't gotta straighten hers," Bessie put in.

Madeline paused, then she jerked my hair even tighter. "It's gotta be tight. That's the only way to make cornrows."

I winced silently, making myself small to avoid Madeline's anger. She continued to work in silence, but I couldn't sit still. The side of my head burned. I stole a glance at Bessie, who surveyed the situation. She caught the look. "Maddie, now that's too tight for the child. You ought to loosen it up."

"My kids can take it. It ain't any tighter than how I do my kids' hair."

"Well, she ain't used to it. You ought to loosen it up."

I stayed silent, afraid to say anything. For some mysterious reason, Madeline's children endured this, and if they did, then I should, too. I felt some confused sense of wanting to be fair, but each time I moved even slightly, my hair pulled. I was starting to get a headache. Madeline had loosened the other braids she'd made, and they didn't hurt. I thought I could stand the persistent pinch at the side of my head just for the glory of those magical braids.

Soon she was done, and Jeanne produced a mirror. A miracle. My head was covered in tiny silk rows of braids, all neatly running next to each other like a cornfield. My eyes beamed delight. Jeanne moved the mirror around the side of my head, and the braids continued all around my head in smooth, unbroken rows. "It's beautiful. Beautiful. Oh, thank you." I stretched out my arms to hug her, but when I moved my head to the right, my hair pulled and my head ached. I was ashamed to admit it. If Madeline's children had to tolerate this, then I should, too. And she'd been angry about something, so I was afraid to ask her to loosen the one braid.

Roxie sat in the chair next and I stood, enchanted, trying to see how Madeline's fingers blended the new hair into her ongoing braid. I still hadn't figured it out by the time she finished. Her fingers moved so fast. We both stood there, elegant in our new cornrows. That's what Bessie called them. Content, we ran off to play Old Maid in Roxie's room. But the left side of my head ached, and I kept fiddling with it while we played.

"You're going to tear your braids out. Stop pulling at your hair," Roxie said.

"But it hurts."

"Then go ask Madeline to fix it."

I shrank into myself. Roxie shrugged and contemplated her hand of cards. She reached for a new one. I started tugging at my hair in earnest. Every time I turned my head, my eyes watered up, and I couldn't get rid of the pinch.

"It's your turn," Roxie said impatiently.

"Oh."

"Come on. Let's play cards."

"But my head hurts."

"Then go ask Madeline to fix it."

I looked at Roxie hesitantly. "Will you go with me?"

"Okay."

"Will you ask her for me?"

Roxie put her cards down with a huff. "Oh, all right."

We descended the stairs slowly, guilty of some unnamed crime, and stole into the kitchen.

Madeline looked up from her ironing. "What you girls want now?"

Roxie looked at me. I looked at the floor. "Caroline says her braid's too tight."

I was embarrassed, defeated. I couldn't take what to Madeline's children was an everyday event, a commonplace.

Madeline looked down and me and clucked her tongue. "All right, then. Come up here and I'll fix it. But you girls have got to stop bothering me after this. Which one is it?"

I pointed to the left side of my head, too embarrassed to speak. Madeline undid the braid, combed it out, and then braided it again, gently this time. "How's that?"

The relief was tremendous. "It's wonderful. Oh, thank you, Madeline." I buried my head in her shoulder and burst out crying.

"Well, child, it's all right now." Madeline patted my back until the tears stopped.

Roxie and I spent the rest of the afternoon in her room playing Old Maid. When it was getting on to be time for supper, I said goodbye to Roxie, then ran down the stairs and stuck my head in the kitchen to thank Madeline. She stood in the middle of the room, pulling a sweater over her uniform. She leaned over and picked up a wrinkled paper bag that served as her purse, then turned to walk out the door with Jeanne. I walked out beside them. "Thank you, Madeline, for fixing my hair. It's beautiful. It's so beautiful."

Madeline laughed at my enthusiasm. "You're welcome, child. Good night."

"Good-bye," I said, then turned and slipped through the bushes, listening to the crunch of gravel as Madeline and Jeanne headed for the bus stop. I ran for my house, excited to show Mother my new hairdo. When I walked in, she was bent over the stove, peering into the deep kettle set in the back, her hand full of noodles.

"Oh boy, spaghetti," I said, immediately forgetting my hair.

"Almost ready," Mother said. "Go wash your hands."

I headed for the bathroom.

"Who braided your hair?" she asked as soon as she looked up. "Come here. Let me see that."

I stopped next to the stove to let her inspect my new pride and joy. She dumped the noodles into the pot, then turned me to face her, tilting my head this way and that. "Well, I'll be. How in the world? Who did this?"

"Madeline."

"Who's that?"

"One of Roxie's maids."

"It's beautiful. Nate, look at this."

My father looked up from behind the evening newspaper and ran his eyes over me. "Looks like a pickaninny."

"It does not. This here is what they call French braiding. The French wear their hair this way."

I didn't tell Mother the maids called it cornrows.

"If the French wear their hair that way, then how'd the niggers learn it?"

"I don't know. Maybe in New Orleans." She turned her back on him and walked me into the light, examining my head closely. "I think it's beautiful."

I kept those braids for two days, but when they worked their way out of my slick, straight hair, I never asked Madeline to do them again.

17

Caroline

"It's not fair, I tell you. She didn't do a thing wrong. Not one thing. Those biddies who run the office at the store are just out to get her. They think they're so much better than the rest of us." Mother glanced down at me confidingly. She'd just gotten home from work. She hadn't had a spell a couple of years, so I'd practically forgotten about them.

"Now they finally did it. Made it look like she was goofing off at work. Taking too much time at lunch, too many breaks. Punching in late in the mornings because she already had a customer. That's why she did that. And she needs this job. More than I do. I don't know how she's going to eat." Mother stretched her feet and kicked off three-inch navy heels.

"Why doesn't she just explain it to them?" I asked.

Mother laughed. "Oh, Caroline, things are just not that simple in the world. She used to sing in this band, you see, and they think it's a bad image for the store."

I didn't know what to say to this. It didn't seem fair to me.

"I've got to get out of this bra and girdle," she said. But she didn't move.

Mother dressed up for work, bottom to top, underneath to the surface layer. I watched the whole procedure, start to finish. She wore black, beige, or white underwear and never mixed themor matched. She was solid monochrome underneath. She had two sets of each color—nylon panties, matching bra with lace, girdle, and slip. Sometimes she even wore underarm shields. She used Mitchum deodorant, which was supposed to keep you from sweating for three whole days. That sounded dangerous and mysterious to me—very grown-up—but when Mother wore certain dresses, she also wore the underarm shields to keep her clothes dry. The number of straps involved was prodigious.

Before dressing any further, Mother proceeded to the bathroom, where she carefully made up her face—first cream to protect the skin. "A woman's skin is her prize possession, the most important thing she has. Don't let yours go, Caroline. You see this cream? This is what you should use to keep your skin young. You don't need it now, of course," she would say, looking down at my young peach face gazing up at her, a flower drinking in everything.

Next, she applied a smooth coating of beige, just a tiny bit darker than her skin tone, a ghost of a summer tan all year round. "We're part Indian, you know," she would sometimes say.

I would look at my blond, blue-eyed reflection and contradict her. She ignored me.

Then rouge, actually a touch of lipstick which she blended in with her fingers. Next, her lips, then she would line her eyes. Her mascara brush scared me. I was certain she'd poke her eyes out, so I held my breath until this part was over. She topped it all off with a dusting of powder, then marched back into her room for the next layer.

Over the armor of bra, girdle, slip, and underarm protectors, she'd slip on a dress. Accessories were next—a pin, earrings, sometimes a scarf, and finally matching shoes. Mother had dozens of shoes, at least it seemed that way to me—navy pumps, black high heels with shiny decorations almost like brooches, white satin heels from a wedding somewhere, beige sandals to show her polished toenails, shoes dyed all colors to match different dresses, penny loafers. She even tried saddle shoes once, but ended up giving them away. My mother was a high heels kind of woman. She still sold shoes at Di Stefano's.

What an elegant place. Crystal chandeliers hung in every room. Mother's customers sat on white chairs, French provincial, I later learned. Plants, thick Oriental rugs, and mirrors filled the store. In the powder room, the gold swan faucet compete with marble basin was the height of luxury to me, but I never could quite get used to seeing that swan with its mouth wide open and water pouring out. Somehow a regurgitating swan didn't seem quite right, but I tried to put away my proletarian prejudices and would spend much of my time when visiting the store enjoying the luxury I knew I had been born to possess.

We couldn't take a shower at our house. Daddy had forbidden it soon after we moved in. The tile was plastic, and the water would slowly melt the glue beneath the tiles, and they would fall right off the wall. Sometimes cutting corners with money wasn't worth it in the long run. That's what Mother said. I figured Daddy got tired of trying to put them back up.

So I was restricted to tub baths. Later as a teen, with hair down to my waist because I had to look like Cynthia Lennon after all, it always went down the drain when I rinsed it under our plain silver chrome faucet. But all that elegant stretching was fun, leaning over until my head was poised under the running water, turning this way and that to rinse every side. I was preparing for the time when my bathroom would have a marble sunken tub with ferns and deep-piled rugs and an enormous gold swan that threw up water into my tub. I would float amid drifts of bubbles, barely visible, but glamourous, successful, and mysterious. I practiced for those days in the bathroom of my mother's store.

I was going on nine when my mother came home spitting mad that day I was telling you about. She stretched out in the chair, her high heels lying on their sides. "It makes me so angry. I don't know what she's going to do now. And there's not a thing I can do about it."

"You should quit," I said, drawing myself up to my full height.

Mother laughed again. "Oh, Caroline, I can't quit. No, that's not going to do any good. No one would pay any attention to that."

"But it's not fair. If she would just explain to them that she needs this job and that she didn't do anything wrong, then they'll give it back to her." I knew people were good and that they always helped each other out. I learned this at Vacation Bible School.

"Honey, you've got to learn sooner or later that the world is just not fair."

"But if she just explained it to them," I insisted. It was a simple misunderstanding that could be easily corrected.

"This kind of thing happens all the time. The world is just not fair."

"But . . ." I couldn't comprehend this. I would not. I resisted it with all the might in my body. Someone should just explain it to the women where Mother worked and they would fix it. But Mother was laughing, explaining to me this kind of injustice happened all the time, that people were deliberately mean to each other, to the point of depriving each other of food and jobs. It was intolerable. Someone had to do something about it. It was then that I knew that I'd been born to change the world, and I told her so.

"Well, I'll fix it."

This brought more laughter. "Just how are you going to do that?"

"I will. You'll see. We aren't going to let the world stay bad like this," I said. "We're going to fix it." I knew this with every fiber of my being.

"We all feel that way when we're young." She tried to placate me. "You'll change your mind and learn to live with things when you grow up."

"No, not me. It's wrong. God didn't want it to be like that. That's why he sent us."

Mother narrowed her eyes, studying me. Probably worrying that the spirits had returned. "Us?"

"Yes, all of us. He sent a bunch of us to fix the world."

"Who?"

I waved my hands around. "A whole bunch of us."

She shook her head. "I don't know where you get these crazy ideas from. I've got to get out of this girdle."

I ignored her. I had discovered the purpose of my life. I had been born, along with a lot of other children, to put things right again—except I couldn't seem to convince Mother of this. A sense of resolve set in, and I quickly went back to being a child. Now that my life purpose was settled, I could play with my paper dolls again.

Mother stayed with this job at the fancy ladies shop for a good long time. The next summer, before I turned ten, Maggie said she was ready to retire, and Mother started taking me to work with her. The dark days of pinching and cigarette burns and diaper pins through the skin were long forgotten. Mother had come into her own, and all seemed well with the world.

Mother tried to replace Maggie, but she just couldn't settle on anybody. So I went with Mother to her job in the morning, and Daddy picked me up on his way home from the underwear factory where he cut cloth. I never went to his job with him. I honestly couldn't say what I did all day at Mother's store, but I remember that swan in the bathroom, looking at the jewelry, going up to the mezzanine to the ladies' lingerie.

In the shoe department, the boxes were stored on two levels in a small space off the main sales floor. Mother taught me to put them away. First I learned how to stuff the paper back in the toes of the shoes, put the long plastic stretchy things back in—not all of them had these, only the expensive ones—then put them back in the box like mirrored opposites, heel to toe, the heels pointing out. After I mastered that, I got to put the boxes back in their place on the shelves, and she'd come check to see if I got everything in the right spot. Sometimes I got to climb the ladder and push a box onto the top shelf. Climbing high was thrilling.

Just past the last of the tall shelves holding the shoes on the second level was a cramped corner with the switchboard bolted to the wall. The operator sat in front of it in a small swivel chair. A shelf protruded beneath that served as a tiny desk. Wan sunshine from a window in back dimly lit the space. The ceiling hung low like an attic corner. I was the only one who could fit back there with her. We would chat—I don't know about what. When the phone rang, she would hold up her index finger for silence, answer the phone with the name of the store, then say, "Just a moment. I'll connect you." Then she would take the wire and plug it into a small hole on the panel with rows of holes. Each had a small white label naming the department it connected to.

Sometimes two or three lines rang at once, and her hands flew, nails red-tipped just like all the girls in the store. They called them girls then. When things slowed down, she would let me plug in the wire. The rule was I had to be quiet when she answered the phone, but I forgot a few times, and some lady who had called the store wanted to know what a child was doing there. The biddies from the office came up—that's what Mother called them—discovered me there, and put a stop to my visits.

A barber shop sat on the corner behind the store just across the alley, next to the bus station, so I took to visiting them. I used to watch the two men clip hair, but most fascinating was watching them slather the men's faces with shaving cream from big brushes. A black man worked in back shining shoes. I visited him a lot. Finally one day he asked me if I wanted to be his girlfriend. He said next time I came in there, he was going to grab me and take me in the back. The men in the front laughed loud and mean. I ran to Mother to tell her, and she came running back with me.

"What did you say to my daughter?" she asked, hands on her hips.

"I asked if she was in love with me."

"How dare you speak to her like that? I could tell my husband, and you know what would happen."

One of the white men came from the front room and said, "She's your girl. Why aren't you taking care of her? We don't want her in here hanging around."

So that put a stop to the barber shop visits. I couldn't go see the operator either. Things were getting dull. Even the lunches at the cafeteria when all the girls gathered around the table to gossip didn't hold my attention. They talked about boring stuff like their husbands, clothes, the other girls in the shop. Mother had favorites. She'd wait for the others to walk back, then stroll out with one of them. Shirley was her best friend.

Mother offered her a ride home one night. She had the car for some reason, and Daddy hadn't come get me. She pulled out a cigarette and offered one to Shirley, who shook her head. Mother told me before we got in the car that her friend had been subdued all day and she knew something was wrong. The whole gang had gone to the cafeteria at lunch, and Shirley worked upstairs, so now was the first chance they'd had to speak to each other alone.

"He's found me," she said right off the bat.

"Oh my God. How?" Mother looked at her sharply, then back at the road.

"I don't know. I thought I had finally gotten away from him."

They looked back at me, and I looked out the window right quick so they thought I wasn't listening.

"What happened?" Mother asked.

"Yesterday when I left work, he was standing outside the store on the other side of the street. Just standing and watching."

"Did he follow you home?"

"For a while. Didn't talk. Didn't try to catch up." She shivered. "Just letting me know he was there."

"Oh, honey." Mother reached over and patted her hand.

"I dodged through that big church and lost him. Then I went into the library and hid in the ladies' room for an hour. When I came out, I didn't see him. But he'll find where I live." She shook her head, shoulders hunched.

"You could move," Mother said halfheartedly, but Shirley had already moved. She'd fled Memphis and gone to Roanoke, then Newport News, over to Raleigh, and finally here. I'd heard her tell that part of the story before, showing me each town on a map, but she'd made it sound like she liked new places, not like she was running from somebody.

"He'd just find me again. He's never going to give up." She was shaking her head, staring at her clasped hands.

We were close to her apartment building. "Can I pull over here?"

Shirley roused herself, looked around, back over her shoulder, across the street. "It looks clear now."

Mother parked the car and lit another cigarette. This time Shirley took one. Her hand trembled when Mother lit it for her. They smoked for a while, then Mother shook her head. "There must be something we can do."

"She can come live with us." They both jumped when I spoke up.

A sad little smile formed on Shirley's face. She turned around. "That's very kind of you."

"I wish you could, but Nate would never allow it." Mother turned around to look at me. "We don't have an extra room, sweetie."

"She can sleep with me," I said.

"He'd come there, too," Shirley whispered. Then she straightened her back and looked at Mother, her face serious. "I want you to know you've been a good friend. The best I've ever had."

"Well, thank you." Mother seemed uneasy now.

"I want you to know you did everything you could. It's not your fault."

A dark foreboding came over me, like the temperature dropping before a big storm. Mother must have felt it, too, because she asked, "Shirley, do you want to come home with us? Nate would let you stay one night."

Shirley's eyes flashed with hope, but the light went out as fast as it had come. "He'll just find me again. I don't want him to hurt anyone else. Thank you for everything, Lily." She reached for the door handle, then stopped. "I love you." Then she scrambled out and hurried, head down, into her apartment building.

Mother and I sat, staring after her, suddenly at sea.

"We should go after her," I said.

Mother snuffed out her cigarette and reached for the door handle. But she stopped. Looking back now, I realize she must have wondered what she could do. If we warned anyone at the store, they'd fire her. We couldn't bring her home. Daddy would want to know everything. He might blame her. God knows, he used to hit Mother enough, but things had calmed down now. She always told the story of when they were first married. She went grocery shopping, so happy to be filling her own pantry, and he beat her for spending too much money. Trying to show her who was boss, she said. I think Mother envied Shirley's courage. At least she'd run away and lived free for a time.

Mother shook her head and started the car. "I'll call her after dinner. See if she's okay." I scrambled into the front seat, reassured. Except Shirley didn't have a phone. There was one on her hallway, though. That would have to do. When we got home, I went in search of my friends and forgot all about it.

Monday morning we all sat at the breakfast table. Mother wore her navy suit with the white piping around the collar and sleeves, all spiffy. Daddy drank his special fresh-squeezed orange juice Mother made for us, although she kept threatening to buy the stuff in a carton. It didn't taste half as good.

Daddy turned the page of the paper and snapped it to straighten out the page. I watched, envious of his skill. I could never do that. I'd tried and tried, but the paper always tore. "Shirley Nelson? Isn't that your friend?" he said all of a sudden.

Mother got real still. "Yes."

"She died Friday night."

Mother jumped up and tore the paper out of his hand. "Oh my God," she kept repeating while she was reading.

"What happened?" I asked, but nobody answered me. They both just shook their heads.

A few days later, Mother and I parked next to the neat rows in God's Acre, what the Moravians called their graveyard, all with their same square marble stones, and walked up the hill into the city cemetery adjacent to it. A hodgepodge of headstones dotted the hill, some tall and obsequious, the names of the dead boldly engraved, others modest, but all with different designs. Some placed too early, before the ground settled, now tilted to one side. On our side, we knew how to honor the dead with restraint and decorum, not gaudy crosses with scrolled edges and florid angels. At least that's how I saw it. "All are equal in death" was the Moravian philosophy.

Mother wore a sleeveless top and pedal pushers. The brown curves of her perm clung tight around her face in the humidity. We found Shirley's small mound of earth. No stone yet. It was too early.

Mother lit a fresh cigarette, her bright red lipstick leaving a mark like a kiss on a valentine. She inhaled deeply, then let the smoke out in a long exhale.

"What happened to her?" I asked for the tenth time that day.

"She just got sick, is all," Mother said again, most of her attention focused on the fresh grave.

"But—" I stopped, trying to frame my thoughts. How could someone so young, so healthy, just suddenly die? And over the weekend? The very night we'd dropped her off? There'd been no extended illness, no hospital visits.

"How did it happen?" I asked.

But Mother wasn't listening. She bent down. "I wish you'd told me," she whispered to the ground. "I would have done something."

"What could you have done?" I asked, still trying to make sense of the riddle.

Mother turned her head sharply, her lake-blue eyes brimming with tears. "You go play for a while. I need to talk to her."

"But she's de—"

Mother shot me a look, more for ignoring our family secret than for stating the obvious. Actually it was our secret, my brother and mother and me. Daddy didn't share the Sight. That's how I'd talked to the spirits, but it had failed us with Shirley.

I walked away, exploring the headstones just down the hill, then, when Mother wasn't looking, I snuck back up the back side of the hill until I could hear her.

"We could have run away together. Maybe we could have moved to France," she said, "found out where they make that perfume you liked so much. Gotten a job selling shoes in Italy. They make the best shoes."

She stepped back and leaned against an old granite cross. Mother always said this graveyard looked like a real one, with angels and family markers. Not like those spick-and-span Germans. She knew, though, she'd be buried in a row over there—shelved away like a can of soup on a grocery store shelf. All neat and contained. That's how she put it.

I wandered down the hill, reading gravestones, picking dandelions and blowing their seeds to the wind. Finally, Mother called me and we left. She didn't talk on the way home, just smoked and wiped an occasional tear.

I stopped asking her what had happened.

Later that year, Mother tried to make friends with Roxie's mother, but it didn't take. We went over one Christmas after I helped decorate their tree. They hung tinsel on theirs. The long silver strands enchanted me. It was the final touch, and her mother handed us both a handful, admonishing us to be careful and not get any in our mouths, eyes, or hair. She'd said the same thing about the angel hair decoration out in the foyer when I first arrived. Roxie separated each strand and hung them individually on a branch, making the tree look like fairyland. I had a hard time pulling the strands apart, so I started to fling handfuls at the tree, where they stuck like globs of chewing gum.

"No," Roxie said, "you have to hang them like this." She deftly pulled off one strand of magic silver and hung it from the next branch up from where she'd just hung the last one. Her side of the tree sparkled, but I was giggling, not solemn like Roxie. I threw another handful that stuck on the branch next to hers.

"Mommy, Caroline's not doing it right," Roxie complained.

Her mother came and took my globs off the tree and started separating them, patiently showing me how to hang them correctly. "Now see how pretty that is?"

But I was feeling rebellious by now, so I threw another handful at the tree.

"No." Roxie stomped her foot.

I giggled.

Her mother took my strands away and told me to step back and watch. Under the family's careful ministrations, the tree turned from an evergreen hung with lights and balls to a magical tree sparkling with silver strands.

The next night, my parents were invited over for drinks. I didn't know what that meant, really. I'd never heard of it before. Mother got all dressed up, and Daddy put on a tie. We walked out of the driveway and they turned up the road.

"We can go through here," I said, darting up the small hill to the hole in the hedge just across from our house.

"No, Caroline, we're guests. We need to go to the front door."

"We can walk around the driveway. Come on."

"No, we're visitors. We have to use their front walk." So we stuck to the sidewalk once we climbed the tar-covered road, hard now under the winter moon, then turned down the walkway, a series of flagstones bordered on each side by close-trimmed boxwood hedges. Full of self-importance, I pointed out the gingko tree, the side screened-in porch. "That's Emma's room. Roxie's is on the side. And there's a back porch off the second floor that leads up to an attic."

"Okay, now pipe down," Daddy said. He rang the bell.

We were greeted by both Roxie's parents. The kids stood to the back, and Madeline took our coats, which she hung in the closet next to the downstairs library. I told my parents about the library, too. "See the tree I helped decorate?"

"You have a lovely home," Mother said. She walked over to the Christmas display in the foyer.

"Don't touch that. It has angel hair, and it will cut you," I informed her.

She laughed, a little embarrassed for some reason.

Bessie appeared, all dressed up in a blue dress with a white apron. I greeted her, but she just nodded at me and stood back, hands folded.

"Can I get you something? Wine, whiskey, eggnog?" Roxie's mother asked, which was funny since I knew Bessie would do the serving.

"I want eggnog," I said.

Mother laughed. "Honey, eggnog has alcohol in it."

"Why don't you children run and play?" Roxie's mother said to us.

Dismissed, Roxie, her sister, Emma, and I ran to one of the bedrooms and started a game of Go Fish. Her brother wandered back to his room. Later, we went down to look at the tree. Our parents were sitting on the two sofas flanking the fireplace, where logs burned festively.

"You know, I'm part Indian, too," I heard my mother say.

I stiffened. I guess she'd gone and told Daddy.

"My people came from upstate New York. My father was a railroad man, so we moved down here. To Gastonia."

"My mother was Cherokee," Roxie's mother said, then turned the conversation on a dime. "Your brooch is lovely. Did you get that at your store as well?"

I snuck a look at Roxie, who was blushing. Years ago when we'd first become friends, I'd stayed overnight. The next morning at breakfast, curious about her mother being part Indian, I'd studied her hard, trying to see it in her face.

"Stop staring at my mother," Roxie had demanded.

I turned my eyes back to my plate, but they stole back to her face. I particularly wanted to see her nose. Indians were supposed to have large, craggy noses.

"Stop staring at my mother!"

Mrs. Jameson roused herself from her newspaper and studied me back. "You heard I was an Indian, didn't you?"

Dumbstruck, I nodded my head.

"And you want to see what an Indian looks like?"

I nodded again.

Roxie threw down her fork and drew a breath to yell at me, but her mother forestalled her. "So, go ahead and look at me."

My eyes feasted on her luxurious brown hair, her lovely face, her round brown eyes, but I especially scrutinized her nose. She turned her head in profile to let me see better. It was a bit of a hook, rising prominently over her cheeks, but nothing like I'd been told about In-

dian noses. It wasn't huge. It just had a little rise in the middle. Satisfied I said, "You look just like everybody else."

She turned her head back and smiled. "I do, don't I?"

"Yes, ma'am. My mother says we're part Indian, too."

"Is that right?"

"But I don't think I look like it."

Mrs. Jameson and Roxie exchanged a glance. I took up a huge
spoonful of grits, stuffed them in my mouth, and we all went back to
eating breakfast.

That evening when my parents were invited over to the Jamesons'
for Christmas drinks, the conversation didn't turn as naturally. After
saying where she'd gotten her brooch, Mother talked about her job
just a little. Daddy asked Mr. Jameson about his work. He was a vice
president at one mill, Daddy a cloth cutter at another. My parents
didn't sound like themselves. Emma went over to the grand piano and
played a few Christmas hymns. We all sang along, Mother's voice rising above the others in her high, sweet soprano.

Afterward, they were offered more drinks, but Daddy politely refused. They made a little more small talk, then stood up to go, ef-
fusing about how lovely the Jamesons' home was and how pretty the
tree. Madeline brought our coats, and we walked home. I don't think
we were ever invited over again, although my mother said on the
short walk home that she was looking forward to getting to know
Mrs. Jameson better.

Roxie moved before she became a debutante, which happens at
sixteen. I remember looking at her picture in the paper. By then I was
old enough to know I would never be a debutante. That wasn't for
girls like me.

I went over to Roxie's new house a few times. It wasn't near as
nice, and I often wondered why they'd left their golden stone mansion. She invited me to her country club, but the other girls refused
to play with us, so we gradually stopped seeing each other.

18

M aggie

Lily kept up our friendship after I stopped keeping her house and her children. Even though I'd worked for her, I still thought of us as friends. She never treated me no different because of my color. Used to bring us hand-me-downs, just saying, "I wondered if either of you or somebody at your church could use these." Brought us special treats. Not condescending like most white folks. We'd sit on the porch or by the fire and talk.

"Too bad you never had children," Lily said one day. "You're so good with them."

I was quiet for so long, she looked over at me. "You okay?"

"Lily, there's something I want to tell you afore I get too old. If my memory goes before I die, then you'll never know."

"Die? Who's talking about dying?" she said, like younger ones always do, denyin' what's inevitable for all of us.

"Once you asked me if the Grayson's ever took revenge for Mr. Winters goin' off to Virginia and not marrying Vera."

"Vera?"

"That was her name. Vera Grayson."

"Well, did they?"

I took a deep breath and told her the whole story. How we was on our own. How I'd become a woman just before. How they broke in and killed my momma. What they done to me. In the middle of the story, I could feel the flames and the pounding of those men on top of me.

By the time I finished, hot tears ran down my cheeks. I pushed my hands hard against my stomach, took a couple of deep breaths. I felt Lily's hand touch my shoulder.

"I'm so sorry," she said. "What an awful thing."

I couldn't speak, so I just nodded.

"You were probably too young to get pregnant."

Hot grief rose from me in a scream. "God forgive me," I sobbed, gasping for breath.

"Oh my Lord," Lily said and pulled me to her, rocking me, patting my back. "Oh my Lord."

I struggled to speak, but she held me tighter. "You cry now," she said, and I did. When I could talk again, I told her the rest.

I remember Charlise's voice waking me from time to time, her hands holding my head up, her voice urging me to drink something that tasted like hog slop. I'd dream of them catching me over and over, the terror of falling and Billy grabbin' me, the hot agony of that first thrust. I'd wake up screaming. Charlise would run in from somewhere and rock me, telling me it was all over now, it was just a dream, that I was gonna be all right.

"I know. I know what you goin' through," she'd say. Then I'd go back to sleep. I caught some fever. Near about coughed my lungs up. I was delirious for—musta been well over a month.

I woke to a musty smell, water dripping slowly from somewhere behind me, and the smell of pine smoke. I reached to push myself up and found straw beneath my hands, rock walls surrounding me. I tried to sit up, and pain stabbed my side.

"Maggie, you awake?" Charlise rose from her place by the fire and came to me. "Easy now. Your ribs is still healin'."

"Where are we?"

"We safe. I knew about this cave. Been used from way back when slaves needed to hide afore makin' they run for the North." She felt along my rib cage. "Take another couple weeks for bones to mend. Your leg might take longer."

Torn sheets wrapped around two splints holding my leg straight. My ankle ached dully. I pulled myself up slowly and looked around. A tripod supported a black kettle over the fire. Something bubbled inside that smelled of potatoes, onions, and some kind of meat. Small wooden crates stacked against one wall held jars of beans and herbs.

Charlise followed my glance. "I set a snare and caught us a rabbit. Mrs. James has been collecting food for us at the church, but she got to be careful. Them Grayson boys, and Leo and Sa-aa-mmy Lee—" she finally spit out the name of her tormenter from a few years back "—are rampagin' through the county, burnin' and rapin'."

I winced away from her words.

"Sorry." She sat down beside me and felt my forehead. "Look like your fever broke, thank the Lord."

I stared at her, afraid to ask but craving an answer.

She saw it in my eyes and just shook her head. "We reckon she's dead. Whole back of the house burnt up. Took her, Ellie, Suzie, and Simon at least. Still can't find Lottie or Old Joe."

I waited for tears, but a dull emptiness filled me.

"Mick was gone with Mr. Winters. Betty made it out. She's hole up in a cabin with a church lady."

I laid back down, straw rustling, and turned my face to the stone. I must have gone back to sleep. When I woke up again, coals glowed from the fire pit and Charlise snored from her pallet across from me. I pulled myself up and found a stool Charlise had rigged up with a chamber pot. I moved quiet as could be, and she didn't wake up.

Leaning against the wall for support, I made my way outside. I found a low stone to sit on and rested against the side of the cave. Through the bare branches, the stars shone like those diamonds old Mrs. Winters from Virginia had worn at that last ball. Hard, glittering lights, cold fire, aloof and far above the sufferings of this world.

I remembered Momma fussing at me to stand up straight and stop gawking. For me and Gladolia to get our behinds into the kitchen and help Ellie. Simon standing straight, his face passive but looking at me with a brief twinkle when I needed a conspirator against Miss Grayson. I hoped they was up there with them stars lookin' down on me and Charlise. I hoped they was out of the pain and misery visited on them in this life, but I still couldn't weep for them. Not yet. I felt a cold, dark hollowness instead.

The days passed, and Charlise fed me rabbit stew until I thought I'd grow long ears. My stomach gradually settled down and stopped rebelling at the smell of it. Every so often she was brave enough to venture close to a farm and steal eggs. Once she came home with Mrs. James's fried chicken, which I tore into until I remembered Daisy telling the story of Charlise's baby being killed. It turned to sand in my mouth, and I pushed it away.

When the birds had started stirring in the tops of the maples around dawn and snowdrops lifted their white heads above the moldering leaves of last summer, my ribs had healed and my splint came off. I was well enough to help Charlise forage for roots and hunt for rabbit and the occasional wild turkey. I found a stream, fashioned a hook from some old wire stuffed in the cave, and took to fishin'. I landed us a few trout one night, and we had ourselves a feast with them and the last of our potatoes that Charlise roasted in the fire.

I picked the bones from the white flesh of the fish and stuffed my mouth. "We haven't been eating that much, but I seem to be getting fat off it," I joked.

Charlise ducked her head and just nodded.

Spring coaxed green from the trees and forest floor, and Charlise started teaching me about the plants there. "Now this here's burdock. The roots make a good soup stock. And you know dandelion. Good for cleaning the blood."

We walked on past the tree line into a little meadow. A deer lifted her head and sniffed the wind. We froze. Too bad we didn't have a bow and arrow or a rifle. Venison would taste real good. Then two fawns burst from the tall grass, chasing each other, and I was relieved. We couldn't take their mother.

Charlise waited for the doe to graze again and crept out. Then she spoke in a low voice. "See this here? Comfry. It's good for cooking and will help finish healing them bones of yours. You pick a mess of these, and I'll look for some red clover. Too early for berries or we could have pie—at least the inside."

"When can we go back to town?" I asked for the hundredth time, but Charlise's eyes darkened just like they did every time I mentioned moving back.

"Ain't safe," she said.

I wondered when it would be safe. The isolation and dark of winter had suited my grief, but spring had made me look outside myself again. It seemed like the trauma had pushed Charlise back into her old nightmare. I was grateful she'd taken care of me, but I wondered if she'd gone wild in some dark place in her soul. She met people at the edge of the woods for supplies, but that was it. She'd gone into survival mode. Maybe for good.

I watched the fawns romping with each other. They came back to the doe and nursed, tugging at her belly so hungrily I wondered it didn't hurt her. A yellow butterfly flitted around the wild strawberry and trillium blooms. Our rough life had its pleasures, but I yearned for a softer bed, cleaner clothes, and more faces around the fire at night. Not just the ghosts of those who were gone.

One night we sat finishing up our rabbit stew, this time spiced up with wild onions. It was then I felt a fluttering inside. I closed my eyes and put my hand on my belly. Then it came again, like a tickle, fingers opening, or a tiny fish flipping over like a flash of silver in a stream.

"There's something wrong with my intestines, Charlise."

"What you talkin' about?"

"Something's moving in there." I looked up to find her watching me with hooded eyes. "What's wrong?"

She set her chipped plate down. "It ain't your gut, Maggie. Don't you know yet?"

"What?"

"You expectin' a baby."

I jumped up, scattering my fish on the ground. "No, it's not possible. I only had that one blood and then—"

No, it couldn't be. Not that. I shook my head and backed away from the fire. Charlise jumped to her feet and came toward me, her hands spread out, palms open, like she was trying to catch a scared chicken.

I tried to back away farther into the cave, but I just took that thing with me—the little worm planted there by the cruel Billy Grayson or maybe Leo Carlson or Sammy Lee or whoever else had savaged me that night. I pushed against my belly. I'd never know whose it was. I didn't care. I didn't want it. I hadn't wanted any of it.

"Now take it easy. It ain't all them, you know. It's half you, some part of your mother, too."

"No," I screamed, my hands in front of me, wildly pushing Charlise and her terrible words away. "No, not Momma."

I pushed past her and ran blindly, branches slashing at my legs, cutting my cheeks. Vines tripped me. I stumbled but regained my feet, limping a little. I ran from her words, from the loss, from the pain, the fire burning in the distance. My home. I ran from the cruel laughs, the grunts of pleasure, the kicks. Water splashed beneath my feet, and I ran down the creek bed. I ran a long way, then scrambled up a hill and tripped over a root. My head hit something hard, and darkness took me.

I woke up with a start. I was tucked in a bed in the front room of a cabin next to a woodstove. I reached up to touch my forehead and found a bandage and a knot underneath that ached when I prodded it. I remembered falling.

A girl maybe five years older than me sat across the room shellin' peas and watching me.

I wrinkled my nose at the smell of my chamber pot. "I'm sorry."

The girl set down her bowl of peas. "You've been sick. The Lord tells us to take care of people in their troubles."

Troubles. Yes, there had been troubles. Memories pushed at the corners of my mind. I shook my head. I knew I didn't want to remember.

She moved closer. "You thirsty?"

Tears burned my eyes. I nodded.

She went into the kitchen, and I heard her pumping water. She brought me a Mason jar full. I gulped some down, swallowing the memories with the cold well water. "Thank you."

The girl settled her blue bowl back on her lap and commenced to shelling peas again. She started humming low, a hymn. The words plucked at my brain but refused to come in clear. I watched her for a while.

"I'm Maggie," I finally said.

She nodded. "I know who you are. I've seen you at church."

I strained to remember her. Seemed like maybe she sang in the choir.

After a while, she smiled. "My name's Paula."

"Nice to meet you." I swung my legs over the bed, but dizziness darkened my vision for a minute. I laid back down.

"I'll empty it for you." Paula set down her bowl again and took the chamber pot outside. After a few minutes, I heard her voice on the front porch. "She's awake now."

Footsteps sounded, and the door pushed open. There, framed against a bright summer sky, stood Mick.

I let out a cry and held out my arms.

He leaned over the bed and gently picked me up, cradled me in his lap on a chair nearby. "Oh, baby girl. You's alive. Thank God you's alive."

I wrapped my arms around him and nestled into his chest. He was big enough that I fit into his lap easily. I felt like a child again. A tear fell on my head, then another. "You poor baby. All our friends gone. Your Momma gone. Our home. You poor baby."

His deep voice rumbled in his chest and filled me, finding the secret hollows of shame and grief, finally piercing the last deep darkness in my heart. It was safe to remember now. Safe to grieve. I wept for Momma. For Suzie and Ellie. For Tim and Simon. I wept for them all.

He let me cry, rocking me, crooning to me like I was the baby I was carrying myself. After a while, my tears stopped, and he began to tell me the story.

"Word reached us up in Virginia in late February, but our Mr. Winters was away on his honeymoon. They went to England and then were headed to Paris, but those Virginia Winters didn't see fit to send anybody down here to see about our people. Said the house was burnt up pretty bad and the new couple could make their home in Virginia." His voice was bitter as wormwood.

"I finally got permission from them sons a—" Paula's head snapped up, and Mick actually growled. The sound made me smile. "Anyway, I hightailed it down here fast as I could. They wouldn't let me take none of my horses. Raised 'em from colts. Thank God nobody questioned my traveling papers. Went out to Salem Spring. The house is in ruins—"

I clutched at him, and he hugged me tight.

"—but the slave cabins are still there. Old Joe made it through. And Betty. You want to come home with me, baby girl?"

I froze.

"Ain't nobody gonna hurt you there now," he whispered.

I didn't know if I could face the ashes, the emptiness. Where were Momma's pearls in all that heap of ruin? I couldn't ever step foot in the field where Billy Grayson and his pack of hyenas had finally caught up to me.

"When you ready," he said, treatin' me like a wild-eyed horse.

After a minute, I asked, "Did you find Charlise?"

"Nobody knows where she is."

"She took care of me."

"That's good. Where were you?"

"In the woods. We lived in a cave all winter and spring."

"A cave?"

Paula had finished her peas and set the blue bowl quietly down on the floor next to the white one full of the shells. She crept into the kitchen and called her momma in a low voice. She and another lady came in and sat down opposite us.

I tried to sit up, but Mick couldn't let me go yet, so I laid my head back on his chest and closed my eyes.

"She say she been in a cave with Charlise."

"Must be Runner's Cave, down by the river. That's a far piece," Paula's Momma said.

"She musta run a long way," the other woman murmured.

I felt Mick nod. "I know the place."

He waited a while, patient as always. I raised my head, and he let me slip out of his lap and sit beside him on their faded green couch. Two of the pillows had been mended with a different material. I looked around and recognized the two ladies from church. One was Mrs. Williams, who directed the choir and had gotten us the miracle of a piano about a year ago from some white family that was giving up on keeping their land. "For a song," she'd said, "I got it for a song." At the time, I'd wondered if that was literally true. The other was June, who loved talking in tongues. I didn't know her last name.

I nodded to them and straightened out my dress. Only then did I realize it wasn't mine. It was clean, for one thing, and decorated with

little embroidered lilacs. Loose around the shoulders but accommo-
dating my growing belly. I covered that with my hands.

"Nothin' to be ashamed of," Mick said in a low voice.

I stiffened and moved a little bit away from him. He didn't move
an inch. I was definitely the latest beaten and abused horse he'd taken
on. Some part of me smiled, but another yearned for revenge. Dark
and dangerous revenge. To stomp Billy Grayson and all his ilk beneath my sharp hooves.

"Paula, why don't you go get us a pitcher of lemonade," Mrs.
Williams said.

Paula picked up her bowls and headed into the kitchen.

"Want to move out onto the porch where we can get some fresh
air?" Mrs. Williams asked. She didn't wait for an answer, but went to
the crooked screen door and held it open. June walked out and sat
on the first chair. Mrs. Williams settled in one of the rockers. Mick
handed me down into another one, then pulled a stump up from the
wood pile in the yard and set it right next to me. He settled onto it,
his large frame somehow fitting.

Paula brought out mismatched glasses and handed them out,
then went back for the lemonade. She poured everyone a glass, then
sat on the steps. Everyone took a sip.

"That sure hits the spot on a warm day, ma'am," Mick said.

Mrs. Williams nodded her thanks. After another minute, she said
to everyone, "We owe Charlise a debt of gratitude for taking such
good care of you, Maggie. I know your mother would be grateful."

At the mention of Momma, I gripped the arms of the rocker.

"Sure would," June said.

"I wish we could find Charlise to thank her. Be sure she's all right
herself."

"Amen," June said, just like we was in church.

"Think we should go try to bring Charlise home?" Mick asked.

I shook my head. "She's gone feral."

Mrs. Williams nodded sadly. "She comes up to the edge of the woods for food. In all this time, she never mentioned she had Maggie. We thought you'd died with your mother."

In that moment, I wished I had, too. I would be spared this humiliation. This grief. I would be with her and my old friends, together in heaven's kitchen, sitting around the table laughing about some silliness, eating Ellie's chocolate cake. Fat tears fell onto the embroidered lilacs on my chest. A moan escaped. Mick wrapped his arm around my shoulders.

They talked about bringing Charlise back again, how maybe Mick should go visit her next time they took her food, tell her there was room for her at Salem Spring, see if he could soothe her back to civilization. I let their talk buzz over me like cicadas on a summer evening.

I must have dropped off to sleep 'cause next thing I knew Mick was shaking my shoulder. I opened my eyes and the light was low. The sun must be going down. "I'm heading back home now, Maggie. I'll come call on you tomorrow. I'll bring Betty. She can, you know, check you out."

I covered my belly with my hands.

"Now none of that. You ain't got nothin' to be ashamed of." When I didn't say anything, he kissed my forehead. "See you tomorrow, then."

19

Maggie

The Williams cabin sat down in a hollow, tucked in behind a grove of maples, hickory, and scarlet oak, pretty near hidden from view. I don't think many white folks even realized it was down there. Mrs. Williams lived in it. Her husband had died a few years earlier. The children was mostly grown 'cept for Paula, but she was coming on sixteen.

"Momma needs me," was all she'd say when people asked when she was plannin' on marrying. I couldn't really see that this was true, but it weren't my business.

I slept on the cot next to the woodstove, which had a little fire from the night before. Even in the spring, it was chilly in the hollow. That morning I helped Paula clean up after breakfast, but I went back to sleep late morning. In the afternoon, Mick brought Betty to see me. She was the closest thing to a doctor we had. A couple of white doctors would come tend to us if there was an emergency, in particular Dr. Dreher. He was one of the Moravian brethren, a small group that had settled Old Salem and a couple of other towns and held to their ways. But most of the time it was Betty or the root-woman, Lila-May. She was still mostly African, and some folks was scared of her, but Betty thought she was reliable. Said Lila-May knew more about plants than she did.

We sat on the porch, me in a rocker, Betty and Mick telling me the news of our old home. 'Cept they acted like they was telling each other 'cause I kept my head down and didn't talk at first.

"One of them men musta turned over the candles in the living room is all I can figure." Betty shook her head. "I'd just gone out to the barn to help with a sick horse, so I hid there."

A tear traced down her tawny cheek. She wiped at it, but more kept coming. "I could hear the screaming, and I wanted to run in and beat those men off them, but I would have just been killed right along side them. Maybe it would have been a better way to go."

"Uh-huh," I said, not meaning to, but it just slipped out.

Betty and Mick exchanged a quick look. At least I guessed they did from the lapse in the conversation.

"George grabbed the men and whatever guns we could find. Then we could see the fire starting up through the roof. It spread so fast."

I thought about my daddy's library—all them books I never read. Momma's clothes, the quilts on the bed, the silver I hated to polish. I wondered if the cat escaped. I couldn't quite think about those women.

"Some of the men ran out of the house screaming. One of them burnt up right there in the backyard. Didn't nobody lift a finger to help him," Betty said.

"George thought he'd just commence to killin' again," Mick said, as if anybody needed an excuse.

"George and a few others told me they hid behind the cabins, and he started shooting at the others, but they was only one rifle. The rest ran out armed with knives, pitch forks, whatever they could find," Mick said. He shook his head. "Most of 'em died fighting. The rest grabbed up buckets and tried to put out the fire."

Mick wiped at his eyes and tried to speak again, but his voice choked up.

"When they headed for the barn," Betty said, "I opened all the stalls and shooed the horses out. I jumped on the back of one of the mares and took off. Child, if I'd known . . ."

I closed my eyes and rocked even harder.

"I escaped to Reverend Terry's. He hid me and went out to get some men together," Betty said. "Old Joe hid in that cabin with the hollowed-out place under the floor. Put the women who ran from the house under there with him. Said one white man run in and tried to ask him some questions, but the man got tired of beating on him after a little while."

I looked up at her.

"He all right now. Broke his nose, is all. Not like it ain't been broke before."

"That's right," Mick said. "The reverend say he got some men together, but by the time they got back to Salem Spring, the fire was slowing down. It pretty much burnt through the back of the house. For some reason, the front piece didn't burn. George say the men was running around in the back, chasing through the woods. They didn't have no rifles, so they put out the sparks that flew to the barn and the cabin. Dawn came pretty soon after that, so they went lookin' for survivors."

"That's when I got back." Betty put her head in her hands and groaned. "We found your dress all tore up. Your underthings. They was footprints all over. Blood. Oh, baby girl, I looked and looked. They killed Old Moses first thing. I found his body at the front gate. I tried to track you myself, I swear. The woods was all tore up with all them crazy crackers runnin' all over."

I reached my hand out to her.

"Baby, I thought they took you off and had you hid somewhere, like they done to Charlise." She started to sob.

"They searched as best they could," Mick said for her. "Everybody had an eye out. Me, too, once I got back."

"That's right," she said, sitting up and wiping her face. "We listened to all them white people gossipin' about how Mr. Winters had it comin', not marrying Miss Grayson, teaching—" Her voice broke. She couldn't say it.

"Teaching his nigger child to read?" I said it for her.

All she could do was nod her head.

"Momma told me there'd be trouble, but I didn't believe her. I thought things had changed. I was too young to know any better."

Betty shook her head, her eyes tragic. "You still too young."

"Not anymore."

After I said this, they was silent for a while. How could they argue? It had been true for them and looked like it was true for my generation. We stared up at the deep green canopy of the trees, listened to the birds flitting around, the creek runnin' in the distance. Paula stirred in her place on the steps. "Y'all want more lemonade? We got some blackberry pie left from yesterday."

Mick made a visible effort to gather himself. "That'd be real kind of you, Miss Paula."

She made her quiet way to the kitchen.

Betty stood up. "Maybe this is a good time to have a look at you."

I hunched in on myself.

"Come on, now. I want to see how Charlise did setting that ankle."

That didn't seem as threatening, so I followed her into Paula's bedroom and sat on the edge of the bed. Betty started with my ankle, talking quiet, her gentle fingers pressing. "Looks like she did a good job. Got a little knot there. Do you limp?"

"A little."

"That might pass. How about your arms? Any breaks?"

"No, ma'am." I held them out anyway. She felt all along my fingers and hands, up my arms. Then prodded my neck and throat, cheeks, nose. "Nothing broken in your face?"

"My jaw was all swoll up for a while. I lost a few teeth." I opened my mouth, and she peered inside.

Her fingers and voice were familiar from childhood fevers and accidents. She soothed me back closer to myself.

"Did they kick you?"

"My ribs hurt for a while."

"Let me feel," she said and lifted my dress simple as that. My belly stuck out, that baby intruding itself between us, but she acted like she didn't notice and felt all along my ribs.

I winced.

"Looks like you broke these two, but they healed up pretty good. You got any pain left when you use the outhouse?"

She slipped this in so easy, I just said, "Not anymore."

"You get ripped up?"

I shrugged. I had been a child until only two weeks before this had happened. I'd never paid no attention to my woman's parts.

"Would you let me have a look?"

I pulled my legs together.

"It's just me, Maggie. I need to see."

I just sat there. She pushed my shoulder a little, and I let her lower me to the bed. She unfastened my underwear and gently pulled them off. "It's all right, now. Let's see how you've healed up."

I trembled at first, but her gentle touch soothed me.

"That looks like it healed good," she said, then moved on to the next spot. "Does this hurt?"

"A little."

"This scar might give you some trouble delivering. I'll bring you some salve you can rub on it twice a day to soften it up. Could help the baby come easier, but I'll be with you."

Hot tears ran down my face. "I don't want it."

"I know, baby, I know, but sometimes there's blessing in pain."

I shook my head. "It'll look like one of them. I can't stand it."

"Could look like you," she answered. "You never know." Then she started pushing on the sides of my womb, seeing how big the intruder was, asking if anything hurt. "Good size for July. You'll probably come to term in October."

I just shook my head. Nobody understood there was no blessing in it. Nobody asked me if I wanted a baby from them men who'd murdered my mother and most of the women who'd tended my childhood—fed me, taught me, corrected me. Loved me. And this squalling white brat was supposed to replace them?

"But it'll be white," I whispered.

"Maybe, but it'll be yours. And your Momma's grandchild."

I just shook my head. Tears ran down my face, and my lips quivered.

"I'm sorry I didn't find you sooner, child. Maybe I coulda took it from you, although I don't much like doin' such things. But not now. I'm so sorry I didn't find you that night." Her voice broke.

I sat up and looked at her. Silver tears made streaks down her cheeks. "If you had, they woulda done the same to you. There was a few of 'em. They might have killed you."

She took me in her arms and rocked us both until she stopped crying. She let me go and wiped her face with her embroidered handkerchief.

"Let's go have some blackberry pie," she said. "Maybe some of it will rub off on the baby."

That made me laugh. "Paula make good pie."

She chuckled. "I'll go ahead. You get dressed."

So we ate pie and drank lemonade, then Mick and Betty told some funny stories about the old days until the sun was low in the sky. He stretched out his legs. "I still got some horses to feed."

"And I got to go help with supper," Betty said.

"Where y'all cookin' now?" I asked before I could stop myself.

"We turned one of the cabins into a kitchen."

"Got a couple more cabins. One with your name on it," Mick said to me.

I just looked down at the floorboards.

"Old Joe can't get around. He'd love to see you."

"Tell him I love him," I mumbled.

Betty dropped the salve off the next day. After that, they came by on Sundays after church. I didn't stay for lunch at church like I used to. I couldn't stand crowds much. Betty brought fried chicken, okra, collards, tomatoes, whatever was fresh in the garden. I looked forward to their visits, but I just couldn't bring myself to go back to Salem Spring and face that pile of ash that was my mother's grave.

One day Mrs. Williams announced, "You're welcome to stay with us, Maggie, but not in the living room." So we packed up my little sickbed, and Paula let me move in with her. She had an old double bed from a donation to the church that was plenty big for both of us. Or all three, I should say. We got to know each other whispering our secrets across the pillows at night. She told me about her father and her siblings, how she loved to read and had wanted to go to college and become a minister, only they didn't allow women, much less colored women, to do that.

"Did Reverend Terry go to college?"

"I don't know."

"You could do stuff at church, though. You could read the passages and teach Sunday school."

"It's not the same."

"You really believe in God that much?"

"I know my daddy is with the Lord."

"You think my momma is?"

She hugged me tight. "I know it."

The baby readjusted itself between us and seemed to lean toward her warmth and goodness. We fell asleep like that, snuggled together.

We talked about other girls at church. I told her about Salem Spring and all the people. About Mick and his horses. All about the Virginia Winters.

"Do you think you'll ever see your daddy again?" she asked.

"Mick don't think he'll come back. Says he's too heartbroken."

"But what about you? He has you."

"He's not like a regular daddy. He's white, and he couldn't really tell nobody about me."

"But you all knew."

"I mean the white people. He can't tell them. I guess this makes it easier."

She wanted to know what it felt like to have a baby inside, and I turned my attention more and more toward the child, my feelings gradually thawing. "It's like when she get the hiccups, I can't hold my breath for her. My stomach jumps."

"You think it's a girl?"

Just at that moment, the child kicked as if in answer.

"Does that hurt?"

"No, but look at my ankles. They're so big I can push my finger in them and the dent stays for a long time."

She rubbed my back and put lotion on my stomach as it sprouted veins and rivers of red marks from stretching for the child.

Paula and I got real close. She soothed many of my injuries, replacing violence with her gentle touch. We didn't think it was wrong.

Come September, after all the tobacco had been picked and the vegetable harvest brought in and a lot of the canning done, Reverend Terry held a service at Salem Spring for my momma and all those that had perished in the fire. I attended, my belly sticking out big for everybody to see. Weren't nothin' I could do about that. It was my first time back, but I didn't walk up near the ruined house with its patch of ashes where rooms used to stand. I stayed back in the old slaves' plot, which had become the black cemetery for our plantation. Mick had commissioned a stone for each person who had lost their life in the attack. He used the money he made from this year's tobacco crop. They'd gone ahead and planted the fields, harvested and cured, then taken it to auction themselves.

"Them white boys gave us some trouble, but we raise good tobacco. The companies know that, and they bought it," George said. He'd survived somehow, too. "As far as I'm concerned, the place belongs to you now, Miss Maggie."

I couldn't help but smile a little. The row of gravestones with names and dates helped me feel a little better about Salem Spring, but I still couldn't turn around and face that field.

"It's good to see you," George said.

"It's good to see you all," I answered, but I got in the wagon Mick had sent for me and went back to Mrs. Williams's cabin and Paula.

20

Maggie

It was Paula helped me most during the tribulations that come in October. The leaves was turning all colors like they do—them reds and yellows and the gold that shines out at you from the woods and lifts your heart right up out your chest. Just like when I was born. Only now the moon was a sliver in the sky.

I just couldn't get comfortable and accidentally woke Paula up a couple of times tossin' and turnin'. Finally she lifted her head from the pillow. "You all right?"

"Feels like somebody's tightening a screw into my stomach," I said.

"You gonna throw up?"

"No, lower." I took her hand and pressed it against my abdomen. Just then my whole belly tightened up. It stayed that way for almost a minute. Then it let go.

"The baby's coming," she said.

"Oh my God. Where's Betty?" I cried.

She flew out of bed, around the woodstove, and into her mother's room. I heard her shaking her mother awake. "Maggie's going to have the baby, Momma. She's pushing already."

"Pushin'?" I heard Mrs. Williams shout. "How long she been in labor?"

"Just now."

"You crazy girl. Let me get up."

Mrs. Williams arrived next to me in her worn terrycloth robe, carrying a candle. "When did you start feeling contractions?" she asked me.

"Contractions?"

"You know, when did your womb start squeezing?"

"Just now."

"You had any other pains?"

"Yes, ma'am. Like something's tightening inside."

"Where?"

I pointed.

"You bleedin'?"

Paula and I blanched. "Bleedin'? I'm going to bleed?" I asked, terror flooding me.

Her face softened. "It's natural. Don't mean something's wrong. Honestly, girl, you never seen nothing born out on that plantation of yours?"

"It ain't mine, ma'am."

She snorted. "You know what I mean."

"Puppies and kittens."

"Well, it's the same thing. 'Cept your baby ain't gonna be born in a sack."

This settled me down a little. Until another contraction hit me. "Oh, oh." My hand flew to my belly, but it hurt to touch. As soon as it passed off, Mrs. Williams got me out of bed. Sure enough, the back of my nightgown had a big red spot on it. I looked at the matching spot on the sheet. "I'm sorry."

She laughed. "Don't you worry none. There's gonna be a lot more of that before this is over with."

Mrs. Williams made up the bed with a wad of old cloth underneath me and set a kettle on to boil. "Might as well make us some breakfast," she told Paula.

The thought of food made my stomach turn. "I don't think I can eat, ma'am."

"No, you can't, but we need it. First babies take a while sometimes." Another contraction hit me, and I winced. "They ain't that bad yet, are they?"

She must be crazy. "They hurt."

"Let me know when there's another one. They get closer as the time comes."

That's how we spent the morning, me breathing through those contractions that got stronger and closer, gritting my teeth, trying not to yell.

Betty showed up close to noon and checked me out. "Don't push now. You don't push until we can see the baby's head."

But the baby's head didn't come, and I'd done soaked through all the old sheets Mrs. Williams had.

"Paula, go up to Mrs. Terry and get us some more rags."

The afternoon passed the same, but by evening I lost track of it all. I was awash in a world of pain and blood and fear, listening to someone crooning to me, hearing Paula's encouraging words in my ear. Later, I screamed for Momma. Over and over, but she didn't come. Not at first. Not for a real long time.

Then I saw a light, like a tunnel, and peace came over me. I heard singing, only not with words, but sounds that soothed and made things whole again and encouraged things to grow. It was like I was coming home, but not to Salem Spring, no. To my real home, to a place I'd yearned for all my life, a place I'd always knowed was there. Not knew in my mind, but in my heart. In my soul. And I started to float up into that light when suddenly Momma was there. My momma. She'd finally come for me. I rushed to her, and she took me in her arms and whispered, "Not yet, Maggie. Not yet. You've got more to do. You got to go back, but we're all here."

I looked behind her and saw Ellie and Suzie. Simon raised his hand, and light poured out from it, and it was like I was being pushed back. A wind blew me backward, and then the last thing I heard was, "We'll be here waiting for you."

I opened my eyes and saw Mick leaning over the bed. "I saw them, Mick," I whispered. "I saw Momma. They say they waitin' on us."

A wonder came over his face. Then he picked me up and carried me like a treasure chest out to a wagon, whispering, "I got you, Maggie. I got you now." But I don't remember nothin' after that.

"You died?"

I looked up to find her rose-tinged ivory face watching me intently, those lake-blue eyes swimming with tears.

"Maybe for a minute," I said.

"What happened to the baby?"

I took a sip of my coffee, but it had gone cold.

Lily reached across the table and patted my hand, then took my coffee cup to the sink, rinsed it out, and poured me a fresh cup. She fixed it with milk and sugar, just like I liked it, giving me time to gather myself. I told her the rest.

I woke up to Dr. Dreher's face hovering over me.

"Welcome back," he said.

I startled and pulled the sheets up to my chin. They felt rough under my hands. I squinted against the harsh light.

"Betty, our patient is awake."

"Thank the Lord." It was Betty's voice.

"Thank the Lord indeed," he murmured. "I'll let you talk to her." He got up and left the room.

"Where am I?" I tried to sit up, but Betty pushed me back.

"You in the hospital."

"Hospital? They don't let no coloreds into the hospital."

"Dr. Dreher insisted," she said, a satisfied smile on her face. "Said the colored hospital was opening soon, but he wasn't going to let you die. Said you'd suffered enough at the hands of white men."

"How long I been here?"

She settled down in the chair next to my bed. "You were in labor for three days. Couldn't shift the child. Couldn't reach him. Nothin' worked."

My hands went to my flat stomach.

She nodded. "So we finally called Dr. Dreher, who came out to the cabin. He said you'd die if we didn't get the child out, so he brung you to the hospital his very self. Made a big fuss so they'd let you in."

"But—"

"You had what they call a cesarean section." She stubbled a little over the name.

"What's that?"

"They had to do an operation. Get the baby out through an incision in your belly."

My eyes went wide.

"Dr. Dreher said something inside got hurt when you was attacked. Made it so that baby couldn't come down." She paused and stroked my hand. "That was two days ago. You been unconscious since."

I opened my mouth to ask, but then closed it again. Maybe it was best not to know.

"It was a boy. You were wrong about that," she said. "but you were right about a few things. He was white as the driven snow. Big blue eyes."

I shook my head, tears welling up again.

"We was afraid you wasn't goin' to make it. We didn't know who could take him in. A baby that white might cause problems for the family. Dr. Dreher, he asked my permission."

"For what?"

She closed her eyes and seemed to brace herself, then looked at me. "He went to Mrs. Grayson."

"No," I yelled.

She held up her hands. "The new one. Not Billy's wife, but the younger son's. Seems she's had trouble havin' a baby. Been two years now. He brung her to see the baby and . . ." Betty stared down at her hands.

"What?" I asked, wanting it to be true and not true all at the same time. I wanted to see him, too. To see that squirming spark of life that had laid between me and Paula.

"She took him home with her."

A savage glee stabbed me. I was free of him, free of Billy Grayson and his ugly red face all screwed up and yelling his pleasure as he thrust himself into my agonized body. But my breasts ached. My heart hurt. My arms felt empty. Some part of me wanted to see my baby. To hold him. Tears ran down my cheeks.

"Did we do wrong, Maggie? We thought you was dying. He needed a mother. And you always said you didn't want the baby."

I nodded. I did feel relief. Plus he was in town. I could watch him in secret as he grew up. Maybe get to know him a little. 'Cept he was a white man and would eventually act like one. This was best.

"It's all right," I finally said.

"One more thing," Betty said, her face cautious. "Doctor says you can't have no more babies. Not after a cesarean section."

I let this sink in. Finally I nodded. It would be all right. I could do what my daddy had trained me to do. I could teach children. They'd all be my babies. Mine and Paula's.

I looked up at Lily. Tears ran down her face. "So what happened then?"

"I've lived in that little cabin with Paula ever since that day I woke up in it after hitting my head on that rock. After Mrs. Williams passed, we kept it. Opened a little school for colored children in an old slave cabin at Salem Spring."

"So you did go back."

"Mr. Winters's son sold it off after his father died. Mr. Grayson, the younger one who took my son, he bought it years later. Rebuilt the house to look just like it had. Well, almost."

"Ain't that something."

I smiled. "Then my boy owned it for a while before it just got to be too much for the family, and they sold off the land piece by piece."

Lily's hand flew to her mouth. "You're kidding me."

"No, Lily. Nate is my grandson."

"That means . . ."

"Yes, that means Old Man Hauser—he's my son."

Lily stared. Finally she took her hand from her mouth. "Does he know?"

"No, and I'll never tell him. Takes after the men who raped me." My eyes filled in spite of myself. "If I'd raised him, maybe . . ."

Lily pushed that away. "They'd never have let you. Just look at him."

I nodded.

"So this means you and Caroline are . . . this means she's your great-granddaughter." Lily pulled me up from the table into a big hug. "Oh, Maggie, I always felt like you were my real family."

She sat back down, then her hand flew to her mouth. "Oh my God, Maggie. That day I made you go talk to him. I'm so sorry."

I just nodded my head.

"What was it like?"

So I told her.

It took me a good while to heal from that surgery where they ripped the child from me. Nobody mentioned him, and I didn't ask. I thought about him, wondered what he looked like, what his life would be like, if I'd ever get to see him or know him. I tried to put it out of my mind. It was the best solution, really. The circumstances of his coming into existence weren't his fault, but I'd always remember it if he was around. I'd never have another child, though. The doctor was sure of that.

Then one day I was walking down to the general store to pick up some medicine for Paula's mother, and I seen Ellie May standing outside with a stroller. I stopped dead in my tracks. Ellie May worked for the branch of the Graysons who'd taken my boy, and I knew he was laying right there in that stroller. A terrible longing came over me. And a heavy dread. I yearned to see him, search his little face for any hint of my own or Momma's. Stroke his cheek, take his hand and feel his little fingers wrap around mine. But I didn't want to wake those gnawing hungers, to feed them. I could never have him, never be a mother to him. Not now.

My feet didn't listen to me, though. They started walking toward him. Ellie May nodded her head, a signal it was safe, and I walked up next to her and stood. She didn't say a word 'cause there was people comin' and goin' from the store. She leaned down and moved the blanket aside. There he lay. Six months old. Little hands waving up in front of him, kicking against the blanket they had him wrapped in. A chubby little fellow. He fixed those blue eyes on me.

"What they name him?" I asked.

"John," Ellie May whispered. "They named him John."

I cooed at him, and he smiled and reached for my hand.

"Ellie May." A white woman's voice cut through us like an overseer's whip.

My heart seized up. My throat closed. A red haze filled my eyes.

"You know you aren't to let anybody play with Baby John, now."

I started to walk away.

"It's for the best, Maggie." Mrs. Grayson's whisper just reached me.

I kept walking afore I knocked that woman upside the head, afore I unleashed all the anguish, the pain of her brother-in-law rutting on me, of them men killing my mother, burning up my home, of the months I laid in that cave, numb and wanting to die. I made it home before I broke down.

I caught glimpses of him from time to time, outside they church one day, playing with the other children. Bright blond hair, toddling after a ball. I tried to avoid the park, looked around real careful when I went to the store and left if I caught any glimpse of Ellie May. She'd stop if she saw me, turn the other way. I knew she didn't mean no harm by it. She was only just trying to keep her job. She had her own mouths to feed.

When it came time for him to start his schooling, though, I'd walk by the elementary school to see if the kids was out at recess. I watched him grow up that way—from a young, awkward child to one in a group of boys playing marbles or baseball. He was a fine-looking youngster.

Once, I ran across him on a path through the woods. I'd been out to see if Charlise would come up to her meeting place and talk a while. She'd gotten old, and we was trying to bring her back to town, set her up in a church woman's house. John was hunting rabbits. Tall, lean, that square jaw his—the Graysons had. He stopped and sneered at me. "What you doing out here alone, nigger?" he said.

A shiver of terror ran through me. His voice sounded so much like Billy's. He smiled real threatening like. I had a wild urge to tell him right then and there who I was, that he'd be called a quadroon in the old days, that I was his mammy, that his daddy was a savage. But I just stood to the side of the path. His hound dog came and sniffed me all over, growling just a little. He could see how scared I was.

"Should I sic him on you, nigger?"

Right then and there any motherly feeling I ever had for him died. I snapped my head up and said, "Go ahead."

But he just laughed, called off his dog, and walked on.

Lily shook her head back and forth. "Lord, help us. What a world we live in. I'm so sorry for you, honey. You didn't deserve none of that."

A tear ran down my cheek. "Still, I thought on that baby now and again."

Lily patted my hand. "Of course you did."

"Paula and me used to have a little cake on his birthday. We'd add a candle each year. She said it was to celebrate me coming back to life, but we always thought about little John. When he was innocent, you know?"

21

C aroline
　　　　Little Rock was the first political event I really remembered, but I was still young and it made only a slight impression—a
line in the sand. I declared they should let the children go to school,
then picked up my bike and went riding with my friends. I'd turned
seven that year.

A couple of years later, our gang of girls rode the bus to a movie
downtown. I wanted to sit in the sideways seat, but the ones up front
were full, so I went to the back. Once there, my friends called me
back, and Polly whispered, "You can't sit there."

"Why not?"

"Because it's for the coloreds."

So I just went back and asked them if they minded if I sat there.
A nice man in a worn blue suit said it would be just fine, so I plopped
down. My friends hunkered down in their seats, pretending not to
know me. The bus driver looked back and at the next red light informed me that I'd have to move.

"But I want to sit on the sideways seats."

"You can't sit in the back of the bus. It's for the coloreds."

"They don't mind. I asked."

The man in the blue suit smiled, and a fat woman with a huge
purse sitting near him laughed out loud.

As soon as the light turned, he pulled the bus over at the closest
stretch of road, put it in park, stomped back to me, and jerked me
up by my arm. "You will sit where I tell you, young lady, and I don't
want no lip from you." He dumped me next to Polly, who whispered,
"I told you so." The man in the blue suit frowned and shook his head.

When one of the sideways seats in the very front of the bus
opened up, I stood up. The driver looked at me in his rearview mirror.
"You sit down, now. Otherwise, I'm going to throw you off this bus."

I stuck my tongue out at him, which caused general hilarity in the back of the bus. I smiled back at my cohorts in mischief. When I got off the bus, the driver yelled, "I hope I never see you on my bus again," but the people in the back, all the colored, that is, waved at me and smiled. I was as innocent of the Montgomery Bus Boycott as Rosa Parks was innocent of a crime.

There was the time I tasted the water in the coloreds-only fountain at the drugstore in the new shopping mall to see if it was different. It tasted the same to me. That same day the stalls in the ladies' room were all full, so I stuck my head in the colored women's bathroom and asked if they minded if I used it instead. Two women in there said it would be fine. The bathroom tile was old and broken in places and the stalls dented. I told them ours was all shiny and new and asked if they wanted to look at it. The two ladies took me up on it. They came in and had a look around, much to the chagrin of my friends. Roxie and Judy thought I had a screw loose.

I think my rebelliousness was because of Maggie. Plus my mother was from New York, where they didn't hold with racial prejudice. She and Daddy were always getting into it.

"That Martin Luther King, Jr. should go home and mind his own business," Daddy declared before stuffing a fork full of mashed potatoes in his mouth. "The people in Montgomery know how to run their own town. They don't need outside agitators stirring the people up."

"They invited him to come, Nate. Besides, I like him."

"No white people invited him. He's an agitator, pure and simple." He stabbed his chicken-fried steak.

The only agitator I knew about was in Mother's new washing machine.

In junior high, all hell broke loose in the country. Or heaven, depending on your perspective. We watched the March on Washington on our little black-and-white television, all huddled together in the family room. Daddy shouted all about how the colored should be patient, that change takes time, while Mother argued back that if they waited for him or his father to change, hell would freeze over first. She seemed to have lost her fear of him.

Walter Cronkite narrated the sea change in our world with dignity and civility, his face in the monochrome of grays and whites. We still had our old console black-and-white TV. Daddy hadn't bought a TV the first year they were out. "Never buy anything right off the bat. Wait until they work the kinks out of it." My brother and I whined and begged.

"Next year," he said and was true to his word. Time passed and my brother graduated high school and went off to the navy, so I was left to beg for a color TV all on my own. Jimmy was on a tanker in the Mediterranean and sent home slides, which my mother eagerly watched on a brand new screen she set up in the living room for each grand showing. Daddy used his purchase of the slide projector and screen as another reason we couldn't afford a new TV. He kept saying he was waiting on a good price from Mr. Smith, who owned the appliance store everybody shopped at. We were neighbors with him and friends with the family, so Daddy was certain of a good deal once the novelty wore off.

We watched King deliver his soaring speech that August in Washington, DC, goose bumps rising on our arms as he told us about his dream, our dream, the dream of equality. We'd been listening to King on the radio and the nightly news as he refused to ride buses in Alabama, marched all over the South, it seemed, and even went to jail. We were soaked in the cadence of his speech, the soaring images, the rhetoric of justice and freedom and nonviolence. That a person should risk everything to stand up to injustice was a commonplace.

Then the Birmingham desegregation efforts erupted in the church bombings, and pictures of three little girls filled the newspapers and our new television. Mother and I loudly condemned the murderers, and Daddy finally threw in the towel. It got to be too much even for him.

Maggie was over seventy now, and Paula needed to be taken care of, so we went to visit them in their little cabin. Maggie was hesitant about all the changes, sure of a backlash, but she loved Dr. King. She listened to him on the radio. They didn't have a TV yet. She mourned the little girls who had been blown to bits, but didn't seem as moved by it all as I thought she should be.

"Maggie's seen a lot in her day," Mother explained to me in the car going home. "Someday I'll tell you her story. When you're old enough."

"Why do we have to keep going over there? She doesn't work for us anymore."

"Work? What's that got to do with it. Maggie's my friend."

"What will she do when her girlfriend dies?"

We were at a stop sign, but Mother didn't move the car. She turned and glared at me. "What did you say?"

"She and Paula are together, aren't they? Lesbians."

Mother reached over and smacked me across the face. Hard. "Don't you ever say anything like that again. Those two women saved your life. They saved me. You will not disrespect them again. Ever." She glared. "Do you understand?"

A car behind us blew its horn.

"Do you?" She didn't move the car.

"Yes, ma'am." I was scared to say anything else.

We never talked about it again.

Then they killed our shining prince. Our great hope. The man who held the reins of power and could make a difference. John Fitzgerald Kennedy. Gunned down in Dallas, and it seemed to me that the rocks themselves would rise up in protest. That the angels would take up the sword of Archangel Michael and punish the wicked. That God would rain down fire and brimstone. Johnson got the Civil Rights Bill passed—we thought it was so the country wouldn't come apart at the seams—and we expected things to calm down. But they didn't. When I was in high school, things heated up even more.

The pressure for desegregation started. It was all talk my sophomore year, but the school counselor chose me to to represent our high school at the meetings mandated by the federal government. They were held at some rich people's house, a white, rambling, modern affair with a swimming pool. The group involved all ages and both races. Rich people and rednecks. I must have ended up with a group of radicals because three black women argued to keep segregation but double the money spent on black schools "until we can catch up."

"But we're supposed to be learning to get along," I said.

"Why do black children have to bear the brunt of white racism while at the same time doing their studies?" She was skinny and intense and had on the pink lipstick everybody was wearing now.

Her two friends nodded along with her.

"But they say the white schools are better."

"Which is why we should have more money for a while to make up the difference."

"But—"

"You're in high school, right?"

"Yes, ma'am."

"Ma'am." She quirked an eyebrow at her friends, and they all laughed.

"We already have some black students, and they have some friends."

"How many?"

I hesitated. "A couple."

They all broke out laughing. "And the rest of the kids? How do they treat them?"

"Well . . ." She had me there, so when the facilitator came around, we told him no integration. More money for the black schools. He duly noted our opinion, but the majority voted for desegregation. My new radical friend, at least I thought of her that way, said the government had already made up its mind. There wasn't any use arguing.

I guess that's how I got my reputation at school. Plus I was friends with Jeremy, a tall, statuesque ebony man who wanted to be a ballerina.

"Is that the right word for a male ballet dancer?" I asked him.

"It's the right word for me," he said and twirled around in the hallway right there in front of everybody.

"Faggot," a passing student yelled out.

"That's why I came to school here. Over at Carver, they beat me up for being queer."

"You shouldn't call yourself names," I said.

"Nothin' wrong with being queer," he whispered in my ear. "Now at this school, they just beat me up for being black."

Outraged, I said, "You should tell the principal."

Jeremy went into peals of laughter.

One afternoon near the end of junior year, Mr. Dutton made an announcement at the end of his American history class. "I'm sure you're aware that next year we're going to combine with Carver High School."

Jeers and boos broke out, but he raised his hands for quiet. "Now, now, I know how you feel about having colored students invade our school. No offense, Denique. You have acted like a lady all this year."

"Thank you, Mr. Dutton," she said, a smile plastered on her face.

"But the Yankees in our nation's capitol have forced us to fully integrate."

"We'll take care of a few of them after class," Ricky, the quarterback of the football team, mumbled, but it was loud enough to catch Mr. Dutton's ear.

"We'll have none of that," he said. "At least not on school grounds."

The boys in the class stirred around in their seats. Some girls laughed. Denique pulled her books to her chest.

"Mr. Dutton, I don't mind going to school with black students," I said. "I think it's only fair."

"We all know you're a nigger-lover, Caroline," Mr. Dutton spit out.

I started to answer back, but he kept on going. "As for the rest of you, I expect you to act like ladies and gentlemen. No fighting in the hallway. No name calling in class. Be polite. We'll show those Yankees that we know how to treat our coloreds, even if they force us together."

"Yes, Mr. Dutton," a few students said, their voices flat. Others sat a little straighter, shoulders back. He had invoked their pride.

"Who knows, Ricky. We might get a few decent tackles out of it. Those niggers have been plowing and picking tobacco for so long they've got some big boys."

Students started gathering their books and pushing back chairs. "Remember, the final exam is next week. Study." He had to shout this last part over the hubbub of chairs being pushed back and loud conversation.

I hung back until most students had left, then walked into the hall where a few football players huddled around Ricky. He glanced up as I walked by. "Guess he put you in your place, Caroline."

"You're a racist," I spit out.

The group burst out laughing. "Nigger-lover, nigger-lover," they chanted.

I hustled down the hall to my next class.

"Girl, you are so brave." Jeremy waited for me around a corner.

"We've got to speak up. That's what Dr. King says."

"Listen, there's this new place opening called The Rap Room. One of the guys involved is just a dream. Will you go with me on Saturday? We can pretend it's a date."

"Rap Room? Like H. Rap Brown?"

"I guess."

"That guy is scary. Why'd they name it that?" We walked past rows of beige lockers, students dodging around us.

"To rap means to talk—like really getting down and telling the truth. They say it's a place for black and white kids to meet and get to know each other."

"They're not going to get many white kids with a name like that."

"Yeah, but you're brave. You'll come, right?"

"I'll have to meet you there. My parents wouldn't let me go with you."

"I'm serving at the country club until eight o'clock. Can you pick me up?"

"Sure."

"Remember to wait at the end of the road. If they see us together, I'll get fired."

The bass vibrated my stomach as soon as we opened the door. We pushed through a few people hanging near the entrance. A strobe light sliced through the dark and illuminated cigarette smoke, rising and swirling in the beams. Jeremy and I edged our way through the crowd and found a table for soft drinks in the back. A whole dollar for a plastic cup with ice.

"That's highway robbery," I said.

"It's a fund-raiser." The girl serving shrugged and handed me a cup.

Armed with cola, we found a wall on the side to lean against. A white band played their rendition of "Light My Fire," the lead singer doing his best imitation of Jim Morrison, which was a bit stiff to tell the truth. Their drum announced their name in big letters, The Collins Rockers. They had a bit of a following around town. A well-mixed crowd filled the dance floor. Two black guys near us laughed about how white people danced, which was practically obligatory commentary in 1967, but the mood was jovial, and everyone seemed to be having a good time. The band segued into "Never My Love," and some couples moved together for the slow song while others left the floor.

Jeremy kept craning his neck to see over the crowds of people.

"You looking for someone?"

"I told you about that guy, remember?"

"The one who asked you out?"

"Sort of. He thought we should go to Twisted."

"Twisted?"

Jeremy rolled his eyes in dramatic fashion, then leaned down and whispered in my ear, "It's a gay bar. Don't you know anything?"

"Why do they want to call themselves bad names?"

"It's a joke," he explained. "Honestly, are you sure you're not from Mayberry or something?"

I poked him in the shoulder.

The band announced their last song and struck out with an attempt at "Whiter Shade of Pale," a questionable offering for at least two reasons I could think of, but it was still one of my favorite songs.

"Want to dance?" I asked Jeremy.

"To this? How?"

I laughed. Many people seemed to agree. Someone had hooked up one of those lava lamps and shone a light through it. Amoeba-like blobs of color floated and eddied around each other on the walls in a sensual display of lazy intimacy. One girl dressed in a tie-dyed dress and about five strands of beads, her blond hair hanging to her hips, swayed in imitation of their movements.

"That white chick is gone," a guy near us said.

"What they call it? Psychedelic?"

"Shit, give me reefer any day."

The song ended and a well-built man with shining bronze skin and a tight Afro took the microphone. "Let's give our white brothers a big hand."

The cheers varied from polite to enthusiastic.

"We'll take a break while our soul brothers, Carolina Blues, get ready to entertain you." His words were lost in a big cheer from mostly the black section of the audience. The right word was "black" now. Only rednecks said "colored" or "Negroes" anymore.

"Who are they?" I asked Jeremy.

He shrugged. "Beats me. I like Jimmy Hendrix. That makes me a freak to these people."

The man at the microphone held up his hands for quiet. "We're glad to see so many of you here at the opening of The Rap Room. We hope that's what we'll do—rap, which means to really talk and get to know one another. Next Saturday, we're sponsoring a voter registration drive, so come on down around nine o'clock—"

Groans erupted.

But I wasn't really listening to him. I was staring at the young man standing next to him, just under six feet, broad shoulders, golden-brown skin, eyes gleaming, head held high. He exuded a quiet confidence. He wore a black leather jacket, dark jeans, and one of those black caps the Panthers favored, which gave me pause, but the rest of him drew me like a feline to catnip.

"Who's that?"

"That's Howard. He's always trying to organize something around town."

"Not him. The other one standing next to him."

"Ahhh," Jeremy stretched the word out. "You like him, do you?"

I flushed.

"All the girls like Tyrell, but he's one of those radicals. He probably wouldn't go for a white girl."

"I never said—"

But Howard's mic suddenly boomed and drowned out my words. "I know that's early," he said, "but this is a good cause, brothers and sisters. We'll carpool to East Winston first and get people to register so we can win this election."

The group erupted in cheers.

"You all know Tyrell. He'll be leading the group."

I wondered if my father would let me sign up to help. I knew he wouldn't. Maybe I'd just tell him I was going to the library. Again.

Jeremy grabbed my arm. "He's coming this way."

"Who?"

"The guy I told you about."

I looked around. A stylish man wearing bell bottoms and a paisley shirt walked toward us. He stopped dead when he saw me.

"I'll catch you later." Jeremy sashayed up to his friend and waved good-bye to me.

I raised my hand to wave back, but he'd already turned around, and the two disappeared into the crowd. I wondered what I'd do now. I supposed if things went well, Jeremy would catch a ride home with his new friend. Or not go home at all.

The Carolina Blues had set up, and the lead singer tapped on the mic. It screeched, and he jumped back, laughing. People stopped talking, so he introduced the band, and they started right off with "Sweet Soul Music." Kids swamped the dance floor, but I stood on the fringe and watched. A couple of guys asked me to dance, but I shook my head. Somebody tapped me on the shoulder. I turned around and found Denique from history class standing there with none other than Tyrell in all his glory.

"Caroline, I wanted to introduce you to my brother. This is Tyrell Davis."

"Pleased to meet you." I held out my hand, but he just studied me.

"Caroline stood up to that pig Mr. Dutton when he said the Yankees were forcing them to integrate next year. Called her a nigger-lover." Denique chewed gum as she talked.

"Are you?" he asked in a velvet-smooth voice.

"Pardon me?"

"Are you a nigger-lover?"

I flushed scarlet from head to toe. "Well, I uh—"

"He's just teasing you." Denique frowned at him. "Be nice."

Tyrell smiled and took my hand that was still hanging out there, limp as a dead flounder. "Nice to meet you, too. Want to dance?"

Dumbstruck, I just nodded and followed him onto the dance floor.

I was grateful the band had moved on to "Standing in the Shadows of Love." Still fast enough. So we danced, close but not touching. Tyrell moved with the grace and deadly self-assurance of a tiger. Or maybe like that fighter, Muhammad Ali. Tyrell ignored the looks we were getting. And the comments.

"Thought you was true to your own," a dark girl said as she moved by us.

He winked at me when she said this. I tried to look around the room and not stare at him, but he captured my eyes and held them. I soon lost my awkwardness and started to move more naturally.

He smiled at me, something secret and suggestive communicating between us, and warmth crept up from my belly, a radiating glow that loosened my muscles and left me languid. It made me want to lay down in the grass with the tiger and stretch out, never mind those sharp teeth.

Then they played a slow song. The strains of "Your Precious Love" filled the room.

"Thank you for the dance," I said.

"You goin' somewhere?" He reeled me in.

My arms circled his neck without consulting me, and he pulled me closer so the fronts of our bodies almost touched, but not quite. This made the glow in my abdomen ignite into a steady flame.

"So you coming tomorrow?" he asked a little sardonically, like he knew the answer would be no.

"My daddy won't let me."

"Your daddy?" He threw back his head and laughed.

"I could tell them I'm going to the library."

For some reason, he found this even funnier. "You go the library a lot?"

I tried for a wicked look. "That's what they think."

"Mm-hmm," he murmured, his voice sexy and low.

My head just sort of fell onto his shoulder, and he closed the small gap between us.

22

The next Saturday, I attended a rally The Rap Room hosted along with a few other organizations working for voting rights in the city. Jeremy told me I was on my own, that he had a hot date. Denique had talked me into volunteering to register people to vote. They had tables set up at the back of the crowd. My mother thought this was a fine thing to do. My father just shook his head. I got there just before the speeches started. The same girl who'd sold me the one-dollar soft drink showed me where to sit, what papers to have the people fill out, and where to put the forms afterward.

A white lady from a Christian group talked about equality and the message of Dr. King. Then I heard a familiar velvety voice. I looked up and saw none other than Tyrell Davis standing at the microphone, his Black Panther cap sitting to the side just right. He had on a T-shirt with the face of Malcolm X, who had been assassinated two years earlier.

He welcomed everyone, then launched into his talk. "Brother Malcolm, Brother Evers—these are only a few of our martyrs. These people gave their lives for us. So we could hold our heads up and be men. So we could go to school and get a decent education. So we could get good jobs and support our families.

"The black man has suffered long enough. We have been demeaned. We've been hunted down by dogs. We've been beaten. Lynched. We've been made to bow down, to take the leftovers, to go to the back of the bus long enough. We've been made to shuffle, to chuck and jive, to say 'Yes, sir' and 'Mas'er' long enough.

"Today I say that is enough. Today it is time to stand up. It's time to claim our power. It's time to vote for politicians who will do right by us. And if they don't do right, we will hold them accountable."

Applause and shouts of approval rose up from the crowd in a roar. I found myself clapping wildly.

"Now if you haven't registered to vote, then today is your lucky day. Just go back to that table in the back," he pointed to us, and his face broke into a smile when his eyes met mine, "and these lovely ladies can get you registered today." He paused and smiled at me. My heart flipped over in my chest.

Next up was Howard, who grabbed Tyrell by the arm as he was trying to leave the stage. "I am so proud of our youth today. They have been born into a world of new possibilities. Let's work to make Dr. King's dream a reality for all these young people." He spread his arms wide, like a shepherd blessing his flock. "Tonight, The Rap Room will be hosting a dance. We're right across from the justice center and the police department, so you parents can be sure your children are safe."

For some reason, a lot of people in the crowd found this funny.

"Now let's give another round of applause to Tyrell."

All the girls at our table cheered madly.

"Today we have a very special guest," Howard said. "Today the head organizer from SNCC, the Student Nonviolent Coordinating Committee, is here with us. Please give a warm welcome to Mr. Stokley Carmichael."

This was exciting. This man had a real reputation. He'd been on the Freedom Rides, had marched with Dr. King. He'd been arrested more times than God. I shouted and clapped until my hands burned.

Carmichael told us about his experiences. He talked about founding the Mississippi Freedom Democratic Party, about demanding to be seated at the 1964 Democratic Convention. He explained how all this had led to the founding of the Black Panther Party, which was accused of violent extremism, but really just gave out free breakfasts to kids. "Children come to school hungry, and they can't learn. They can't concentrate when their bellies need to be filled."

He explained now was the time for everybody to register to vote. "They used to give us these ridiculous tests that were so hard the crackers giving the tests couldn't pass them." This got a big laugh.

"Now you can register to vote. At last, you can exercise your right as a citizen of this United States of America. At last, we can make a reality what it says in the Bill of Rights, that all men are created equal. Now get back to those tables and register."

We didn't have time to applaud after that. We were busy for two hours with five lines registering people, giving them information on where to vote and who the candidates were. Denique worked at a table near me. When things slowed down, I looked up to find Tyrell sitting backwards on a chair, one long leg stretching on either side, his chin in one hand, watching me.

I blushed.

"What a pretty shade of pink," he said.

I turned red.

He smirked, then ambled over to the table. "You coming tonight?"

"I guess so."

"Good," he said. "I've got meetings all afternoon."

"With Stokley Carmichael?" I breathed.

"The very same." He settled his cap on his head at a better angle. "But later on I was hoping we could . . . spend some time together."

A delicious tongue of flame licked its way up my belly. "Uh, okay."

He winked and sauntered away.

I told my parents that I was going to a dance with my friend Beverly from school. They didn't have to know she wasn't going. I was sure somebody named Beverly would be there. My one rich uncle who had retired from GM and moved back home had given me a VW Bug for my birthday. I painted a little sign that said "Flower Child" for the front where there was room for a license plate. I jumped in the blue Bug and pointed it toward The Rap Room.

The place was loud and smoky and smelled of patchouli and sweat. By now I'd gotten to know some of the regulars, so I danced with a few friends, all of us in a big group so nobody was with anyone in particular. I went to the booth where the records were stored and picked out a few albums, tried to convince Steve to play them. He just wrinkled up his nose and played what he wanted. Then I went back to the soft drink table and helped out for a while.

That voice that sent my skin into fine pinpricks spoke from behind me. "Would you be so kind as to give me a Coke?"

I turned around so fast I sloshed the drink over my hand.

"Whoa, easy, girl." He laughed.

"Here you go, Tyrell." Debbie, another regular, handed him a soft drink and pushed out her chest just a little bit.

"Why, thank you, sister," he said. He gulped it down. "Planning a revolution is thirsty work."

I couldn't imagine what they'd talked about all afternoon, but I wanted to hear.

"Didn't you promise me a dance?" he asked me.

I followed him to the dance floor and abandoned myself to the drums and his moves. After a few fast numbers, we both needed a breather, so he steered me out the door to the side of the building. I leaned back against the still-hot bricks and looked up at the stars, catching my breath, pulling my long hair up off my neck, arching my back in what I hoped was a provocative gesture.

He stood in front of me for a minute, then leaned in, took me in his arms, and kissed me. His lips were satin warmth, full and insistent, claiming my mouth. He pulled me closer, his broad shoulders engulfing me. The tip of his tongue slipped between my lips and met mine. I gave a soft moan and opened to him. His hands slid down my back and tugged my shirt from my jeans. His thumb brushed the skin on my back and a wave of dizziness hit me. He pulled me tighter. "I've got you, baby," he mumbled against my mouth.

I leaned into him, turned my head away, trying to catch my breath, but he bent my head toward him again and kissed me, his mouth questing, demanding, yet soft at the same time. I'd never been kissed like this before. I'd only experienced the wet mouths and fumbling hands of boys in the backs of cars at drive-ins. The lip smacking and tongue probes of high schoolers after a date. This was something entirely different. This was the kiss of a man, I thought, a man who knew what he wanted in the world. A man who knew what he wanted from me.

An alarm sounded way back in my brain somewhere. "It's late," I said.

He shook his head like a swimmer emerging from a pool. "Late, you say? I think it's early."

"My parents will ask too many questions if I come home much after midnight."

"It's only," he looked at his watch, "twelve thirty."

"I've got to go. Where'd I leave my purse?"

He laughed. "You shouldn't leave your purse lying around here."

"Why? Can't people be trusted?"

"Only so far. Come on. We'll get it for you." He led me back inside to the office, where I retrieved my purse from a pile of them in the bottom of a file drawer. I pulled out my keys and headed for the door, but he reached for me again.

"When can I . . . see you again?" he asked.

I just stared at him, at his golden skin, his dark, brooding eyes, the firm line of his jaw. "Next weekend?" I said, not knowing what was happening but certain something would be.

"So long?" he asked.

Awash in tides of heat and desire, I couldn't find words.

"I'll walk you to your car."

I'd parked just half a block down. I moved like someone in a dream, like I was underwater, my body warm, my joints somehow loose and molten. We reached my car, and I pulled out the keys, then hesitated. I yearned to move closer to him.

As if in answer, he pulled me tight and kissed me again, his lips searing mine, his body strong, but his fingers gentle and deft. I came up from the kiss gasping.

"Maybe that will keep me until then," he whispered, then nipped my ear.

I jumped back, a little surprised, then raised my hand good-bye. He kissed my palm, and I somehow managed to get in my Bug.

The next Saturday, there was another dance. I hung with Steve, helping him put on records, then served up drinks, all the time waiting for Tyrell to show up. A girl named Jacy, who helped with organizing and was a year or two older than me, slipped into the chair beside me. She didn't beat around the bush. "What you doing dating Tyrell anyway?"

I froze for a minute.

"Don't you think black leaders should stick with their own women? It don't look good, him hanging around you."

I remembered what Tyrell had told me to say, so I repeated it. "You should talk to him."

"I think I will." Her eyes were hard behind her heavy eyeliner. She stared at me for a full minute, then left.

A while later, Tyrell slipped into the same seat. "What she want?"

"Told me you shouldn't be seeing me."

He looked around. "That right?"

"I told her what you said to say."

"What's that?"

I paused, surprised he didn't remember. "To talk to you."

"That's my girl." He tugged my hand, and I followed him to the dance floor. But I was self-conscious now, looking around at who was watching, wondering what they were thinking.

"What's wrong, baby?" His warm breath in my ear sent a shiver through me.

"I don't want to upset people. You do serious work."

"Which is why I need you."

Just then another slow song came on, and he pulled me to him. The room darkened. His arm held me steady, a strong protection against the outside world. He moved closer to me, started humming in my ear. I leaned into him. He gave a grunt. "Come with me, baby," he said, and led me off the dance floor.

We slipped around the corner into the conference space where people had meetings and made signs and phone calls during the day. Nobody seemed to notice us. I leaned against the wall, and Tyrell pushed against me, claiming my mouth with his skilled lips, his hands moving up my back, then down again, tugging at my dress.

I pushed him away. "Somebody will see."

He groaned in frustration, then opened a door to a room where we stored extra clothes and blankets and such that we gathered for needy families. I followed him inside. He leaned me against the now closed door and kissed me again, his strong hands moving over me. The heat in my belly burst into a fire, sending waves of heat through me. Tyrell held me firm with one arm, and his other hand stroked down over my rear, down my leg, then started to move up my thigh. I moaned, half in desire, half in protest.

"But somebody will come in," I said against his insistent mouth.

He locked the door.

His finger moved up under the elastic of my underwear, stroking my low belly, then moving up more, parting my lips and finding wet.

I gasped.

He grunted again, an almost animal sound, wet his fingers, then started to stroke. The waves of pleasure shocked me, took my breath. I clung to him, and God help me as hard as I tried, all I did was push against his fingers and open my legs wider.

"Yeah, baby," he said, and slid his fingers inside me. I laid back against the door, but he moved us over to the wall. Reached up and pulled my panties off.

"Tyrell," I said, weakly trying to push him away, but wanting nothing of the sort. I closed my eyes and heard his pants dropping to the floor. Afraid to open my eyes, I reached for his mouth again. He kissed me thoroughly, stroking that magic spot more with his fingers. Then something firmer, but with silky soft skin, took their place, and he wrapped his arms around me, still pushing against me. The tension grew to bursting, and I spasmed against him.

Embarrassed, I pulled away, but he pulled me back. "Yeah, baby, that's right."

While I still gasped, he lifted one of my legs and cradled it in his arm, then guided himself with his other hand a bit lower and pushed, gentle at first. I felt a burning sensation. I shifted away, but he reached behind and held me. Then thrust harder. I felt a sort of tearing sensation and a gush of something. I buried my head in his neck and filled my mouth with his flesh, trying not to yell. He didn't stop, but kept thrusting inside me. He found my mouth again and kissed me, deep, commanding. Then slowed his movements and crooned to me, but now I was dry and the thrusts burned. I squirmed away. He built up speed and pinned me to the wall, grunting. His back arched, and he let out a guttural sound of deep satisfaction. He held still for a minute, then slipped out of me.

He let me down slowly. Stood back. "Damn, girl, you something."

I stared at him. "Oh my God."

"I knew we'd be like that," he said.

I looked down and found my panties. Tyrell handed me a box of tissues and I cleaned up, throwing them into the trash can, seeing a bit of red in the dim light. I'd take them with me and flush them in the bathroom. I finished dressing.

"Oh, baby, you're the one all right," he said.

23

Tyrell and I spent a smoldering summer together with Denique as our go-between. At least it was for him. I had some pleasure, but not like they write about. I kept wondering if there was something wrong with me. But I didn't have the sense to stop. I was following a script, doing what girls were supposed to do, trying to make my experience match what the world told me it should be. My only rebellion was in the color of our skins.

I introduced Denique to my mother as a friend from school. "We're helping with voter registration."

"Good for you." Mother approved, even if Daddy didn't. But he'd mellowed, so he let me go be a "do-gooder," as he put it. Our group did political things, ran The Rap Room. We held dances, attended rallies. At the rallies, Tyrell put Jacy on his arm, and I hung with my white friend Tod, who was another supported of The Rap Room's work. But my nights belonged to Tyrell in the back of his friend's apartment or in his room when his parents were away.

By September, I was to go off to college in Greensboro, that town made famous by the lunch counter demonstrations, thirty miles east. I told him he should come see me, that we'd find a way to be together.

By November, I realized I was pregnant.

"What are you going to do about it?"

"Me? What am I going to do about it?" I closed the door of the phone booth in the dorm.

"Well, yeah."

"What about you?"

"Baby, you know I love you, but I'm working in the movement. I got national connections. I want to get out of this hick town and make something of myself."

I looked around to see if anyone else had come into the room. I was still alone. I wanted to close the room off, but there was no door.

"I'm in college, Tyrell. I can't have a baby."

"I can't either. I'm organizing. They want me to come speak in Atlanta."

"Atlanta? That's great."

"With Lewis Jackson."

"My father's going to kill me. He'll shoot you."

"Shoot me? Whoa, baby."

"I'm not kidding."

"You want him to shoot me?"

"I never said I wanted that, but if he finds out . . ." I twisted my hand in my hair and leaned on my elbow against the wall. "You've got to help me."

The operator interrupted us. "Please deposit a quarter for three more minutes."

I did it, and the connection cleared.

"You want it?" he asked.

"Want what?"

"The baby? You want to keep it?"

"What are you saying?"

"I know a guy. He does abortions."

That sounded serious. It would hurt like hell. "Does he know what he's doing?"

"He worked in a hospital."

"What, mopping floors?"

"Oh, so black men don't do nothing but janitorial work?"

"Tyrell, you know I didn't mean that. This is serious."

"So you want me to ask him?"

"Where does he do them?"

He hesitated. "He works in a funeral home."

I was stunned. "A funeral home?"

"Yeah."

"So, what? He does them next to some corpse?" My voice was getting higher and higher.

"Look, it's an option. I know people that have gone to him. They're fine."

"I don't know, Tyrell. That sounds creepy."

"You could go to Mexico."

"Mexico? How am I supposed to get to Mexico?"

"Drive? Fly?"

"You're crazy." Mexico might as well have been Mars as far as I could imagine.

"Fine, then let your father shoot me."

I sputtered out a laugh.

"You're at a women's college. Surely somebody there has had a similar predicament. I'll bet you somebody knows something. Ask around."

"All right." We hung up.

That night, a girl a girl in my biology class knocked on my door. "Can I come in?"

"Sure."

She settled on the empty bed in my room. My roommate's very white parents had forced her to move when I'd stood up for one of the maids in our dorm. "Word is you have a situation."

"Situation" was the word that was used in the white community to say a daughter was pregnant out of wedlock, a disaster for her chances at a good marriage, still a permanent stain on her reputation.

"How did you know?"

"I just heard. Listen, I have a connection, but he's with the mob. You call this guy. He has a few doctors on call. You set up an appointment."

"Do they do it in their office?"

"No, a hotel room."

That beat a funeral home by a country mile. So I made the appointment. Two o'clock next Tuesday at the Hampton Inn on Friendly Road.

But when Tuesday rolled around, I sat in my dorm room and kept getting up and going to the door, then turning around and sitting back down on the bed. Two o'clock came and went. Then three o'clock. I'd known I was pregnant the next morning when I woke up with Tyrell snoring beside me in the cheap hotel room we'd rented. I'd known you were a girl.

The next day, I got paged to the phone room, and the guy reamed me out. "You owe me $250. That's how much I paid the doctor. He showed up. You didn't."

I hung up on him.

He called the next day and went through the same routine.

"I don't have the money."

"Look, bitch, I'm with the mob. I can call them in on this."

But he was talking to the wrong person. I'd been threated by the KKK. The police had followed me around after I started working with The Rap Room. Stopped me on dark streets and asked me where I'd been, where I was going, what was wrong with me. For some crazy reason, he didn't scare me.

"So call them." I hung up.

I went to the school psychiatrist. That was the only way to get a legal abortion. I thought maybe in a hospital I could go through with it. I sat waiting on the split plastic covering on the seat in the student health center. He listened, then told me he'd seen women go through psychosis and come out the other side in time to deliver a healthy baby.

I called Tyrell. "I can't go to a funeral home . . ." I closed the door to the phone booth firmly. "I found a mob guy."

"Great, when you doing it?"

"I'm not. I just can't go through with it."

He was silent a long time. Finally he said, "I can't marry you, Caroline. An up-and-coming black leader just can't marry a white woman. I'm sorry."

When I didn't answer, he said, "I love you."

I hung up and sat there for a long time, ignoring the dingy woman who kept knocking on the door telling me she wanted to call her boyfriend.

I finally called my parents.

The Hetty Sorrel Home for Unwed Mothers stood across from the hospital in Charlotte, an unmarked two-story brick colonial with a basement for crafts and laundry, plus a big rec room with a TV. A chapel squatted next to the back walk, a secret brick building hidden in a grove of trees with beautiful stained-glass windows. Most of us attended services because it broke up the monotony. A few seemed devout. A very few.

The first floor held reception, a large living room for visitors, and offices for the social workers and nurses, plus a library that doubled as a smaller TV room. Across from the nurses' station was the mothers' room, where the girls who had just given birth came back from the hospital to recover—without their baby. The babies were collected by social workers from the various cities we came from on the third day and taken to their adoptive families. The mothers' room held about eight beds. At least two of them were full at any given time, usually more. Dorms were on the second floor, three girls housed in each room. I put the psychedelic John Lennon poster at the foot of my bed on the side of the dresser and settled in.

Integration had not quite arrived at the Hetty Sorrel Home for Unwed Mothers. "Some of the girls would be uncomfortable," the intake lady explained. The black girls had their own room. There were three of them, each from well-to-do families. I was a bit surprised given the African-American attitude toward adoption, but these families aspired to being accepted into the white community, so they embraced the idea. One of them, Joanna, worked with me when I first arrived.

We all had chores, and my first assignment was laundry. "Before you get too far along to do it," my social worker explained. "When you're in your ninth month, we'll give you a lighter job. The last two weeks, you don't have any chores. After breakfast, which is at seven, you come down here and do the sheets and towels. No personal laundry. The girls have to do their own clothes."

I looked around at the row of white washing machines and the two industrial dryers.

"You don't mind doing laundry, do you Lucy?"

"No, ma'am."

We went under aliases at the home so nobody would know who we really were when we got out. To keep our precious reputations intact. I'd picked Lucy from "Lucy in the Sky with Diamonds." Somebody had already taken "Celeste" from Donovan. "Lucy" was cooler anyway.

The girls still in high school went to classes during the weekdays, so they didn't have to work. The rest of us did our chores and then were free for the day. We were allowed to go to the drugstore next to the home on our own, but we had to have a buddy for any other excursions. We were encouraged to walk in the park nearby, which had a lake complete with ducks and other birds, plus families and women with strollers, from which we carefully averted our eyes. Well, most of us.

A few volunteers taught crafts. I painted a Madonna figurine baby blue, although it was suspiciously foreign to me since I'd grown up a Protestant. Mother wrinkled her nose at it when I presented it to her as a gift after I got home. "You made this for me?" she asked. "We don't worship Mother Mary, you know." She held it at arm's length and studied it. "I don't know what I'll do with it, but thank you," she said unenthusiastically. But it had been the most interesting statue to paint and fire. The others were dogs and horses, that kind of thing.

Another woman came on Thursday nights and played games that she made up. She drove all the way from Chapel Hill, which seemed incomprehensible to me. Three hours on the road? Then three hours back? We never drove that far unless we were going to Myrtle Beach on vacation, which was my father's limit. I tried her games but got bored. I read a lot. Watched TV.

We got regular checkups from the maternity interns in the nurses' station. Many wished for the dreamy Dr. Bird, the youngest and most handsome, to deliver their baby. We still sleepwalked under the sway of romantic myths, even though we were the victims of them. Feminism was just stirring—again—but we thought for the first time. Not many of us had awoken from the hypnotic 1950s. Father still knew best. Dr. Bird had a jocular way about him and treated us like working girls, although I didn't realize it then.

I got a few visitors. My father came every two weeks. He would sit with his hat in this hand, staring at his shoes, shame filling him. Mother came twice, the last time to announce she was divorcing my father, that she couldn't believe I'd made this horrible mistake. She wore a royal blue suit with a hat like she was going to Easter service or something. It reminded me how she'd dressed up when she came begging at my aunt's door after my father had taken me away from her. "I'm taking Jimmy to Florida. He can get well there." My brother had suffered a nervous breakdown in the navy. "I gave your father the best years of my life. I can't give him anymore. Or you."

The minister of our church showed up, much to my surprise. Touched by his kindness, I let him pray over me.

The biggest surprise was Tyrell's parents.

"Let us keep the baby."

"What?"

"It's our blood. We'll keep it. We'll raise it. You can see it whenever you want."

This was beyond my cultural depth. Single girls gave their children up. It was just how things were done. Then we knew the baby had the best chance of a good life. The social worker had already picked out a family for us, the first black CEO of a company here in Charlotte, the mother a nurse. "Both with advanced degrees," the social worker had stressed. "Your baby will have an excellent family."

"I'll talk to my parents," I said, tears filling my eyes. Could it be possible I could keep you? But I knew one of Tyrell's brothers was shooting up heroin and another had taken up robbery as a profession. The CEO sounded like a safer bet. Except I'd never see you again. Could I make this sacrifice? Was it the right decision?

My father forbade it. "You'll be over there all the time. You'll never get away from those—" He stopped himself from saying "niggers." "If you do this, you'll have to leave my house. I'll never speak to you again." Tears ran down his cheeks, but his hands gripped the arms of the chair he sat in until I was afraid they would break. After that, even he stopped coming to see me.

I waited.

24

Y ou were born on a warm May afternoon, just after one o'clock. No snow for you, but flowers, lots of flowers. I was in labor for twenty-four hours. It started in the afternoon, a sharp stab followed by thirty minutes of silence, then another. The contractions came, regular and steady, all afternoon. Then I sat up and watched the late shows, walking the floor from the TV room to the nurses' station, back and forth. The nurse called the doctor, and he said to wait until I was four centimeters, so I walked back to watch Johnny Carson, swollen ankles, protruding stomach, and all. When Johnny said good night to his last guest—I can't remember who—and there was nothing left to watch, the loud hum came on, and a pattern projected on the screen that looked like a target. I walked back to the nurse, who checked me again. She called the doctor to announce I'd arrived at the prescribed number of dilation, and we walked over to the hospital, just across the block. She carried my overnight case. I carried you.

Time blurred for me as the night ticked away, my world shrinking to the bed, the pain, and the nurse who finally sat with me as the light from the window got brighter. I thought you'd arrive soon, but the hands of the clock kept moving, although it seemed like the same moment to me. After the last visit of the doctor with his large hands and white gown, the nurse said simply, "Your baby has quite a head of hair."

"You can see her?"

"How do you know it's a girl?"

But I always knew, from the first moment I realized you were with me, the morning after I'd spent the night in that hotel with Tyrell. It was like I'd been alone all my life and woke up with company. So they wheeled us into the delivery room, and finally there you were, a little blue, topped with soft, dark brown curls. I begged to see you, and finally the nurse took you from the clear plastic bassinet and held you up to me. "Seven pounds, three ounces," she said. "A healthy baby girl." But they wouldn't let me touch you. Not until later that day when they brought you to my room to let me feed you.

With you came every black woman who worked on that floor. They lined the wall to watch us, the white hippie girl and her mixed-race baby. It was 1968. I didn't mind. It was nice to have some company after that long night. They put you in my arms, and you opened your eyes, and I put the bottle in your little mouth, and you wrapped your tiny hand around my little finger, closed your eyes, and drank, content. So was I. After a few swallows, you opened your eyes again and took a good look at me.

I'd never been looked at like that before. You trusted me. Completely.

And it terrified me. I didn't think I could be trusted. Not like that. You felt my fear and frowned, so I started to sing, and you smiled.

I grew up with that look.

I realized I really did have to give you up because I couldn't let anyone hurt you. I never wanted to say those words my mother had said so many times, "If it wasn't for you . . ." And for some reason, infants scared me. I was afraid I would hurt one for some nagging reason that I couldn't quite remember. Not until much later.

But I wanted you more than anything, to hold you, feed you, let your sweet weight rest in my arms. I had nowhere to rest with you, that was the thing, nowhere to take you I thought was safe. The Klan had threatened us so many times my father changed the one phone number we'd had all my life to an unlisted one. Tyrell's mother had nine children in two bedrooms and by now two sons shooting heroin. She knew nothing about that. You were perfect, too precious to risk being hurt by all that. My father had rejected you from the beginning.

One of the women in the room interrupted this reverie. "Now don't let her drink too much the first time."

I pulled the bottle out of your mouth, and you grunted a protest. I held it up and checked how much you'd drunk. "Just a little more," I whispered, then looked up at the nurse's assistant who'd spoken. "She has blue eyes."

"They'll turn," someone said who was leaning against the wall. "They're all born with blue eyes."

I opened your little fist and looked at your fingers, creamy with light brown in the wrinkles around the knuckles. "Will she get darker?"

"The color there." The closer woman pointed at the wrinkled skin in the crease of your elbow.

"Isn't she beautiful?" I said.

The women murmured among themselves, nodding their heads and smiling. "They all are," someone said.

"I wish Maggie could see you," I whispered.

"Who Maggie?" someone asked.

"She took care of me when I was little. She lost a son when she was younger than me." My mother had told me the story when I told her I was pregnant.

"Where she from?"

"Winston-Salem, but they sent her somewhere down here to be with a friend. She's forgetful. Kept wandering off from the lady who keeps older people."

"Wait, what's her last name?"

That stopped me. "I don't remember," I said. "I was a kid, you know."

"Could it be Maggie Winters?" someone asked.

"Maybe," I said. "I think that was her father's name." Could she have kept that man's name?

"I'm gonna go see something," one of them said, then ran out.

You gave a strong kick as if to object to no longer being the center of attention. I stroked your forehead and hummed a tune. You widened your eyes as if that would help you feel more.

All of a sudden the nurse hustled back into the room pushing a wheelchair. "Hop in. I got a surprise."

"Whatchu doin', Matilda?"

"It's a surprise."

Between the group, they loaded me into the wheelchair and put you into my arms. One stood lookout and waved us out when the head nurse went back to her desk. They surrounded the chair to hide me, it seemed like, and hustled me onto the elevator. We rode up two floors. They rolled me into one of the rooms and there, laying tucked into starched white sheets, almost gray, her eyes closed, was my Maggie.

I gave a little cry, and Maggie stirred, opened her eyes.

She smiled at me. "That you, Paula?"

"It's Caroline," I said.

"Just agree with her," somebody whispered in my ear. "She's wandering in the past now. Probably won't come back."

Maggie's eyes fixed on you, and something in her switched on. "Is that him?" She struggled to sit up, moaning with eagerness. One of the nursing assistants went over and pulled her up higher in the bed.

"Oh, Charlise, is that him? Is that my baby?"

My eyes filled with tears, remembering the awful story. "Yes, Maggie, this is your baby."

"Let me hold him." She reached out pitifully thin arms, her face lit with an otherworldly light.

I was wheeled closer to the bed, and one of the women held her arms out, a question on her face. I held you up and she took you and snuggled you in Maggie's arms. Maggie wasn't strong enough, so the attendant supported you beneath Maggie's arms.

"You came back," Maggie whispered. "You came back to me. I'm so sorry. I loved you in spite of your daddy. It weren't your fault."

Maggie looked up at me, her face awash with wonder, her eyes glistening with tears. "He came back to me. He forgave me."

We sat like that, Maggie feasting on your presence, stroking your forehead and nose and cheeks, soothing you just like she'd soothed me that night when I was a terrified, lost child whose mother had turned on her too many times.

After a while, Maggie fell back on her pillow, exhausted. "Thank you, Charlise."

"You're welcome," I said.

Maggie never recognized me, but it didn't matter. I'd brought her something precious.

Peace.

Peace at last.

I heard Maggie passed later that night. I got to feed you three more times the next day before they took me back across the street and you off to your new family. I never saw either one of you again. At least, not until today.

"Please put your seatbacks and tray tables back to their full up-right positions. We'll be landing in Charlotte shortly."

I found you in Charlotte. The Adoptee Rights people traced you in two days after I gave them your birth information. Imagine my surprise that you live in the same town you were born in.

"Ma'am, you might want to put that paper away. We're expecting a little turbulence. Is your seat belt fastened?"

"All right."

I guess this is it. I can tell you all about the rest in person. I just want you to know I love you.

I stuff these sheaves of paper into a large manila envelope. Then I realize maybe I should wait a while to give them to you. It might be a little much for a twenty-one-year-old. I'll wait and see after I meet you. I've tried to be faithful to that story.

I put the diary in my carry-on for safe keeping, then shove the bag back under the seat before the flight attendant gets too excited. The wheels touch down, and I sit with my eyes closed, letting everyone else get off the plane.

"Ma'am, are you all right? Do you need any help?"

I open my eyes to an empty plane. "No, I'm fine." I grab my bag and walk down the aisle, fear fluttering my heart.

What if you reject me? I wouldn't blame you. I gave you up to other people. I thought you'd be better off, but were you? Can you possibly understand? Does it even matter how you feel about me? I learned that first day I saw you that you are the only one who really matters.

Maybe you're just curious to see me once, then you'll go on with your life. Your letter said you are married now. Have a two-year-old. You're a responsible parent. Not like me and Tyrell.

Maybe you want to yell at me for making your life miserable. Maybe your adoptive parents treated you badly. You never know how people will turn out. After I found you, I tracked down Tyrell to a prison out west. He was in for possession and intent to sell.

I don't care what you are or how you feel about me, though. I'll always love you.

I push my feet down the Jetway where you're waiting for me. I get to the end. Walk out to the waiting area.

There you stand. A little taller than me, wavy dark hair, eager eyes searching the crowd.

I step forward. "Violet?"

Your adoptive mother changed your name. She grew up in Louisiana, your letter said.

You step forward. Your hazel eyes light up. "Caroline?"

"Oh my God. It's you." I open my arms, and to my great delight, you come to me, after twenty-one years, and I wrap my arms around my child.

You pull back and study my face.

I drink you in. Then I say, "I'm so sorry."

You just shake you head.

"I have so much to tell you." I wave the manila envelope I'm holding. "I wrote some of it down."

Acknowledgements

My thanks go to those who have helped with this manuscript. First, the Moravian Writers' Conference and Beverly Donofrio, in whose workshop parts of this novel were born. Also readers, including Peg Brantley, Beatrice Bruno, Sandra Maresh Doe, Cynthia Kuhn, Lorna Hutchison, and Lauren Hughes.

My deepest thanks go to Stephen Mehler for his unwavering support and enormous heart.

About the Author

Born in Winston-Salem, North Carolina, Theresa Crater grew up in the middle of the civil rights movement, an experience that left her believing anything is possible. At the age of seven, Theresa Crater announced to her parents she was going to be a writer. They promptly told her no one could make a living doing that. But like most kids, she didn't listen.

Now a best-selling author, Theresa brings ancient temples, lost civilizations, and secret societies back to life in her visionary fiction. Her novels include The Power Places series, *Under the Stone Paw* and *Beneath the Hallowed Hill, School of Hard Knocks, The Star Family* and *God in a Box*. Her short stories explore ancient myth brought into the present day. *The Star Family* won best fiction in the Indie Spirit Book Awards in 2015. She blogs here, and is a member of the Visionary Fiction Alliance, Sisters in Crime, and the Independent Authors Network. She also teaches creative writing, British literature, and does free-lance editing.

She lives in Colorado with her Egyptologist partner, who writes and leads tours to Egypt, and their feline overlords. She's been to Egypt four times so far, and also traveled in Central and South America and Europe. This year she hopes to add Cambodia to her list with a trip to Angkor Wat.

Also by Theresa Crater

Books
The Power Places series
Under the Stone Paw
Beneath the Hallowed Hill
Return of the Grail King (coming soon)
Stand Alones
The Star Family
God in a Box
Short Stories
The Judgment of Osiris
Bringing the Waters
White Moon
Solstice
Still Shots

Made in the USA
Coppell, TX
10 January 2021

47949920R00154